# THE CHRISTMAS PARTY
An addictive psychological thriller with a
jaw-dropping twist
Mikayla Davids

'**Absolutely a 5 star book**! **WOW**... There are **so many twists** in this psychological thriller... They really do come at you thick and fast towards the end... **an absolutely brilliant novel** from an exciting new author. It is fast paced and engaging, full of tension and it drew me right in!' Goodreads reviewer, 5 stars

'**Really packs a punch and the plot twists were just brilliant! I absolutely loved this book**. Davids smashes it right out of the park! Read in one sitting as I could not get enough! If there is one book you need this year, *The Christmas Party* is the one! Davids is definitely an author to watch!' *Once Upon A Time Book Reviews*, 5 stars

'**Utterly gripping**... **I was hooked right from the start** with this murder mystery and **I couldn't put it down I read it in one sitting**... Full of action and atmosphere and I loved the setting of the Christmas party... **There were so many twists and turns in this book and I was on the edge of my seat for most of it, I loved it**.' Goodreads reviewer, 5 stars

'**Wow! Wow! Wow!** Every time I thought I knew what was coming next, I was wrong! This **addictive** story kept me gripped until the final jaw-dropping twist. **Five huge stars!**' Goodreads reviewer, 5 stars

'**I couldn't put this book down! I was gripped from the very beginning**... **The story twists and turns**... I'm so excited to read more from this author!' Goodreads reviewer, 5 stars

'**Obsessed**... a massive success... Let's just say **I was so far on the edge of my seat I might have fallen!** Oh this book was written with lots of detail and in such a way that it felt like you were right there. **The twists were so clever**... **absolutely brilliant and a definite must-read for the holidays!**' *naturalbri_books*, 5 stars

'**I absolutely loved** this compelling thriller filled with family drama, secrets and scandal. It is fast paced... **genuinely surprised at the plot twists**... the setting was perfect... reminded me of a modern day Agatha Christie mystery where all the family gathers and one gets bumped off.' *lovetoread42*, 5 stars

'**A thrilling murder mystery with lots of shocking twists. A page turner that I was unable to put down**... **completely shocked** by a jaw-dropping twist at the end. Secrets, lies and backstabbing make for a great family reunion. I couldn't get enough of this **I absolutely devoured it. A gripping psychological thriller.**' *leannebookstagram*, 5 stars

'**Loved this book, full of twists and turns**, and the "jaw-dropping twist" tagline definitely doesn't disappoint! If you're a fan of Lucy Foley books you'll love this!' Goodreads reviewer, 5 stars

'**Fantastic**... **I loved**... I read this book in one day and every time I tried to put it down I had to pick it up again to find out what happened next! An **excellent** book and **a must read for all thriller fans**.' Goodreads reviewer, 5 stars

For my family

# Prologue

I spin with my sister in the middle of the dance floor, our hands clasped tight, whirling round to the music just as we did when we were children. The DJ is playing yet another classic Christmas tune and we both shout along at the tops of our voices, smiles wide, eyes bright, mirroring each other. Rainbow-coloured disco lights shine across the vast room and the crowd around us shimmers and sparkles.

The moment I've been hoping for is finally here. After ten long years, my family are together under the same roof again. My two sisters, my mother, our children and our husbands. We're reunited after a decade of not speaking. But I don't want to think about the terrible night that shattered our family because I've waited for this day for a long time.

As the song ends, I stagger, wobbling on my high heels and putting a hand to my throbbing head. I feel a steadying arm loop through mine and I'm guided along the edges of the friends and family gathered here to celebrate in this exquisite hotel.

Everyone else seems to be enjoying themselves, lapping up the festive atmosphere, but I'm on edge and I can't seem to properly let my hair down, despite the champagne that's flowing. A huge Christmas tree dominates one corner of the room, while the warm gold and red colour scheme spills out across the rest of the space and throughout the multitude of plush rooms beyond. Everything looks perfect on the surface. But, right now, I need to get away from the party.

When I exit through the double doors, the noise instantly dims and I feel like I can breathe properly again. I make my way along a winding corridor, my sister's hand in mine, and then we swing open another set of double doors into the grand foyer. This is the dazzling focal point of the building, with its curved marble staircase and sweeping gallery complete with a glittering crystal chandelier.

The first thing I notice is the strange silence. The music from the party shut out by the soundproofing.

The second thing I notice is the dead body. Lying spread-eagled on the white marble floor, a pool of dark red blood surrounding the head like a halo.

I'm stunned, surely this can't be happening? But my sister inhales sharply next to me so I know I'm not imagining this.

This is not a horrible dream. It's real.

My heart is hammering in my chest and my mouth feels dry. I lift my chin and make myself look once more at the person lying on the floor. I immediately recognise the broken figure at the foot of the steep marble staircase.

And I scream...

# Chapter One
# Erin
# Now

It's the first of December and I feel excitement bubbling up inside me as I sit at my desk, looking out at the crisp, cool winter's morning. I've always loved this time of year: it's a time of hope, a time of joy, a time of promise. For me, the beginning of December marks the start of a new chapter and is a far more exciting month for fresh starts than dull and dreary January. December is a month of connecting with others, with memories to be made and good times to be had. As my manicured fingers run along the fold of the gold envelope I smile to myself. It's taken a long time to work up the courage to do what I'm about to do, but I'm finally ready to put my plan into action.

I slide the gilded invitation into the envelope and then seal it. Picking up my silver fountain pen, I write the familiar name and address with a flourish. I sit back, surveying my handiwork and I feel a calm settle over me. I haven't seen my mother or my two sisters for the last ten years. Making any kind of contact with them is a really big deal for me. But I think the time is right to mend broken bridges and my therapist agrees.

So I'm inviting them to our annual Christmas party. The one me and my husband Aaron throw every year at our gorgeous country hotel. We spent years remodelling the place and I've poured everything into making this building a beautiful hotel as well as a successful business. It's taken a lot of hard work to get here so it's an amazing feeling to be able to use the space for celebrations. Our Christmas party has become part of the festive calendar for many of our friends and Aaron's family. I adore playing the hostess, choosing the perfect food, the perfect decorations, the perfect entertainment and then welcoming all of our guests. Except, I've always felt like something is missing. Because even though it's our Christmas party, it's really all Aaron's nearest and dearest who fill the hotel every year. We've been together for over nine years and his friends are also my friends by extension. But no one comes just for me.

I've decided I need to change that. Whatever happened with my family in the past, I'm sure we can all move on from it. After having children of my own, my darling twins Ophelia and Jasper, I've realised just how important family is. Christmastime is the ideal moment for forgiving and forgetting.

'Here's your tea.' Nia, one of our waitresses, and my most trusted member of staff, comes into the room and puts a teacup down on my polished oak desk.

'Thank you. These need to go out in this morning's post.' I gesture at the expensive invitations and Nia immediately scoops them into a tidier stack to take with her.

'Is there anything else you need?'

'There's a couple coming in for a wedding consultation at noon, it's in the diary. Could you be on hand for refreshments?'

'Certainly,' Nia replies, flicking her raven hair over her shoulders and taking the bundle of gold envelopes with her as she exits the room.

All I have to do now is wait for the replies. I've included photos of Ophelia and Jasper as well as a heartfelt letter to each of the women I'm desperate to be reunited with: my mother Nadia, my older sister Sasha and my younger sister Leah.

I gaze out of my big bay window. I love this view of the gardens; it's the reason I chose this room to be my office. The terrace, dotted with rattan garden furniture, gives way to a rose garden. The flowers have already withered and died for this season, but we have some colourful winter shrubs blossoming at the moment. The pops of purple, pink and blue cheer up the outdoor space in the absence of the roses at this time of year. Sometimes I almost have to pinch myself because I can't believe that this life is mine.

Beyond the terrace we have an extensive lavender field. In the summertime, the scent is simply divine and the purple rolling field is such a pretty picture. It's a big part of the attraction for couples wanting to get married at Burcott House; they love to have their photoshoots against the blanket of lavender flowers. We also have a team of staff employed to make all sorts of lavender-scented products — from soap to gin — and there's a steady stream of sales through the year. Our guests purchase our lavender-scented gifts as a memento of their stay, the locals in the nearest village adore the lavender honey we make and our online sales are on the up as well.

The lavender enterprise is just one of the many projects I've been working on since Aaron officially let me take over the management of the hotel when our twins went to school and our profits have quadrupled in that time. It's a dream come true to have a career of my own. During the children's early years 'a Mum of twins' became my job title as Aaron wasn't keen on me working while they were little. I get to enjoy the perfect balance of work and motherhood these days. I can work towards my goals for the hotel between the hours of 9 a.m. to 3 p.m. and then after school I throw my energy into spending time with Ophelia and Jasper.

Curving alongside the lavender fields is a narrow road that leads to the cottage where we live as a family. I can just about spot the top of the roof from here. We do sometimes stay in the hotel if the rooms aren't booked, for a change of scenery, but it's wonderful to have the quaint four-bedroomed cottage to return to after a busy day. It helps me separate myself from work demands and gives me the chance to switch off in a way I can't if I stay at the hotel. Although I'm lucky that my commute is only a ten-minute walk along the charming lane between the two buildings.

We're miles away from the nearest village and the rural, tranquil location is such a draw for our returning customers. A haven away from the hustle and bustle of the world. I find looking out at the scenery surrounding the hotel so soothing and I need that right now because I'm on edge. What if my mother and sisters don't reply? What if they say no and refuse to come? But I can't think negatively, I just have to wait and see what happens. In the meantime, I'm going to get on with my party planning. There's so much to be done.

Because I want to make sure this will be a Christmas party that none of our guests will ever forget.

# Chapter Two
# Sasha
# Now

'Mummy, look at this!' My nine-year-old daughter bounds through into the kitchen, waving something in her hand.

'What is it, sweetheart?' I ask as I hurriedly spread a thin layer of jam across several slices of toast.

'It's a gold envelope,' Freya says excitedly. 'What do you think is inside?'

Freya dumps the envelope on the worktop amidst all the breadcrumbs. I glance down at it. My name, Sasha Bailey, is handwritten in black, curly font. There's something familiar about it and I chew my lip as I try to think whose handwriting it is. But nope, it's too early in the day for my brain to kick into gear.

'Can you open it, Mummy?' Freya asks, looking up at me with her big green eyes.

I glance at the clock. We're still on track for this morning's school run but even just a few minutes can make the difference between a leisurely walk to the school gates versus a sweaty sprint to get Freya into her classroom before the bell rings.

'Um, I'm not sure we've got time, Freya. Have you got everything ready in your bag?'

She nods in response, still looking up at me. Anticipation shining in her eyes. How can I possibly say no to her?

'OK, here's your toast. Sit down and I'll open it while we're eating our breakfast.'

We both settle down at the little breakfast bar, perching on the too-high stools. I take a bite of my toast and nod at Freya to encourage her to do the same.

'Let's play a game,' I suggest. 'Can you guess who the letter is from?'

Freya answers immediately, through a mouthful of crumbs. 'Santa!'

'Ah, so that's why you're so keen for me to open it,' I chuckle, suddenly seeing the envelope from my daughter's perspective. 'Well, you only just sent off your Christmas list. So Santa might not have had time to reply just yet.'

Her smiling face drops. Every year we've got into the tradition of sending off a letter to Santa on the first of December. About a week later, Freya then receives a letter back telling her to be a good girl and wishing her a Merry Christmas. I'm not sure how many more years she will be willing to believe in the jolly, red-clothed Christmas figure. I know she's heard kids at school debating whether or not he's real. So I've got to make the most of it this year. My little girl is growing up fast.

'I'm sure we'll get a reply soon though,' I reassure her. 'Any more guesses?'

She chomps her way through another mouthful of her food before saying, 'The tooth fairy? The King of England?'

I laugh. 'I guess this does seem fancy.' I turn the envelope over in my hands. It feels quite weighty. Like there's more than just a single sheet of paper in there. It's probably just a round robin from an old friend or marketing from some company who's decided to deliver the personal touch.

'Are you going to open it then?' Freya asks.

I take a slurp of my cold tea. 'Yes, of course.'

'Don't tear the sparkly envelope.'

I peel the paper open as carefully as possible. I'm sure my daughter already has an arts and crafts project that she will want to reuse this for. I ease out the contents to reveal a matching gold rectangle of stiff paper. I'm just thinking to myself it must be a posh postcard, when a sheaf of paper and a photograph fall onto the worktop in front of me. All face down.

Freya has cuddled close beside me, eager to glimpse the mystery contents. I turn over the photo and gasp. It's a picture of two children standing by a big oak tree. A little boy with reddy-brown hair and a girl who looks exactly like my Freya. I take in the auburn curls and the big green eyes; this child is the spitting image of my own daughter. It's like looking at her double.

'Mummy!' Freya squeals. 'Is that a picture of me?'

'No,' I say.

My hand shakes as the realisation of who this might be from suddenly dawns upon me and my stomach begins to churn. I turn over the thick, gold cardboard. It's an invitation to a Christmas party. I gasp out loud again when I see who the invite is from.

Erin Bailey-Scott.

The sister I've not seen for ten years.

I take in the details. It's an invite to a Christmas celebration on 22nd December at somewhere called Burcott House. It's in the county next to ours.

'A party!' Freya claps her hands as she reads the information.

I don't know what to say to her. I pick up the letter and start to scan the contents. Erin is asking for a family reconciliation. A chance to put the past behind us all. She has children now, twins Ophelia and Jasper. She wants us all to meet.

My mind spins.

'Mum, are we going to a party?' Freya shouts with glee, completely oblivious to the emotions running through me right now. I'm so thrown by this. It's come entirely out of the blue.

For years I longed to speak to Erin, to sort out our differences and move forward. I tried multiple times to contact her but she always froze me out. Never wanting to talk about what happened on the night that everything changed between us. Ignoring my heartfelt, pleading messages. So I'd got used to the idea that the two of us might never speak again. I had thought any kind of reunion was out of the question. I grew angry with her instead. Angry that she could be so heartless as to not even listen to my side of the story. And angry that she could walk away from me, from the rest of the family, so easily without even a backward glance.

So to hear from her now has turned my world upside down.

Freya is dancing round our tiny kitchen. She loves music so the word 'party' is all she needs to make her happy. But can I accept? Can we really just pretend all these years haven't happened and move on from them?

'Hey Sasha, you OK?'

My husband Jesse has just walked into the room, his short blond hair wet from his shower, humming a song to himself.

'It's half past seven, shouldn't you guys be on the way to school?'

Before I know what I'm doing tears are streaming down my cheeks. I'm sobbing at a rate that will make my mascara run.

'Hey, hey.' Jesse looks bewildered, he's never been very good at dealing with tears. 'What is it?'

He comes over to where I'm sitting and I pass him the invitation.

'Wow. Wasn't expecting that.' Jesse pulls a face. 'Must've been a shock, huh?'

'You can say that again,' I murmur, grabbing a tissue and dabbing away my tears.

I glance at the clock. 'We're going to be so late!' I exclaim, feeling panicked. 'Freya, get your shoes on! We need to go now.'

I rush around grabbing my bag, keys, and phone. Then I tap open Google Maps to see how busy the route is. I need to drop Freya at Breakfast Club today before driving to my own place of work. I'm an assistant headteacher at a primary school on the other side of town so I have to be on time.

'Oh no,' I groan. 'The route is solid red; it's saying it's going to take me forever to get anywhere.' My pulse speeds up. I hate being late; it makes me feel physically sick. Leaving even a smidge behind our usual time in the morning leaves us open to sitting bumper to bumper in traffic and I just can't afford to be behind for my first meeting of the day.

'Jesse, can you walk Freya to school for me please?'

My husband is taking two eggs out of the fridge and audibly huffs.

'Jesse, I'm really not going to get to work on time if you don't help me out this morning.'

He likes to make a leisurely protein-fuelled breakfast before cycling to the health and wellbeing centre where he works as a personal trainer.

His work is a lot more flexible than mine and yet he doesn't do much to help with the pressure of the morning school run.

'I've got a new client starting today. I wanted to—'

'Jesse, do you need to be at work before nine?'

'No.'

'Then please just take Freya this once.'

'I can walk myself,' Freya pipes up.

'You're not old enough yet,' I tell her. We've had this conversation several times already in the last few weeks. Freya is keen for more independence but her school is on the other side of a main road and I'm just not ready to let her do the journey by herself yet.

'OK, sure. Let's go now then,' Jesse says, turning to Freya. 'If we run, I might still have time for my eggs before I go.'

I hold my tongue and don't say anything. Jesse doesn't give me a hug or a kiss or any kind of reassurance, despite me being a ball of nerves after receiving the invite from my sister. He's blind to how I'm feeling.

I stand at the door and wave goodbye to my husband and daughter and then I'm left alone in the house. I've got only a few minutes to gather myself, to sort out my make-up and make myself presentable again. So I shuffle everything back into the gold envelope and put it on top of the microwave. For now, I've got to put this out of my mind and get myself to work.

That of course is easier said than done.

As I drive along the familiar route to my school, all sorts of memories from the past come flooding back. Happy memories of birthdays, family days on the beach, and laughing with my two sisters until we doubled over. Tears start to form once more; I wipe them away.

Then I see the reason for all the traffic: roadworks. Steering the car into the inevitable queue, my mind wanders to the later, not so happy memories. The arguments. The betrayal. The hurt. My decision is made. Too much has happened. Too much has been lost. I'm not going to see Erin again. I'm going to ignore her just like she did to me over and over again.

There's no way I'm going to that Christmas party.

# Chapter Three
## Erin
## Now

'Erin, I've just checked the business account. How much money are you spending on this party?'

Aaron strolls into my dressing room as I'm brushing my shoulder-length, copper-coloured hair. I stare at his reflection in my mirror and take in the man who is my husband. He's sleepy-eyed and tousle-haired, a complete contrast to the sleek, smart exterior he portrays to the rest of the world. At the moment his brow is furrowed and, as always, his top-of-the-range phone is in his hand.

'Sweetie, it's nothing we can't afford,' I reply, winking at him and allowing the sleeve of my satin night-attire to slip down my shoulder. With any luck, I can distract him from his precious accounts.

His frown deepens, his attention still on his mobile device. 'It's not a question of whether we can afford it. I'm talking about whether this is the most sensible use of our resources.'

I turn around in my seat and face him. 'Aaron, you know how important this event is to me. It's not just our annual celebrations this year. It's much more than that.'

Aaron looks at me properly then. 'Have you had any replies from your family yet?'

I hesitate for a beat and then respond. 'No, but the invites only went out at the start of the week. I'm sure I'll hear from them soon.'

'OK, well update me when you do. I know you want this to be the party of the year, but we can't keep upping the spend each time as well. Put your business head on and lower the costs. We own the best venue in the town so surely you can do a bit of negotiating. Get a new florist on board in exchange for becoming one of our recommended wedding suppliers or something. That sort of thing.'

I purse my lips in response and remain silent.

'There's no need to look at me like that, Erin. We've got twins to send to a private secondary school soon. That's going to cost.'

I can tell my husband isn't going to soften this morning, so I just nod and sashay past him.

'I need to get changed,' I say before dropping my silk robe and walking towards our large ensuite bathroom. We've got more than enough money to afford this party, so why does he have to be such a Scrooge?

'Erin—' I hear Aaron call. But it's too late. He's blown his chance for any further interaction this morning. It didn't used to be like this between us, but weekdays in our household now tend to be a tense affair. Aaron always seems to have an important business deal occupying his attention and we only have time for short exchanges around our busy work schedules.

I switch on our waterfall shower and set the lights to a deep, warm purple. I'm thankful that our home is a spacious cottage set in the grounds behind Burcott House. It means we can keep our family life separate from the hotel but still be close enough to be on hand any time day or night. We do have staff who are employed twenty-four seven to deal with the day-to-day running but it's good to be nearby in case of emergencies or any particularly high-profile guests who might need an extra bit of attention.

The job is constant but I'm doing something that gets me fired up. However, I have to find ways to switch off, both from my husband's demands for perfection and the fast-paced nature of the hotel business. That's why I love this room. I designed it myself, my dream bathroom. Not only do we have the waterfall shower but there's also a huge, clawfoot bathtub as well. This is the place where I prepare myself for each day because, in the circles I move in, I have to be immaculate. It's also the room where I relax most at the end of a long day.

After I've showered and dried, I go back into the bedroom, a fluffy white towel wrapped around me. Aaron's routine is like clockwork and he will be downstairs with the children eating breakfast by now.

I think about our conversation. My husband definitely holds the keys to our shared bank accounts. He likes to be in control of everything, especially our finances. But that's OK, because what he doesn't realise is that some of the suppliers we're paying aren't real businesses. They're companies I've invented in order to bolster my private bank accounts. It's not that I don't trust my husband, but given all the wealth we have, he isn't very generous with the money that comes my way. If I were carrying out the kind of role I've been doing for the hotel on a salary, I'd be taking home far more for myself. So I'm just evening things out really. Aaron wouldn't see it that way but a girl's got to have an escape fund just in case she needs it.

Besides, I've earned it. I've helped to launch a desirable, exclusive hotel that's booked up months in advance. And that's not all. After we started hosting weddings last summer our profit margin increased phenomenally. It's true when they say a wedding is the most expensive celebration you'll ever have. This year's Christmas party isn't a patch on the money I've seen some couples spending for their special day.

I blow-dry my long copper locks until they look salon-fresh and then dress in my white power suit before applying my make-up, adding a dash of my trademark red lipstick. Then I go downstairs. Aaron is sitting at the breakfast bar with the twins. My husband has finished eating his overnight-oats but the children are still making their way through their cereal. Pale early morning sunshine is filtering through the skylight and everything in this white-washed room looks pristine, nothing is out of place. Just how Aaron likes it.

'Hi gang,' I say, placing a hand on my son's shoulder. 'How are we all doing this morning?'

Jasper responds by giving me a hug while Ophelia has her head in a book and doesn't reply. I'm not sure she's even heard me.

'Ophelia, did you sleep OK?' I ask as I start to make a black coffee from our high-end barista-grade machine.

'Yep,' she replies, eyes still on the page in front of her. She reminds me so much of my older sister Sasha, who was a total bookworm at that age as well.

'Right, I've got a meeting first thing,' Aaron announces, scraping his chair back. 'So I'll leave you to it. See you later.'

Aaron drops a kiss on Ophelia's head and ruffles Jasper's hair. As he passes me he gives me a perfunctory peck on the cheek.

'I'll see you for our eleven a.m. meeting,' Aaron says to me and, before I can say anything back, he's disappeared into the hallway. A minute later, I hear the door closing.

I have wondered lately about all the early-morning meetings he's been having, and the late-night ones as well. Not to mention I've been feeling more and more like his secretary in the last year than his wife. There's definitely been a shift in the dynamics of our marriage but then we have been together for over nine years, so it's not necessarily going to be all hearts and roses any more. I know that, but I also know Aaron inhabits the kind of world where a little fling wouldn't be out of the ordinary. The stories I've heard from the wives of his golf friends have been enough to make me paranoid.

I push the thought from my mind as I sit down at our large dining table and check my phone. I've had plenty more RSVPs for the party from our friends. But so far, there's been no response from my family. The invitations went out on Monday in the first-class post and I calculate that they should've arrived at least a day or two ago. So why haven't I heard anything from any of them yet? I can't wait to see them again, my mother and my two sisters. There's so much I have to tell them; there are so many years to catch up on. I'm not going to worry just yet though. The invites would have been a big surprise. So I'll just have to sit tight for a few more days.

After all, I've already waited this long.

And I'm sure this reunion is going to be worth it.

# Chapter Four
# Nadia
# Now

I pick up the photograph that takes centre place on my fireplace. It's one I've looked at so often over the years and the image is imprinted on my brain like no other. My three girls, together. Sasha with her dark curls, Erin with her long auburn hair and Leah with her short, blonde bob. The three of them couldn't be more different, in appearance and in personality. The picture is one from Erin's twelfth birthday party. She always liked to be the centre of attention and that day was no exception. In the image she is in the middle of the group, hands on her hips and her head held high. Sasha is fourteen years old and standing awkwardly behind her two younger sisters, while little Leah, only eight years old, has her head turned slightly away from the camera, eager to be on to the next thing, to find her next adventure. I've always treasured this photo in particular because it sums the three of them up in such a natural way.

I put the picture frame back where it belongs. Turning around, I peek out the window. There's no sign of any cars on this quiet back-street so I busy myself in the living room, straightening cushions and throws. Some days I find the silence in this house deafening. It once used to be filled with the voices of three loud children and then three even louder teenagers. There was always shouting, singing, laughter and music. Nowadays, it's mostly just me here. I tend to pop to Sasha's house to see her and my adorable granddaughter Freya, as it's easier to go to them and slot into their busy lives.

It breaks my heart that my family is so splintered. I always imagined big Sunday lunches, with lots of us crowded round the table as I entered my golden years. Instead I haven't heard from my middle daughter, Erin, for ten long years. Not since the devastating night that changed everything for all of us. And Leah, my youngest, is off globe-trotting. I don't begrudge her at all – she always was the adventurous one. Although I wish I could see her more than just a few fleeting times on a video call each month. It would be even better to see her in person, to spend some proper time with her. Whenever she does return home in between trips, it only seems like five minutes and then she's gone again. Chasing awe-inspiring sunsets, sandy beaches and the perfect Instagram image.

I hope all that's about to change because finally Erin has reached out to us. Yesterday I received an invitation in the post to a Christmas party she's hosting, along with a photograph of two grandchildren who I never even knew existed. I was stunned to hear from her. After so long thinking I'd never see my middle daughter again, reading her handwriting has stirred up all kinds of emotions. It also pains me to think of Erin pregnant and without her mother. Just like it pains me to think of her juggling life with twin babies. When Freya was tiny I was at Sasha's house morning, noon and night. Jesse wasn't much help during the baby years so Sasha relied on me for advice and childcare and I was happy to be there for her. As a single mother of three chil-dren, I've experienced how hard raising your children without help can be, so I hope Erin has been OK. Deep in my bones, I believe she will have managed because she's a survivor – like me.

I wander over to my letter rack in the kitchen and pull out the gold invitation again. By the looks of it, Erin seems to be doing well for herself and I'm curious to see what her life is like now. The guilt of letting her go has never left me. Choosing between your children has got to be the hardest thing a mother can do, but circumstances forced me to do just that. I had to do what was right and stand by Sasha and Leah. I've endured a number of tragedies in my life but losing Erin has been the hardest.

Pacing back to my front room window, I peer through my curtains again. My visitor still hasn't arrived. So I slump down on the sofa and switch on the TV, flicking listlessly between the channels, my mind still on other things. I hear a phone ringing, which at first sounds like it's coming from the TV programme I've settled on. Then I realise it's my own ringtone and I race to retrieve my mobile out of my handbag. I manage to get to it in time and swipe the green call button.

'Hello love,' I say.

'Hi Mum.' It's Sasha's voice down the line. 'I need to talk to you.' Her voice comes out in a rush. 'Did you receive an invitation in the post?'

'Yes, I did. From Erin.'

'Me too,' Sasha sighs. 'I can't believe she's got in contact after all this time.'

Sasha sounds stressed and I dig my nails into my palms, waiting to hear what she's thinking.

'I can't go, Mum. I just can't.'

There they are, the words I was hoping my eldest daughter wouldn't say. Because this means I will have to choose again. I'll have to decide between Sasha and Erin.

Her sentences hang in the space between us and I'm not sure how to respond. Too afraid of saying the wrong thing and losing someone else I love.

'Mum? Are you still there?'

'Yes... Why don't we have dinner together and we can talk about it? Just me and you?'

'I can't tonight. It's Thursday. Freya has drama class.'

Sasha sounds distracted: I know how busy she is and hearing from Erin will have knocked her sideways. We need to have a proper chat about the invite though, so I try again.

'Could you pop round here when she's gone to bed? Will Jesse be home to watch her?'

'He should be. I'll message you later and let you know.'

'OK.'

'I've got to go.'

'Sasha, I love you.' But my words come too late. She's already gone. I hope that's not a sign of things to come and I pray Sasha will understand how I'm feeling.

Because I've already made up my mind. I am going to see Erin. I desperately want to see my flame-haired daughter and the grandchildren I've never met.

I'm going to the Christmas party.

# Chapter Five
## Erin
## Ten years ago

'You can't tell me what to do!' I'm yelling at the top of my voice and my throat is red raw. I'm sick of being told what I can and can't do by my meddlesome mother. I'm twenty-six, I know my own mind and my own heart. I want to make my own choices in life.

'If you do this, it will be the biggest mistake of your life.' My mother is standing two steps above me on the stairs in her little terrace house, her arms folded across her chest.

'At least it will be *my* mistake!' I shout.

I flounce down the rest of the stairs and hastily shove on my shoes. I bang open the coat cupboard and rummage around for my own jacket.

'Where is it?!' I cry. It's just typical that I'm trying to make a dramatic exit but I'm being thwarted by the fact I can't find my coat amidst the number of items in here.

'Just cool down,' Mum says behind me. 'Let's sit down, get a nice cup of tea and talk this through.'

'Don't you get it?' I whirl around to face her. 'I don't want to talk things through.'

She looks so taken aback that I stop myself. Perhaps all this is going too far, I need to pause and think. I breathe in deeply and try to push down my anger.

'Erin, I'm sorry but I have to step in and say something. Your sister—'

'What about me?' I retort, instantly furious once again.

'Oh Erin, just listen, you don't know what you really want. You're forever bouncing from one thing to another. Your sister—'

I throw my hands down in frustration, I still can't find the damn coat.

'I don't want to listen to any more of this.' I fling the peeling yellow front door open and march out into the night. It's cold and it's raining. I wish this argument had never started and that I could just go back up to my room, curl up in a ball and go to sleep. But it's the same argument I keep having with my mother on repeat and I've had enough.

I moved back home six months ago because I'd had a bad break-up. At twenty-six, I'd thought my life would have got going by now but I can't seem to find the right track to go down. I need to get away and to think things through, decide on a proper plan for going forward. I need to get away from this house.

I jam the key in the car lock and open the door to my battered red Ford Focus.

'Erin, don't go!'

# Chapter Six
# Sasha
# Now

I step inside my front door and the sound hits me. Christmas music is on full blast and I can hear giggles coming from the front room. What on earth is going on?

'Jesse? Freya?' I call, but there's no way my voice will be heard.

I dump my bags, shoes and coat and swiftly make my way towards all the noise. I find my husband and my little girl energetically jumping and twirling around our postage-stamp-sized front room. Freya is giddy with excitement and, as I come into the small space, she bumps into a side table, spilling an almost-full cup of blackcurrant juice across our fawn-coloured carpet.

'Freya!' I shout sharply, but still she doesn't hear me. So I'm forced to shout, 'Alexa, stop!' At the top of my voice, before Jesse and Freya finally notice me.

'What are you doing?' I point at the blackcurrant which is quickly saturating into the carpet. 'That's going to leave a stain.'

I hate myself for sounding so boring when I've interrupted a father and daughter moment of fun. But I've been working all day long; I've got a banging headache and now the carpet is probably ruined.

'Sorry,' Jesse says breathlessly. 'That only just happened. I'll go and get something to clean it up.'

I take a deep breath and then follow him into the kitchen. Jesse's not well acquainted with the cupboard where we keep our cleaning products, so I'm going to have to fish out the carpet cleaner for him.

'Sorry,' he says again, looking a little sheepish. 'We were just having a dance.'

'Yes, me and the whole street heard,' I snap as I hand the correct cleaning bottle over to him. Again, I hate myself for turning into the wife who gripes about the music levels in case it offends the neighbours rather than being the woman who jumps into the mosh pit and joins in with the dancing. But one of us has to be the responsible parent.

We both re-enter the living room and Jesse sets to work on cleaning up. Freya rushes towards me and gives me the biggest cuddle and instantly my annoyance melts away.

'Were you having a dance-off?' I ask, trying to shake off my stuffiness.

'Yes!' Freya bounces up and down before me. 'Because we're going to a paarrttayyyy!'

Oh no. I've gone over and over the invite situation in my head today and each time I came to the same conclusion. I'm not going to the party. I wasn't even planning on replying to Erin. Somehow, amongst the rollercoaster of emotions I'd experienced today, I'd completely forgotten that Freya had seen what was in the post.

'Freya, sit down for a second,' I tell her. 'The thing is, the invite was from someone we don't really know any more. So we're not going.'

Jesse stops scrubbing the floor at this news and stands up.

'I want to go,' Freya says, looking to Jesse for support. 'Daddy said we could.'

'What?' I glare at Jesse, praying this isn't true.

'Um...' Jesse flounders, and it's obvious he has told Freya she can go to the Christmas party.

'Freya, Mummy and Daddy just need to have a little chat.'

Freya swings her focus from me to Jesse and back again.

'Can you go up to your room and get ready for your drama class.'

'We are going to the party though, aren't we?'

'Freya, do as your mum says, upstairs.'

Freya exits the room and I give Jesse a hard glare. 'What were you thinking?' I say. 'Why did you tell her we could go to the party?'

'She wants to go, Sash, she's seen the invite. She's also seen that photo of her cousins. She's excited. She doesn't have any family her age.'

'Uh.' I shake my head. This is worse than I thought. 'So you just said we'd be going?'

'I didn't say that we weren't...' Jesse comes over to me and takes my hands in his. 'Seeing Erin again will be hard but you've wanted this for so long. I know deep down you miss her. You can't all carry on like this, not talking. It's not right.'

I snatch my hands free from his. 'You have no idea how I feel about Erin.'

'OK, but let's think about the bigger picture here too. What about what Freya wants? What about what your mum might want? And what about what I want?'

'You want to go?'

'It's a party in a big, swanky hotel. What do you think?'

I sigh. For a nanosecond, I thought Jesse was going to say something profound. Like he wanted to go to help our family get back together again. His reply is exactly what I should've expected because Jesse has never really grown up in the time we've been together. I fell for him because of his good looks and spontaneity. He's always been the life and soul of the party, that's what I loved most about him. But throw in twelve-hour working days, a hectic calendar and making life choices for our child without support and that love wears thin. If I'm honest, Jesse's never really stepped up. He's just left me to manage everything, while he still spends the majority of his week at the gym. It's true that he has some clients but a lot of the time when he's at the health club, he's not working: he's socialising. I try not to be resentful, it's just who he is. Except lately it's dawned on me that Jesse's way of life is causing me to lose myself to the daily grind of working and adulting.

I check my watch. 'I need to take Freya to her club. Will you be in to put her to bed afterwards? As I need to go and see my mum.'

'I was planning to—' Jesse starts to reply and then sees the expression on my face. 'Yeah, I'll be here.'

I head back to the kitchen to grab a drink of water and a snack before leaving the house, as I'm not going to have time for dinner today. Freya thunders down the stairs and we go out to the car together. She clips herself in and I start the engine. The radio station comes on, playing the same song she was dancing to fifteen minutes before. The song I turned off. Freya starts singing away to the lyrics.

I study her in my rear-view mirror and I have a sudden thought that makes my head spin. Maybe Jesse is right for once? Freya has plenty of friends, she's popular at school, but there is something different about having playmates who are also family. Despite how things have turned out, I was lucky to grow up with two sisters. Jesse and I tried to conceive again for a number of years but we didn't end up falling pregnant again. He was so hopeful for a boy, but it wasn't to be and we stopped trying a year or so ago. I'm edging towards forty now and our lives are busy enough. So Freya is an only child.

But Erin has twins, and they're around the same age as my daughter. So there's an opportunity for a new generation to help bring us all back together. I feel a flutter of optimism at the thought. Perhaps there is a chance we can put the past behind us and move on?

Maybe there is a future where my sisters and I can be friends.

Maybe we can all be one big happy family again...

# Chapter Seven
# Leah
# Now

'I'm back!'

The familiar smell of home – the hint of orange and cinnamon in the air, my mother's two favourite scents – hits me straight away when I walk through the door.

I place my Chanel travel bag on top of the matching suitcase and gently roll my aching shoulders. It's been a while since I've come home to England. I've been in Australia for eight months. I'm tanned, relaxed and full of new stories from my travels. However busy my work calendar is, I always aim to get back to England for Christmas, as my mom appreciates me being around for this time of year. It's important to her. And it's always good to see my big sister Sasha and my cute niece Freya as well.

'Leah!' Mom appears at the other end of the hallway and in a heartbeat she's wrapped her arms around me.

'I can't breathe!' I joke.

Mom finally lets go and stands back, looking me up and down. She does this every time I come home and I can predict exactly what she's going to say.

'You get more and more glamorous every time I see you. And look at that tan!'

'Mom, you saw me on a video call last week.'

'It's not the same though, is it?'

'Oh Mom,' I give her another cuddle in response.

'I love it when you call me Mom.'

I smile. She used to complain that with three girls shouting out 'Mum' all the time and sounding similar, she never knew which one of us it was. So I started calling my mother 'Mom' in my teenage years because we loved American TV. *The Gilmore Girls* was our favourite programme to curl up and watch together. It stuck and became my way of letting her know it was me calling down the stairs to her. Growing up in a house full of girls, I had to find ways to stand out and my mother thought it was sweet and endearing, so it was a win-win for me.

'What's for lunch?' I ask cheekily.

'Well, if you'd told me you'd be arriving I would've whipped up something special,' Mom says. 'So it will have to be soup and bread, I'm afraid.'

'I could do with warming up. It's freezing.'

'I do have a batch of freshly made cookies, if you want one while you're waiting?'

'Do you even need to ask?' I reply. My mom was never a great baker when we were growing up – she barely had the energy to shove food in the microwave. Since retiring, she's had more time on her hands and, as a result, she's discovered a talent for cooking.

In the kitchen, I settle down at the little round table with the coffee Mom has just made and select the cookie with the most chocolate chips from the tin.

'Mmmm, delicious,' I say. 'I might just have to have another one or two.'

I watch Mom as she cuts thick slices of her freshly cooked home-made bread. She's looking well. Her short, spiky blonde hairstyle suits her and she seems happy as she puts our lunch together, filling me in on the latest with the neighbours and her friends. I'm glad she's keeping busy, as I often get a pang of guilt when I think about all the places I've been to while she's here on her own.

All of my latest journeys are well-documented online. I began blogging about my travels when I first went on my gap year ten years ago. I only started it as a way to share my photos with friends and family. To my astonishment, the blog quickly gained momentum so I rolled out content across all the popular social media platforms at the time. I didn't know much about social media but I've learned a lot along the way and enjoy being able to share my passion for photography. Luckily, my following on Instagram exploded, giving me star influencer status, and I haven't looked back. The gap year still hasn't ended, thanks to the money I make from my advertising and brand partnerships. I do daily videos now and my TikTok fans can't get enough of my content. I'm grateful to be able to fund my travels around the world – it's everything I wished for and more.

My phone vibrates and I open the screen to check it. Although when I read the message that's just appeared I really wish I hadn't. I bite my tongue. I thought coming back to England would put an end to all of this. It seems changing phone numbers and continents isn't enough to shake off some people.

'Is everything OK, love?'

I look up and I realise I've been grimacing as I stared at my phone screen.

'Yeah, yeah. All good.' My life is far from good right now, but I don't want to get into my latest romantic entanglement with my mother.

An idea occurs to me and I suggest it immediately. 'Would you like to do a little trip with me, Mom? It doesn't have to be far, maybe somewhere in Europe?'

She turns around, her eyes glistening with emotion. 'Leah, that would be wonderful – as long as I wouldn't be cramping your style?'

'Of course not.' I feel a fresh wave of guilt. Why haven't I suggested this before? 'We could go for Christmas? Perhaps catch a flight to Berlin and see the German Christmas markets?'

'Oh, we couldn't go over Christmas. Little Freya would be so disappointed and, besides, I've ordered all of the food for Christmas dinner now.'

'Does all of that matter? Just for one year?'

'It's too short notice, Leah. How about we go just after New Year for a January break?'

'It's a deal,' I say. Even though inside my stomach is doing somersaults. I'm not sure I can risk hanging around here until the New Year. Not if a certain person has already worked out where I am. I'll agree for now and will think things over later.

'Besides, we've all been invited to a Christmas party.'

'Oh really, whose party?' I'm intrigued.

'Erin's.'

I was expecting to hear the name of an old school friend or work colleague. I wasn't expecting my estranged sister to be mentioned at all. Not after all this time. Not after what she did.

'Erin? She's been in touch?'

'Yes, I got this the other day.' Mom slides an envelope across the table.

I open it and study the contents. The invitation looks fancy, like the kind someone wealthy would send. Not like something someone from a run-down suburb would post. Not like an invite from someone from our family.

My mind is whirring and I'm wondering exactly how Erin's life has panned out over the last ten years. The location of the party is Burcott House, which sounds bigger than your average semi-detached. I also notice that Erin has signed the invite 'Erin Bailey-Scott', so she must be married. It's interesting that she's double-barrelled her maiden name. I assume this is because she thinks a double-barrelled surname sounds posh. But maybe using Bailey as part of her surname shows she hasn't forgotten us completely. I unfold the letter and skim over the words.

It's really smulchy stuff. There's lots about how she loves and misses Mom. She says she wants us all to meet her kids, her twins. My jaw drops: I never imagined Erin with twins. It doesn't escape my notice that Ophelia and Jasper are upper-class names. It also doesn't escape my notice that not once does Erin apologise in the letter she has written. This saddens me. Despite the heartache she has caused, she still can't even write that she's sorry. So I very much doubt she will be in a hurry to actually say those two important words either.

I sigh. This was not the Christmas I was expecting to come back to. Usually coming home is safe and familiar. As if I don't have enough problems right now.

'That was a big sigh,' Mom comments, her voice low and soft. Her eyes are glistening with emotion once more.

'Look, these are Erin's children.' She shows me a photograph of two flame-haired children.

'Oh! The little girl is so much like Freya!' I exclaim, surprised by the uncanny similarities between the child in the photo and the niece I adore.

Mom tugs the photograph from my hand. 'Maybe a little bit,' she says in a non-committal voice. The voice she uses when she wants to change the subject.

Instead, a tense silence hangs over us. I wait for Mom to say something else but she doesn't. She puts the soup and the bread down in front of me and sets about eating her own. I follow suit but then, when I can't stand the elephant in the room any longer, I ask the question burning on my lips.

'So, are you going to go?'

'I've thought about it a lot over the last couple of days. I wanted to talk to you and to Sasha first because I would like to see Erin again and those little ones too. I don't want to upset you or Sasha but this family feud has gone on for too long. I'm getting older and I want to make peace before it's too late.'

'Don't be silly!' I cry, jumping up and going over to her side of the table to give her a reassuring cuddle. I scoot into the seat next to her.

'You've got years left, Mom, don't be thinking like that,' I say. Her words have rocked me a little. My mom is fit and sprightly; she may be sixty-five but she's healthier than I am. I hate that she's been thinking like that.

'God willing,' she murmurs. 'It has gone on too long though. We need to at least try to be a family again.'

I study my mom, who is still clutching the photograph, and think about how heart-wrenching this must be for her. Not only has she not seen her middle child for years, she's also never met two of her grandchildren. I wonder how it came to this.

I clear my throat, frightened I'm going to cry. Because if I start crying, I might never stop. This whole situation happened because of me. If only I'd taken a different path that night. To be fair, Erin's behaviour and the way she reacted to the situation were the hammer blows. Her actions and the nasty things she said in the aftermath of the accident were the real reason everything erupted. She could have said sorry and made amends. But instead she left.

'You should go,' I say quietly.

'What?' my mom says, an expression of disbelief on her face.

'You should go,' I repeat.

'Really?'

'Yes, really. Like you said, you only have one life. You'll regret it if you don't.'

'Thank you Leah,' she says, squeezing my hand, and then gazing back down at the photograph of the two children. 'I want you to come too.'

'Me? No, I think you should see Erin first. I don't think me being there would be helpful. Besides, Erin might want to see you but I don't think she'd be happy to see me.'

'She does want you there. She sent you an invitation too.'

Mom goes over to one of the kitchen drawers and hands me an envelope identical to hers.

I take it and hold it in my hands. I feel weirdly unsettled. If Erin has written me a letter, what does it say?

There's only one way to find out.

# Chapter Eight
# Sasha
# Now

I still can't get my head around the fact that Erin has reached out. I mean, it's been ten *years*. Not ten days, ten weeks or even ten months. *Years*. When she first left we thought she'd come round. Come back to apologise. I thought we'd all kiss and make up soon enough. But the silence stretched on and on. I tried to speak to her. I called and texted but she changed her phone number. I sent messages on every social media platform I could find her on. I never had a reply. My own sister ghosted me.

Now she's expecting us all to come running to her. Jesse searched 'Burcott House' online and we were both gobsmacked by the size of the place. Burcott House seems to be a swanky hotel, with a big price tag, set on some kind of estate with acres of land. I can't even imagine how Erin went from her life with us to where she is now.

'Here you go, the next size up.'

I wince and then pull the changing room curtain to one side.

'Thank you so much,' I say, plastering on a smile as I take the dress from the helpful shop assistant before folding myself back in the too-small room with its glaring, unforgiving mirror.

I've been here for over an hour trying on different dresses. I had to give up on my usual size as it quickly became clear that I need the next one up. I tried to tell myself the sizing in this store was unrealistic but it's been a long time since I last went shopping and, truthfully, I've stretched all of my current leggings and jeans to their limit. Waistbands digging into me is something that's become the norm of late. Just another thing that seems out of my control.

Behind the closed curtains I shake my head with embarrassment, before holding my breath as I step into the black, sparkly dress. It's my last hope. I think I've tried just about everything else on. It's not really my style, I'm not a sparkly sort of person, but it seems I don't have much choice now thanks to my expanding waistline.

I drag the zip up my back and, to my relief, it reaches the top. I stand and survey myself in the mirror. My face is pale and puffy in contrast to my dark curls and the dark dress. I'm going to need a truckload of make-up to pull this off. Thankfully, my bingo wings are just about hidden by the capped sleeves. The dress reaches my knees and the whole outfit just makes me appear cuddly and frumpy. I hadn't quite realised that my weight gain in the last year had gone this far.

I curse myself for not getting more into shape over the summer but I can't do anything about it now. My life is busy and self-care is the last thing on my priority list. Besides, I've birthed a child and I'm getting close to the big four-zero and all the hormonal changes that come with that. This dress is covering my lumps and bumps as much as it possibly can so I try not to worry and be thankful for what my body can do. But I also vow to commit to the soup and salad diet between now and the 22nd December. We all come in different shapes and sizes, but for me, shifting a few pounds could help me feel a little more like my old self again.

Of course it doesn't help that my stunning younger sister is back in town. She's a natural beauty with long legs and high cheekbones. As a top social media influencer, she has the pick of the latest coats, bags and shoes thanks to her partnerships with various fashion brands which means that she always looks trendy and fresh. Beauty and wellbeing is at the centre of her world; every day she posts a new video across her social media platforms explaining her look. She tells her followers how she put her outfits together, where to buy them and goes into the most minute of details, even suggesting which eyeshadows to pair with an ensemble. Her lifestyle is so glamorous and Leah always looks sensational but I don't know how she does it. It looks exhausting putting that much thought into what you wear every day. But then again it's her whole life and it also pays. She rarely has to buy her own clothes and make-up and she gets enough sponsorships and freebies to allow her to have multiple changes of outfits a day. And that's only the half of it, she has partnerships with a plush hotel chain and a celebrity restaurant and she's always being asked to go on holiday to do travel reviews. Her life is a constant cycle of new photos, ads and video content on her blog feed. I love Leah to bits, but I do feel like a bit of a dinosaur next to her. I barely use Facebook these days, let alone have accounts on all the latest platforms.

I take the dress off and pull my bobbled, pale blue sweater and my trusty old jeans back on. I'm not exactly making the best of myself right now. I should really give my wardrobe an overhaul but the thought of trying on more clothes that aren't going to fit me doesn't fill me with joy. Instead, I decide to pay for the party dress and then head to the make-up counters in the department store. Perhaps I can sink into one of the chairs and get a makeover to make me feel better.

I'll then have to pay a high premium for the overpriced products that they'll use but I've been buying supermarket brands for years. It's time to treat myself.

I weave through the perfume aisles, dabbing on a bit of my favourite scent as I go, and then I work my way towards an available cosmetics counter. I don't think Jesse will be splashing out on Christmas presents this year, as he hasn't bothered buying me anything special for the last couple of Christmases, so this will be my present to myself instead.

As I sit in the chair and let the make-up artist work her magic, my mind runs through all of the things I need to do today. Freya is at a friend's house, so I have a rare Saturday afternoon to myself. I shouldn't really be sitting here getting pampered; there are presents to wrap and cleaning to do at home, but it's not like I do this all the time – or ever, even. I feel so tired I could nod off here while my face is primed and painted.

I've had trouble falling asleep for six months or more. Things have definitely got worse in the last few days since the gold envelope arrived in the post. I'm ashamed to admit that last night, as well as my sleeping pill, I also had a few glasses of red wine. I shouldn't have done, I was far too dozy this morning as a result, but I was also more chilled out than I've been in ages.

My mind drifts as my eyeshadow is added and my blusher applied. The thought of facing Erin when I'm looking so tired and chunky fills me with dread. But I feel as though I'm fighting the inevitable, which is why I came shopping for a dress. Jesse and Freya want to go to the party and Mum couldn't hide her emotions when we had a heart-to-heart about it so I know she does too. I don't want to be the stick-in-the-mud, the person who prevents this family reunion from going ahead. Instead, I decided to prepare myself and make sure I've got the tools to help me get through this. My battle outfit and my war paint.

Leah will be the deciding factor. I don't know what her reaction will be. Usually she runs from anything confrontational or difficult. She was still so young when the argument to end all arguments happened. It may all come to nothing. If Leah holds out and decides not to go, then I will stand shoulder to shoulder with her. Just like I did last time.

The make-up artist presents me with a small mirror and I'm relieved to see that she's brought some colour back into my face. The crow's feet that have started to form around my eyes are still there but the rest of my face is smoother and brighter. The magic of cosmetics. I thank her politely and buy everything she's recommending, crossing my fingers this will help me to transform from the dowdy woman I've become into a shinier version of myself.

As I leave the department store, I pray Leah makes the decision that will mean I can stay at home on the 22nd December and not have to worry about reunions, or waterproof mascara, or confronting the past.

But I've got a sinking feeling I'm going to end up at Burcott House...

# Chapter Nine
# Leah
# Now

I make my way upstairs, past the three school photographs still hanging in the hallway where they've been for what seems like forever. I open the door to my bedroom, which is largely unchanged from my teenage years, except all the popstar posters have been taken down, leaving tacky marks in random places over the walls.

Throwing myself down on my narrow single bed, I stare up at the ceiling. Memories rush through my mind of me and my sisters. The games we used to play, the songs we used to sing, the way we told each other everything. So many moments bonded us together. We used to be the three amigos, us against the world.

Don't get me wrong, I'm not viewing the past through rose-tinted glasses. We used to fight and argue and steal each other's clothes too. When we were younger allegiances used to change a lot. Sometimes on a daily basis. But it was always me and Erin ganging up on Sasha. Or Erin and Sasha, together lording it over me. It was never me and Sasha against Erin. So when Sasha took my side in the incident that split our family apart, I was shocked. My eldest sister could often be quite distant from me. I guess with the six-year age gap between us that was only natural. I must admit, at first, it did feel quite weird to have Sasha on my side. I guess she felt protective of me.

The truth is, I haven't really repaid Sasha for sticking up for me and then helping me to recover in the long months following the accident. I've hardly spent any time with her alone at all in the last few years. I do try to help out with Freya when I'm home. I love to play the fun auntie, taking my niece ice skating or to the cinema. The last few times I've seen her Sasha has looked so stressed that I think she's just been grateful that Freya has been entertained so she can sneak in a nap or put her feet up for a change. Sasha has always been like this though, the typical older sibling overachiever. Always taking on more than she can handle. I observe her manic life, juggling a demanding full-time job and parental responsibilities, and I know I've definitely made the right choice for me. I can do as I please. Go wherever I want and not have anyone to answer to.

Of course, the only reason I took a gap year in the first place was because I felt responsible for causing the major rift in our family. I still feel so guilty about it...

No more though, it's time to face up to things. I rip open the envelope to find my own party invitation. It's identical to Mom's but there's a different photograph of Erin's twins included; they're hanging from monkey bars in a play park. They both look more dishevelled and natural in this image. Their distinctive red hair stands out against the grey sky in the backdrop.

On the back of the picture, Erin has written: *To little duck, here are my own little ducklings, I hope you will meet them soon x*

I choke out a sob. I wasn't expecting this. I thought Erin might write me a letter warning me off, telling me not to come with Mom. Instead, she's said the sweetest thing she could. She always used to call me *little duck* when we were younger. Somehow, I'd forgotten that.

I read my letter. It's shorter than Mom's but her tone is warm: she's done fighting, she misses me and wants to be friends again. I take a deep breath. Maybe I'm finally ready to move on?

I did a lot of running away from my problems during my twenties. Being back home usually makes me feel anxious and uncomfortable. The awful flashbacks have calmed down in recent years but the past still feels like a weight on my shoulders. I hit thirty a couple of years ago so I really need to confront all the family drama once and for all. There's no way I can seriously think about moving home until I've tried to patch up my relationships with my sisters. Then again, I'm not sure settling down is for me. I enjoy my lifestyle so coming back to England permanently isn't necessarily on my agenda right now. It would be nice to have the option though.

'Mom,' I say as I wander back into the living room. 'I'll come with you.'

My face is tear-streaked but Mom will understand why. She opens her arms at my words and we're hugging again. We've run through a lot of emotions tonight but I feel weirdly zen and ready to face Erin again.

As we're sitting watching an old favourite on the telly together, I sip a warm mug of tea and flick through my social media apps. It's cosy in this room, fairy lights are strung around the fireplace and the comforting smell of one of Mom's winter-scented candles is making me feel sleepy. I upload a few photos I took today in the airport and schedule some updates for tomorrow. I'm so engrossed in what I'm doing that I jump slightly when I get a message notification. One sentence flashes on the screen:

*YOU CAN'T HIDE FROM ME FOREVER.*

I delete it immediately. A wave of anxiety floods through me. I've received a number of messages like this since I left Australia, so I would be a fool to think the sender won't be in contact again but I don't have the mental energy to think about it tonight. As the film dialogue I've seen a zillion times before plays out on the screen in front of me, my mind strays. Perhaps Erin really is living the high life. Maybe she is rich now? If so, it wouldn't be such a bad thing to become best buddies again. Money can solve a lot of things.

And I could do with some help to get me out of the latest mess I've got myself into...

# Chapter Ten
## Erin
## Ten years ago

I don't look back, I climb into the driver's seat and rev my engine. It's really lashing down now, the rain all of a sudden much heavier. The windows are all steamed up and I can't really see properly but I just want to get away fast. I'm so furious about the heated words I've just had with my mother.

I flick on the window wipers and the heater and then swing the car past our front hedge and into the quiet road. I put my foot down, my anger fuelling my desire to increase my speed.

I need to get away; I don't know where I'm going but I jam the car quickly into third gear. The windows are just starting to demist but it's pitch black and there's no street lighting on this road. And then I hear a sickening thud.

I slam on my brakes and jerk to a halt.

Something – or someone – has just hit the bumper of my car.

# Chapter Eleven
# Sasha
# Now

As I drive down the dark, winding country lane I can't stop thinking that agreeing to this evening was a bad idea. I finally accepted Erin's invitation after Mum said she was going to the party and she pleaded with me to go with her. I've thought of nothing else in the last couple of weeks, the idea of going to this country manor fills me with apprehension. I want to be at home, cosy in my favourite set of pyjamas, making my way through a box of chocolates and watching an old Christmas movie. Instead, I'm squinting into the fog and gloom and praying that I don't scratch the car's paintwork on the overgrown hedgerows that seem to be closing in on us the further down the road we go.

'Come on Sasha, you're barely clearing second gear,' Jesse grumbles in the passenger seat. 'I said to you I'd drive.'

The only thing worse than me driving as carefully as I can down this narrow, unknown track is Jesse screeching round sharp corners while I cling onto my seat with white knuckles. Jesse is far too cocky when he's driving. In fact, he's cocky in most situations. He's got this natural confidence that often means he breezes through life, but on a few occasions his attitude has got him into trouble. So I'd much prefer to be in control of the wheel – especially when our daughter is sitting in the back of the car.

'Sasha, did you hear me? Shall we just swap, this journey is taking twice as long as it needs to.'

'No,' I snap back at him louder than I intended. I glance in my rear-view mirror, hoping Freya hasn't picked up on my tone, but she's fully immersed in her iPad.

Jesse sighs heavily and fidgets in his seat.

'Just let me concentrate,' I say under my breath. 'We left in plenty of time and we don't want to be the first ones there.'

Now it's Jesse's turn not to respond. Our interactions tend to take on a stilted stop-and-start pattern these days. Neither of us prepared to smooth things over. I wish Jesse would ask me how I'm feeling, maybe ask what he can do to help make the meeting with Erin tonight a little easier. But he doesn't.

'Well we don't want to miss out on the free booze,' Jesse mutters.

This is more typical of my husband's line of thought. I glance at him out of the corner of my eye and, not for the first time, I wonder what I saw in him all those years ago. He used to make me laugh until my stomach ached, I used to feel so carefree with him. But eventually life took us on a path that meant I had to get a proper job, learn how to parent a child and run a house. Jesse has never really grown up since the days in which we used to go on endless nights out, lying in bed until midday before heading out for leisurely dinners. In fact, he still goes on those nights out with the same set of friends he's had since his teenage years. They're still all so immature: their idea of a good night out involving necking as many pints as possible and playing silly pranks on one another. It completely contradicts his healthy, clean eating and focus on exercise the rest of the time. Jesse says those friendships allow him to let his hair down, which I'd be fine with if the get-togethers weren't quite so frequent. It's become a repeated source of arguments between us. I'd love to have a weekend away with my husband or even a night at a pub but, lately, whenever I suggest this he always seems to have something planned with one of his mates.

'Sasha—'

'Don't,' I snap back at him again. 'I'm stressed enough about tonight without you making this drive harder than it already is.'

I try to keep my focus on the road, wishing we'd ordered a taxi instead. It would've been much easier than navigating these unknown roads. Except, I didn't want to feel like I was trapped at Burcott House, on Erin's territory, without an escape route if I needed one. I can't help it; the negative thoughts have been overtaking the positive ones. I feel like I've been railroaded into this evening by Jesse, by Mum and by Freya. Even Leah seemed enthusiastic about tonight. So why do I feel so different? Why do I have such an impending sense of doom about this whole thing?

'Just chill,' Jesse says, his voice softer now.

'I'm trying to,' I say with gritted teeth. 'I don't know why we had to meet at this damn party. It all feels so wrong. We haven't seen each other in years, there's so much to be said, to be worked out. A venue full of other people hardly seems like the place for us to meet again.'

I can see out of my peripheral view that my husband is shaking his head.

'Listen, maybe Erin was trying to make sure your first meeting was a fun one. With other people around there might not be as much tension.'

'Maybe you're right...' I want to believe this but I'm so frazzled that I can't think straight.

'Wait a second, did my wife just say I'm right?' Jesse laughs and fist-pumps the air.

'Well, let's see how the evening goes before you take this as a win. I really hope you're right though.'

My sentence hangs in the air between us until the satnav cuts in to tell us Burcott House is round the next bend.

'Are we nearly there, Mummy?' Freya pipes up from her seat behind me.

'Almost!' I say, trying to make my voice sound jovial.

'Yay!'

Her response is so simple and so sweet. Sometimes I wish I could step out of 'adulting' just for a day. It's made me far too serious.

'Wowzer, look at this!' Jesse says as we pull up to a large pair of wrought-iron gates, decked out in twinkling lights.

'Where even is the house?'

I stare wide-eyed at the scene in front of me as the gates swing open to let us in. There's a long gravel driveway that disappears into an avenue of trees and we drive along slowly. Snowflakes are falling lightly but the way ahead is well-lit with twinkling lights entwined in the tree branches above us. We curve left and come out from the canopy of trees and the house suddenly comes into view.

It's an enormous country house, like some kind of National Trust palace or a minor royal's home. There's ivy twisting around some of the windows, a huge wreath on the door and the roof is covered in snow.

It's my turn to express my awe at the setting now. 'This is huge, I can't even imagine how many bedrooms it has.'

At first, we thought Erin might have hired Burcott House for the occasion, which still would've cost some serious money at this time of year. But Leah did some cyber stalking and Erin's social media accounts aren't as private as they once used to be. Leah's online snooping also pulled up a web page for Burcott House which confirmed that Erin and her husband Aaron are indeed the owners. The Bailey-Scotts, as Erin has styled her family, are now living life on the next level.

'This is amazing!' Freya squeals, already hastily unclipping her seat belt.

'Wait, we need to park,' I say, gripping the steering wheel tightly.

The house is all lit up and there's clearly lots of movement going on behind closed doors. I shiver, despite the car heating being on. When I voiced my concerns about meeting for the first time in a party setting, Mum came up with a solution. She messaged Erin's number and asked for a phone call as a first step. They apparently chatted for over an hour. Mum looked like she was walking on clouds when she relayed the conversation.

She told me Erin suggested we arrive an hour before the party began. She was hoping the party itself would provide a good backdrop to our first meeting, not too much pressure. And she also said she hoped it would be the start of many more family gatherings.

'Let's park then,' Jesse says, jolting me from my thoughts. 'Otherwise Freya will burst.'

As we draw closer, I see there's a waterfall feature positioned near the front of the house, with two unicorns in the middle, lit up with a multitude of colours. They're just as mesmerising as the Kelpies in

Scotland but on a smaller scale. I follow the road that curves around the side of the building and I can't help but notice the depth of this place is just as expansive as the frontage. I'm curious to see what inside is like.

We pull into a parking bay and I exhale deeply. I'd been holding my breath for most of the tense journey. I'm not looking forward to the drive back, but I can't say I'm looking forward to the next step in the evening either.

Freya jumps out of the car as fast as she can and Jesse isn't far behind. I flip the mirror in the car down and study my face. I've gone for the full works with my make-up to try and hide how tired I am. I breathe in and out, trying to remember the advice on my wellbeing app.

'Come on, Mummy!' Freya cries, and she's tugging at my hand, propelling me out of the car. I stumble and, for a second, I think I'm going to fall. But Jesse is next to me, saving me from crashing down towards the ground.

'Woah! And you haven't even had a drink yet!' My husband jokes.

I lean on Jesse's strong, reassuring arm and straighten myself out.

'Thank you,' I say, my voice sounding shaky. Despite our recent marital problems, I'm glad to have Jesse by my side tonight. We've been together a long time and, although I may feel exasperated by him at times, there's no doubt I still love him.

As we stride forward, my stomach is fluttering and the world around me feels unreal. The darkness, the grandeur, the twinkling lights are all somehow working together to distort normality. I feel like I might faint. I reach for Freya's hand, her warm fingers curl around my own and this small action helps soothe my nerves.

Jesse is a few steps ahead of me and he confidently knocks on the cherry red door. Immediately, it swings open.

And I gasp as I see the person standing before me.

# Chapter Twelve

# Jesse

# Now

As we walk along the impressive driveway to the biggest house I've ever seen, it's mind-blowing to think this is where Erin is living now. It's a proper millionaire mansion and then some. It's like something out of a big budget movie. I try to count how many windows there are and give up as there are so many. I can't even imagine how much this gaff costs but it's more than I'll ever earn in my lifetime. It's weird to think of all of this belonging to Erin and her husband.

I look out of the corner of my eye at my wife, her shoulders are high and hunched, the tension running through her body plain to see. If it wasn't for the fact that Freya was in the car with us, I would've lost my cool with Sasha by now. She's been driving me insane recently with her overactive imagination and her ability to worry about anything and everything. I keep telling her she needs to have a break from that job of hers. It's too much, too many hours. She never gets to kick back and relax. Always hopping on her laptop to reply to one more email. It's no wonder she's exhausted.

I've been telling Sasha for months that she needs to go to the doctor. The sleeping tablets she's on aren't working. She needs a different medication or a higher dose or something because she's tossing and turning all night, unable to rest, but she won't listen to me. She just keeps saying it's fine, she can manage. When it's obvious she can't.

I puff out a sigh. I wish she'd let me help her but she just keeps fighting everything I suggest. I can't make her go to the doctor. Just like I can't make her take time off work. At the end of the day, she's her own person and she's got to make those decisions. I've tried but there's only so much I can do; she has to want to change the way she's living her life.

It's fair to say the two of us have grown apart over the last few years. Sasha doesn't confide in me in the way she used to and I've retreated from our conversations as well. I've got to look after my own wellbeing and there's only so much I can take of Sasha's high-octane stress. I also don't want my Freya to follow the hard path in life that her mother is taking. I want Freya to appreciate the little things, to laugh long and hard, to be healthy and happy. When she's older I want Freya to work to live, not live to work. So when Sasha is working late, I watch silly TV shows with my daughter, I let Freya stay up past her bedtime, and recently we've got in the habit of going for a bike ride together after school. Freya is my world and, like any father, I want the best for her.

The journey here was awful. I said I would drive but Sasha insisted and got into the driving seat before me. I knew that navigating our old car down the small country roads in the dark wouldn't help with her anxiety this evening. And I was correct. I've tried to take over several times, but instead I had to sit balling my hands into fists, trying not to criticise how slow she was going. It's a miracle we haven't ended up in a ditch.

Sasha didn't want to come tonight but everyone ignored her moody reaction to the idea of accepting Erin's invite. Freya was thrilled at the idea of meeting her new cousins, I'm never one to say no to a party, Nadia is desperate to heal the family rift and, surprisingly, even Leah was game. I guess everyone opposing Sasha's objections has made the whole thing worse for her. I wasn't sure she would actually make it out of our tiny terrace house as she was really dragging her heels, but we're here now. I hope she loosens up a bit when we get inside.

As we walk along the gravel driveway, I can feel the excitement building in me. I get the impression this is going to be a proper party, no expense spared. It's not every day you get to go somewhere like this. So I'm going to make the most of it.

I'm aware that Sasha is still scowling next to me but I'm not going to let her emotions get to me. Tonight is for second chances and new beginnings.

I knock on the bright red door of the enormous house we've spent the last hour driving to. I can't wait for the evening to begin.

# Chapter Thirteen
## Sasha
## Now

Before us stands a woman in an elegant, sparkling gold dress. She looks like Princess Catherine attending a film premiere. She radiates beauty, her fiery locks sleek and straight, tied back in an elegant chignon bun, her green cat eyes shining. The years fall away and I see my sister Erin.

I try to open my mouth but I find I cannot speak.

'Erin! So good to see you!' Jesse and Erin hug, so naturally, like this whole thing isn't a big deal.

Freya is beside me, admiring the flawless woman in front of her, and I can tell she is enchanted. Erin bends down, so her face is at the same height as my daughter's.

'You must be Freya,' Erin says, with a stunning smile. 'I'm so glad you came.'

'I love parties!' Freya declares. 'Your dress is pretty.'

'Thank you, sweetie.'

'Can I meet my cousins?' Freya's eyes are big and round and hopeful.

'Absolutely.' Erin gives my daughter another wide smile and then stands up, turning to me.

'May I hug you?' Erin asks me tentatively, some of her confidence slipping away.

I nod, aware that if I speak right now I'll probably sound all croaky and emotional.

Erin leans in and puts her arm around me. Her perfume is strong, an unexpected scent, so unlike the Erin I used to know. I stand awkwardly and stiffly, feeling as though the overwhelming smell of the perfume might suffocate me.

Stepping back, I try not to cough.

'Are you OK?' Erin asks.

I nod.

'This is mad,' she says in a whisper. 'Thank you for coming.'

Time has stood still and I'm gazing at this grown-up version of my little sister, still wracking my brains as to what on earth I can say to bridge the gap of the last ten years. I stutter, struggling to fill the silence.

'Let's go and get a drink,' Erin says, hooking her arm through mine, like she used to do when we were younger. Everything about her is so familiar and yet so different.

I take in my surroundings and see there's the most gigantic Christmas tree I've ever laid eyes on taking up an entire corner of the reception room that we're in. It's like something you'd see in a department store, too polished and too fake. Nothing like the kind of Christmas trees we have at home. Real ones that are forever shedding pine needles, each branch weighed down with baubles and decorations that represent so many memories. I can see them all so vividly: the star Freya painted at nursery, the papier-mâché globe we created together last year, the little robin given to me by my nana.

There's a reception desk in the lobby, reminding me that Burcott House is a hotel and not Erin's actual home. Although I'm sure wherever she lives is bound to be as stylish and sumptuous as this. Erin sweeps us through an incredible foyer, which is absolutely spectacular, from its white marble floor to the gigantic chandelier sparkling above us. The black wooden bannisters contrast with the gleaming white of the rest of the room. A natural tinsel decoration is entwined along the spiral staircase and there's another enormous Christmas tree in this space, its colour scheme matching the tree in the reception entrance. The effect is magical and shows off just how big this place is. I notice there are at least three floors above us.

Erin guides us along several wide airy corridors into a smaller room with a large roaring fireplace and several squishy armchairs. Freya and Jesse follow us. There are rows and rows of shelves running around the room, stacked with books. Not quite a library but not far off.

'This is the Snug,' Erin tells us.

'It's like *Beauty and the Beast*!' I hear Freya saying as she chatters beside me.

We walk through another large room, which holds a sleek, fully stocked bar.

'Nice! What a place.' I can hear Jesse behind me, and I don't need to see his face to know how impressed he is.

Erin nods at the bar staff who are busy stacking glasses and cleaning down the already shining bar tops.

'Everything OK, Nia?'

She pauses as a member of her staff asks her about the ingredients for a particular cocktail. My sister replies and I take the opportunity to peel myself away from her. I reach out for my daughter's hand and pull her close to me. When Erin has finished her conversation, she strides forward on her four-inch heels with the three of us in her wake. I follow, wondering what tonight will have in store for our family.

Erin leads us into the next room, where I can hear voices; Mum and Leah are sitting on an L-shaped sofa, looking so small in this big space. The jet-black grand piano in the corner contrasts tastefully against the white walls and there's intricate plasterwork on the arches, along with an ornate ceiling rose and swirling patterns on the high ceiling above us.

'Sit down, make yourselves comfortable.' Erin ushers us towards Mum and Leah.

We do as she suggests while Erin gracefully perches on a conveniently placed armchair. I have an overwhelming, ridiculous urge to start singing: the way we're sitting makes me feel like we should be auditioning for a music show and Erin is the judge.

'Did you have a good journey?' Mum asks, leaning forward to catch my eye.

'A few hair-raising corners,' Jesse answers, 'but not too bad.'

'Ah, I'm afraid those lanes are the price we pay for being out here in the sticks,' Erin says wryly, as though she's living on a remote farmstead rather than a country mansion that's a stone's throw from the nearest upmarket village.

'Where are my cousins?' Freya pipes up, undeterred from her quest.

Erin laughs. 'They'll be down in a minute or two.'

Mum claps her hands together, the delight on her face matching Freya's.

'We've all had a nice chat,' Mum says. She clearly arrived super early, so eager to be here and see her own flesh and blood.

For so long it's just been my mother and me, our world having shrunk to the two of us and Freya and Jesse. To have both Leah and Erin in the same room with us after all this time is surreal.

Freya takes centre stage, telling everyone about her Christmas nativity play and even acting little bits out for us. She was so excited to be one of the three wise men this year and practised the songs over and over in the run-up to the performance.

The waitress Erin was speaking to earlier, an exceptionally attractive woman with long, raven hair, comes into the room to take our orders. I can tell that Jesse has noticed her good looks as well. I fold my hands neatly in my lap, trying to keep them still. But really I can't wait for a drink to quench my nerves. As soon as the glass of red wine is in my hand, I'm knocking it back like it's water.

The lives Erin and I are living are poles apart. If she has the resources to run a hotel like this and to have bar staff at her beck and call for a party, then it dawns on me she will have a gardener, a cleaner and who knows how many other staff employed to create this perfect illusion.

What did she do to get all this? How has she risen so high?

We make small talk, asking safe questions that aren't too probing. Freya chatters away about dance class and school and all her friends. She entertains us with her childish anecdotes and it's exactly what we all need. An icebreaker.

'Here they are!' Erin smiles, standing up as her twins come into the room. They're not bounding energetically, as children usually do before parties. They're walking in a way that makes me think they could be catwalk models, aware of their audience, chins high and backs straight.

'Oh, my goodness!' My mum is crossing the room, unable to wait a few further seconds for an introduction.

'I'm your nana,' she's saying. Before we know it, there are tears tumbling down her face and her words are all coming out in a rush.

Leah springs forward and produces a wad of tissues from her bag, circling her arm around our mother's waist.

'It's OK,' Erin is saying in a high-pitched voice. 'Ophelia, Jasper, this is your grandmother. She's been looking forward to meeting you.'

I close my eyes briefly, to shut out the scene unfolding before me. I can't help but analyse every word. *Grandmother* sounds so formal. And to say she's been looking forward to seeing them is the understatement of the century.

'Sorry, sorry,' Mum is saying, her cheeks pink with embarrassment. 'I didn't mean to cry.'

Ophelia and Jasper are obviously wary of the strange woman in their home who they have absolutely no connection to. The two children are spotless in their party outfits. Jasper is in a suit that makes him look older than his years and Ophelia has on a white dress that looks brand new. There's no way I'd let Freya wear a white outfit; it would be dirty in minutes.

Erin propels them forward and they give my mother awkward little hugs. Jasper falls back silently and I can see Ophelia wrinkling her nose, as if the whole situation displeases her. As I watch I think what an odd expression it is for a child to pull. Like her brother, she seems very mature and I wonder what kind of childhood these two have had. Presumably money is no obstacle for the Bailey-Scott family but, as the saying goes, too much of something isn't necessarily a good thing.

Freya bounds forward, unable to contain her joy.

'Hi!' she says, smiling widely. 'I'm Freya, I'm your new cousin!' She is gushing, so full of happiness at this first meeting. Unaware of the tensions running between the adults behind her. I chew my lip, hoping she doesn't get rejected.

Ophelia raises her eyebrows, another grown-up expression on a young face. 'I know,' she replies. Then, to my relief, my niece stretches out her hand. 'Come with me, I'll show you where the party is going to be.'

Freya takes her cousin's hand, before glancing back at me to check if this suggestion is OK.

'Go have fun!' Erin cuts in before I can say anything.

I nod in agreement, not wanting to sound too overprotective or stuffy.

Freya gives a little whoop in celebration and the two girls go off through the door into the next room. Poor Jasper trails behind them.

'Aww, so cute,' Erin says, unaware of our mother standing watery-eyed next to her, watching the grandchildren she's only just met disappear after such a short hello.

My mum comes and sits back down beside me. 'Don't worry,' I whisper to her. 'There will be plenty of time to get to know them.' I only hope I'm right. The whole set-up feels so staged and unnatural.

I guess we all have different ideas about what works for the backdrop to a family reunion. A full-on, glitzy party would not be top of my list but we have a little bit of time to talk before Erin's other guests arrive. I'm intrigued who else will be turning up. It's odd to think of Erin with a whole social circle we don't know about. We used to be so close. Her friends were my friends and vice versa. We shared everything, all our hopes, dreams and secrets. Now she has a whole other world that doesn't involve the rest of the Bailey family at all.

Although I'm sure we will find out all about Erin's new life soon enough.

# Chapter Fourteen
# Erin
# Now

'Welcome, welcome!' I exclaim with an exaggerated brightness to my voice.

My older sister is standing before me and I'm shocked at how different she is. She used to be my idol, the one I looked up to in my teenage years for fashion and make-up advice, encouragement with my school exams, career choices and everything in between. I can remember going through a stage of wanting to be exactly like Sasha. I hated my red, noticeable hair. I didn't know any other redheads; I stuck out and just wanted to be like everyone else around me. Sasha has these luscious dark locks that cascade down her back in magnificent curls. I envied her so much back then.

Now her face is pale; life has worn her down. I've found out already that she has a daughter and is an assistant headteacher. I can imagine her life is busy and stressful. Is it wrong that I feel a little smug in comparison? I've been working out for months to look my absolute best for tonight. I was already in decent shape but I feel on top form now, my arms toned, my abs defined, my skin glowing with good health. I selected this dress carefully, from an exclusive Italian designer, to show off my toned physique. It's important I appear every inch the perfect hostess. I also didn't want to risk any possibility of someone else turning up in the same outfit. The embarrassment would just be too much.

For a moment, I'm thrown by seeing Sasha again. But I quickly brush this feeling aside and switch into hostess mode.

'You must be Freya.' I bend down to Sasha's daughter. 'I'm so glad you came.'

I usher in Sasha along with her husband and child. The little girl is sweet, full of confidence. With her long red hair and big green eyes she looks a lot like my own Ophelia.

'Let's go and get a drink,' I say, hooking my arm through Sasha's, just like we used to do when we were younger.

My heart is beating at a faster pace than normal but I manage to keep myself composed. Guiding Sasha and her family through the entrance rooms, I walk expertly in my latest pair of Jimmy Choos. As I lead the way through the striking foyer, my favourite space in the house, I'm checking everything is as flawless as it can be. We had a truckload of new Christmas decorations this year to ensure the colour scheme was perfectly matched, right down to the very last bauble. I can see Sasha looking round in awe, her mouth gaping at the bar and the staff I employ to run it. I'm confident the life I built with my handsome husband, two adorable children, successful business and a house to die for is going to be incredibly impressive to my estranged family.

'This is the Snug,' I say, feeling like I've really made it now and I'm some sort of host on a property TV show. Sasha and I used to watch *Cribs* together when we were teens and we'd dream about living in a big mansion instead of the little terrace house that often felt claustrophobic. I wonder if she remembers too.

We reach the room where my younger sister Leah and my mother are already ensconced. Seeing my family in the flesh is stirring up all kinds of difficult memories. Now she's here, I can't quite bring myself to think of Nadia as 'Mum'. She lost the right to that title a long time ago. Although I try to make sure I'm saying 'Mum' when addressing her as I don't want to offend her and make things awkward. But it's going to be hard to remember.

I've thought of my estranged family a lot over the last decade and I've paid a fortune in therapy sessions over the years as well. It was my therapist who suggested I think of my mother as 'Nadia' to view her outside of her role as my parent. I'm sure the therapist was trying to get me to empathise with the tricky situation my mother was put in, but thinking of her in this way actually helps me to distance myself from her. I had wondered if seeing my family might help to melt away all of my remaining resentment towards them but instead my head is all over the place.

'Sit down, make yourselves comfortable,' I say, still grinning like a Cheshire cat. My face is going to ache from all the fake smiling by the end of the party.

A stilted conversation begins between the adults until Freya takes centre stage and removes some of the pressure from us all. She tells us all about her Christmas nativity play. I'm quite taken with the little girl; she reminds me of myself as a child. I always relished the opportunity to be the star of the show in school performances.

I arrange for the first generous round of drinks to be served. I've chosen our best waitress Nia to be on hand for this part of the evening. I interview new staff and it's also up to me to hire them and fire them. So I take a keen interest in who is excelling in their role and who is not. Nia does her job reliably and I'm sure she will help things run smoothly.

Nia takes the orders efficiently and returns swiftly with everyone's drinks. In my own glass there is only tonic water and lime. I've got to keep a clear head tonight but I'm hoping once the alcohol starts flowing for everyone else they will feel a little more relaxed. Sasha drains her first glass very quickly. I top it up and make a mental note to make sure one of our servers is particularly attentive to my elder sister. From her body language it's obvious she needs to unwind.

Sasha isn't saying anything. I take this as a win, if she's lost for words then I'm starting tonight with the upper hand. Everything is going to plan.

I wanted to see my family for many reasons. I want to right the wrongs of ten years ago. And I have genuinely missed them all. It's been so strange not having them in my life, but it also feels bizarre for all of them to be before my eyes right now. But I want them to know I've made it in the world and achieved my dreams. All without any help from them. Everything I've done in the last ten years is to prove to myself – and to them – that I could survive without them. And there's another reason I've gathered us all together tonight as well...

'Here they are!' I jump up as my children enter the room. Ophelia is wearing an exquisite white dress with a silver bow tied at her waist and another silver bow in her red hair. Jasper is wearing an adorable light blue suit. He looks so grown up in it.

Before I can do any introductions, Nadia has flown across the room, tears streaming down her face and arms outstretched. Ophelia and Jasper both recoil away from her and I don't blame them. They've never seen this woman before, so I can understand why they're taken aback. I feel cross with Nadia for being so over the top. Surely she must realise this is a daunting situation for a child.

I'm also surprised at the outpouring of emotion from my mother; she must've realised there was a possibility that I'd have children of my own? And that she'd miss out on their lives as well as mine? Or maybe she's never considered it. I expect she didn't think I would amount to much – or maybe she didn't think I was the type to marry and have children. Maybe she's feeling bad for taking my sister's side over mine. I hope so. My therapist tells me this kind of thinking isn't healthy but I can't help it, not after everything I've been through.

I encourage Ophelia and Jasper to say hello. It's a lot for them to take in, a group of new people who are the family they've never met. I've briefed my children on how to behave, what I expect of them. Much to my husband's dismay, Jasper is a shy boy, so when he hangs back and keeps his expression neutral I'm expecting it. But Ophelia follows my instructions to the letter. She holds out a hand, gives a glimmer of a smile and invites Freya to go and see the main rooms where the party will be held, just as I asked her to. Her white dress is pristine; she looks so neat and well-turned out. My heart swells with pride. She's such a good girl – the model child.

With the children out of the way, I can give everyone my proper attention. I play the dutiful hostess, nodding and agreeing with the observations being made about the three youngsters. I make sure to top up everyone's wine glasses again. Sasha drained all of her second glass in a few short minutes.

Then, at precisely the right moment, my husband walks in.

# Chapter Fifteen
## Leah
# Now

I'm not usually a wine drinker but, as that's what's on offer, I sip the cool liquid slowly. I feel shaken up by how upset Mom was at seeing Erin's twins. Mom used to be so tough when I was younger but she seems to have mellowed in recent years. I knew tonight was going to be hard, and I was right. The voice inside my head telling me this whole situation is my fault hasn't let up since we got here. I'm fed up with carrying this burden of guilt all the time. So I've made my mind up to say something, to mention the unmentionable and get it out of the way. It'll either clear the air or stop the evening in its tracks before it's even started. I'm prepared to risk it, because at least then we won't all be pretending. Like we are now, sitting round a table full of drinks, acting like nothing ever happened.

I wish there were some spirits on offer. A quick shot of vodka might give me the courage I need. My right leg twitches restlessly, I listen to Jesse and Mom direct the conversation and I wait until there's another pause so I can say my bit and then move on.

The room falls silent and I realise this is my chance. 'There's just something I wanted to say...' I start. But my words fade away as a man comes striding into the room and everyone's attention is pulled away from me.

The man is shorter than average but his presence fills the room. His movements are deliberate and confident. He is dark-haired and classically attractive, with a chiselled jaw and brooding grey eyes. He's wearing a tailored suit that's surely designer and he's obviously at ease in his surroundings. This must be Aaron, Erin's husband.

'Darling!' Erin says, springing forward to stand by the man's side. She clutches his hand in hers and does a round of introductions. Aaron stares at me a beat too long and I blush under his intense gaze. I look away, with the knowledge that he is the sort of person you want to notice you. He's handsome, he's rich and, as he speaks to us all, it's apparent he is also very charming.

Watching Erin standing next to Aaron, I can see they make the perfect couple. They look beautiful together – I can almost picture their wedding day photos. The two of them have everything: the perfect marriage, the perfect children and the perfect house. It's hard not to be a little envious.

Aaron sits down amongst our group, effusive in his welcomes. He seems genuinely pleased to meet his wife's family. I wonder if he knows why Erin fell out with us all. My cheeks burn red at the thought. It's only natural that Erin would've told him her side of the story. And not the whole truth.

'Leah, you were about to say something?' Erin says, staring at me expectantly.

'Was I?' I lie. 'Oh, I can't remember.' Another lie.

Erin smiles sweetly at me. I swiftly change the subject. 'How long have you been living here?'

'About seven or eight years now,' Erin replies. 'We actually live in the cottage in the grounds. Burcott House is a boutique hotel.'

When no one says anything, Erin continues, 'I run the hotel business, but it makes a good venue for a party as well!'

Erin's laughter is tinkling, nothing like the raucous laughter I remember. Her accent is more polished too; perhaps she's had elocution lessons to fit in with Aaron? Or maybe she's just a good actress.

Aaron joins in the conversation. 'Erin is too modest, Burcott House is an award-winning hotel, thanks to her. I confess, I was unsure what to do with the old place until Erin came along and breathed new life into it. We remodelled and she's picked out every last detail of the decor and the furnishings. I'm so proud of her.'

He leans over and kisses his wife. Erin bats her eyelashes coyly at him.

I turn away from the fawning that's going on over my sister's interior design talents and catch Jesse rolling his eyes. He's sitting back, arms draped along the curve of the sofa, legs splayed wide. He sees the look on my face and we give each other a little smirk of joint understanding. I'm happy for Erin but the showing off from Aaron feels a bit over the top.

'This is such an amazing hotel,' Mom says. 'You'll have to tell me all about how you refurbished the building. The rooms are just so lovely.'

Erin talks at length about how she designed this particular room. I tune out as much as possible, still catching words like 'mood board' and 'complementary colours' as I let my mind wander. Normally this kind of discussion would be right up my street but I zone out, taking in my surroundings.

I glance at Aaron again. The Rolex on his wrist, the leather shoes on his feet; even if I wasn't sitting here in the luxurious hotel owned by the pair of them I could tell how wealthy he was. I think about the guests who might be arriving soon and assume they are all of a similar class.

Excellent. This might be just the opportunity to find my own Prince Charming. To find someone who can whisk me away from my troubles and open the door to a life like the one Erin is living.

'Who else will be coming to the Christmas party?' I ask, keeping my tone as casual as possible.

'Aaron's family, our friends, work contacts...' Erin begins to list.

'Don't worry, there's plenty of eligible bachelors,' Aaron says, with a twinkle in his eyes. He's seen straight through me.

'Good,' I respond. 'Perhaps you can introduce them to me.'

Aaron chortles at this; clearly it wasn't the answer he was expecting. 'It would be my pleasure.'

'Looking forward to it.'

'Leah, this is a family gathering!' Mom exclaims. 'Not one of the dating shows you watch.'

'Don't worry, I'm married to a Bailey woman. You know what you want and I admire that.' Aaron picks up Erin's hand and kisses it, her spectacular engagement ring catching the light and shimmering. 'Honesty is a trait I approve of, above all others.'

A curious look comes over Erin's face. For the first time tonight, I wonder if everything really is as perfect as it seems between the two of them. Erin laughs, but it's a second too late and sounds forced.

Another waitress comes in and places little bowls of olives and nuts on the low table in front of us. Jesse immediately reaches for a handful of pistachios at the same time as I do. Our fingers brush past each other and I bat his hand away playfully.

Aaron is still talking and Jesse subtly pulls a face to show me he's bored of the other man's boasting. I stifle a giggle. It's always been this way between Jesse and me. We have a knack for silently communicating our thoughts to each other and we've got the same sense of humour. It's got us in trouble more than a few times with my Mom and Sasha, who tell us we behave like naughty children together. I know that Jesse is likely to liven up the party and I'm glad, as an evening out with him is always memorable. I'm just starting to think tonight might turn out better than I expected when I feel my phone vibrate.

I don't even need to open it to know it's another message. And I know exactly who it's from. My stomach flips. I thought that by coming back to England I could leave my past mistakes behind me. But I don't think it's going to be that easy...

# Chapter Sixteen
# Erin
# Ten years ago

I sit still for a minute, straining my ears. I can't hear anything. Maybe I just imagined it? But no. That was a solid thunk on the front bumper. It might have been an animal of some kind. Maybe it caught a glancing blow and has run off now?

I'm tempted just to drive on and pretend nothing happened. I can't though – whatever I hit might be lying in the road. I gingerly take off my seat belt; the impact and the sharpness of the brake meant I was thrown back into the seat.

Opening the door, a rush of cold air and rain hits me. Then I walk round to the front of my car and see there's definitely something there in the road but it's so dark I can't make out what it is.

I fumble in my pocket for my mobile and then flick on the torch. Stepping forward, my breath hitches up a notch as I shine the light towards the bundle on the ground.

'Damn!'

I drop my phone and it clatters to the floor, landing in a deep puddle.

I'm shaking.

There's a person in the middle of the road.

And they're not moving.

# Chapter Seventeen
# Sasha
# Now

Erin's husband is impressive – and he knows it. In the short time since Aaron made his entrance, he's managed to slip into conversation his love for his wife and children, his talent for languages, his extensive property portfolio and his grand plans for building a golf course near Burcott House. Yet he is not a bore, or a know-it-all. Far from it. He is charming, courteous and very likeable. He somehow has us all captivated as he tells us a funny story about his children before moving on to mentioning the selection of delicious canapés that will be available this evening.

I'm relieved to hear there will be food as I'm aware that I've knocked back my first three glasses of red wine a lot quicker than I normally would. The alcohol has already started to work its way into my blood stream, making my limbs feel less tense than they have done all week.

Leah is sitting beside me. I've seen her briefly a few times since she's been home but not as much as I would've liked to; the end of the school term is always so busy. And I haven't had the chance to speak to her alone.

'You OK?' she asks under her breath.

'Fine,' I reply, nodding my head.

'This is so weird, isn't it?' Leah says in a whisper, fiddling with a strand of her short blonde hair.

'Just a bit.' I take a sip of my drink.

'Are you going to stay here?' my little sister asks.

'Apparently there's a room if we want it but I drove. I'm not planning on staying long.'

Leah raises her eyebrows and I feel like I'm missing something. She's wearing a figure-hugging red dress, looking far more elegant than I do right now.

'How many of those have you had?' Leah questions, pointing to my glass.

I groan. 'Too many.' I was so nervous about being here that I didn't even think about needing to stay sober enough to drive. Which is so unlike me. My head swivels towards Jesse, but it's too late, he looks as though he's already gone through a few glasses as well.

'Staying here then?' Leah smiles.

'No.' I shake my head vigorously. 'I'll get a cab.'

I'd kept my voice low, but Aaron has zoned in on our conversation. 'There's no need to get a cab back,' he protests. 'Stay, that way you don't have to watch your drinks. The kids can go to bed when they're ready as well then.'

'Oh no, I couldn't possibly...'

Aaron turns to Erin. 'There's a room made up for them, isn't there?'

Erin nods. 'Yes, room twelve. It's there if you'd like it. The keys are behind the bar, just ask one of the staff for it and they can show you where it is. It's on the second floor.'

Aaron is nodding, 'There you go! No need to be thinking about cabs the moment you've arrived. The night is young!'

To my dismay, Jesse adds his voice to the conversation. 'Thanks, we appreciate it. We'll stay!'

Aaron and Jesse clink glasses, Mum and Erin lean in and do the same, so Leah and I both stretch forward and join in as well. It would be rude not to. But I don't feel like celebrating. I'm annoyed at myself for slipping up with the drinks. Staying here is not something I want to do but, yet again, I've been railroaded into making a decision I'm not happy with. I guess I really am in it for the whole night now.

Aaron stands up. 'More guests will be arriving soon. I'm going to go out front but it's been a pleasure meeting you and I'll find you all later. As Erin said,' he puts his hand on Erin's shoulder as he's talking, 'we really hope this will be the first of many gatherings.'

Erin smiles and nods in agreement.

'I'd better go and check that everything's ready,' she says. 'Feel free to go to the bar and order whatever you'd like. The main room will be filling up soon, so I'll see you in there in a bit.'

'Thanks love,' Mum says. 'This has been really special.'

Erin exits the room behind her husband. I'm glad that's over with. With any luck, we won't have to interact too much more. I'm sure they will have far more interesting guests arriving. If I have to stay here then my plan is to fade into the background and be out of the hotel as early as I can in the morning.

'More drinks?' Jesse suggests.

Everyone nods so he takes our requests and heads towards the bar. No doubt he'll be a while, he's bound to get chatting to one of the bar staff. Jesse's like that, he's much more sociable than I am.

'Want to go and freshen up?' Leah asks.

'Good idea.'

I follow her to the ladies' toilets. We both touch up our make-up in front of the well-lit mirror and discuss how things are going.

'I really didn't want to come,' I admit. I'm so relieved the initial meeting is over and that it went as smoothly as it could. Although I feel like I'm just waiting for something bad to happen.

'Well, I wasn't exactly keen. But I did it for Mom,' Leah tells me.

I nod. I should've made the effort to talk to Leah and find out how she was coping. Maybe we could've put our heads together and avoided this. Instead, here we are.

'I was about to speak my mind before Aaron arrived,' Leah is saying.

I finish applying my lipstick and stare at her. 'You were?'

'Well, it's stupid us all pretending. I wanted to say my piece and be done with it. Now I think the opportunity has gone.'

'It's probably a good thing. I mean, look at the life Erin has now. We may never hear from her again anyway. This is probably just some kind of empty gesture to make herself feel better. There's no need to stir everything up when we don't know how all of this is going to pan out.'

'I still feel so terrible though.' Leah's voice is trembling as she speaks and I realise just how much she means this.

'Leah, you've nothing to feel bad about.' I pull her into a hug.

Leah's shoulders sag and the strap on the left-hand side of her dress slips down her arm.

'Look, Erin made her own choices and she brought everything on herself.' My words come in a rush and sound harsher than I intended.

I want to reassure my little sister; her face looks so sad. 'Stop beating yourself up about it.'

Leah looks at me, a faraway expression on her face.

'Why do you think she did it? Why do you think she left us?' Leah asks, holding my gaze with her big blue eyes.

'Erin? I think she walked away from us because she was selfish.'

'There must have been something else though... The accident... it was awful but I always had a niggling feeling there was something else that pushed her away.'

I shrug my shoulders. 'Who knows what was going through Erin's mind at the time.'

'It's weird, but I've always felt like there was a distance between Erin and me and then, after what happened, there was no going back.'

I look down at my shoes and sigh.

'I just wish there weren't so many secrets in our family.'

'I know what you mean...' I take in my younger sister's expression. 'Leah, there's something you should know...' The words come spilling out of my mouth before I know what I'm saying, the alcohol making my tongue loose.

'What?'

'I probably shouldn't tell you... but you have a right to know. You're old enough now.' I feel reluctant to be the person saying this but she has to find out at some point. I can't stand all the secrets either.

Leah throws her arms up in the air and turns back towards the mirror. 'I'll always be the baby of the family. No matter how old I get. You guys will still be saying I'm too young, even when I'm in my eighties!'

I laugh at this. 'I'm sorry Leah, I didn't know you felt that way.'

Leah meets my eyes, her facial expression harder now. 'So, are you going to tell me or not?'

I shouldn't be revealing family secrets in this elegant, la-di-dah bathroom but I feel so bad for Leah. It's true, there's a lot she hasn't been told over the years.

'Sit,' I order, directing her over to the set of two armchairs at one end of the room – who has a bathroom so big they put furniture in it?

Leah does as I suggest and sits down.

Gently, I say, 'Simon wasn't biologically Erin's father. Or my father.'

Leah crosses her legs, repeating my words. 'He wasn't Erin's father or your father... But he was my father?'

'Oh yes,' I say in a rush. 'He was your father.'

I see the penny drop and Leah puts her hand to her forehead. 'What? Wait. That means I have a different dad? We're not proper sisters?'

She's hit the nail on the head. Leah's father, Simon, died from a tragic road accident when he was only in his late forties. Nana, Simon's mother, stepped into the breach to help our own mother bring us up. Erin and I were never told that the man who raised us for most of our early years, and who was Leah's biological father, wasn't in fact our own daddy.

I grasp Leah's hands in mine. 'Yes, we are. We grew up together, I will *always* be your sister. It doesn't matter about how we got here. But it's true. Erin and I have a different father.'

'You and Erin are full siblings?'

'Yep, I drew the short straw!' I snort, trying to bring some light into the situation.

'Right... and no one thought to tell me this before because?'

'Mum didn't want you to know. She felt ashamed. She never meant to hide it from us but it just never came up. We all assumed.'

As soon as I see the expression on Leah's face, I know this is all coming out wrong. This was not the time or the place to have this conversation.

'Why wasn't I told? How come you know?' Leah's voice is becoming more and more agitated.

'I wasn't supposed to know. I overheard Mum talking to Nana about it, years and years ago. It wasn't my secret to tell. We only spoke of it once, after Nana died.'

'I see.' Leah's mouth is downturned, she's taking this harder than I thought.

'All this time,' Leah says slowly. 'All this time I've felt bad that Erin left because of me. And yet you and Mom have been keeping the truth about our fathers from me!' She's on her feet now, gesticulating with her hands.

'Leah, it wasn't like that,' I say, standing up too and trying to reason with her. 'We were just trying to protect you. I'm sorry. I got it wrong.'

'Yes you did.'

Leah storms out of the bathroom, slamming the door shut behind her. I'm reminded of her teenage tantrums. She always did like slamming a door to get her point across.

I rush after her, my stomach churning with anxiety. Leah deserved to know that Erin and I are her half-sisters.

But it wasn't my truth to tell.

# Chapter Eighteen
# Erin
# Now

The room falls silent. Leah and Sasha have both made a swift exit. And I'm sitting here in the toilet cubicle alone, wondering what just happened. I heard every single word of the exchange between my two sisters. I'm stunned. Stunned to hear how much Sasha hates me and stunned to hear Sasha telling Leah she is my half-sister. I sit with my head in my hands, trying to sort out my jumble of thoughts.

When I think about everything Sasha just said, it makes my blood boil. Sasha, as the first-born, always seemed to get the better deal – new clothes, new toys – while I got her hand-me-downs, her second-hand stuff. It wasn't so much that things weren't brand-new that I had an issue with, it was the fact that I was shaped into a mini-Sasha, wearing all the clothes she'd picked out and being told to play with the things she liked.

As the middle child, I was forever trying to carve out my own identity, to show everyone I had my own interests and my own personality. Even as we got older and Sasha realised I'd end up with her things, she never chose anything with me in mind – and neither did our mother. Nadia never really listened to us; it was her way or nothing. She was a tough cookie back then and it strikes me that she seems somehow softer tonight.

By the time it came to little Leah, Nadia had got rid of a lot of the baby things or the cheap clothes were just too worn-out after they'd been used by two children, so Leah's wardrobe and playthings were also more tailored to her preferences. So for the two of them to label me as selfish, when for my whole childhood I was the little girl who always felt like second-best, makes me feel furious. It wasn't easy being sandwiched between the golden girl elder sister and the sweet baby of the family. Maybe that's why I always strived to break the mould, including my flexible thinking on abiding by rules. Although the thirst for making something of myself has certainly worked out. Just look at all I have now.

There's no point in going over it all again. At least I've found out how they really feel about me. I dab at my eyes with a tissue, not wanting my mascara to run. I've spent far too long in here, going over everything. My guests will be starting to arrive now. I need to take a deep breath and carry on.

I run my wrists under the cold tap to cool me down and then take my mini hairbrush from my Mulberry handbag and draw it through my long copper hair before tying it up. Scrutinising myself in the mirror, I'm sure I've managed to stay composed and presentable.

I can't see any sign of Sasha or Leah as I emerge back into the hallway, so I head towards the entrance where my husband is busy greeting a number of our business acquaintances. He whispers under his breath to me, 'Where have you been?'

I can tell by his tone that he's not pleased. He expects me to be an exceptional hostess, given the hospitality business we run together.

'Geoffrey! Tallulah! How are you?' I beam, putting my game face on as I stand next to my husband and give both of them warm hugs. 'Thank you so much for coming.'

Geoffrey is an important client for Aaron and also one of his most trusted friends from his private school days. Tallulah is Geoffrey's new girlfriend, a good twenty years younger than he is. Geoffrey recently caused a scandal by separating from his long-suffering wife, Mary, and moving Tallulah into his ancestral home only weeks later. A lot of my husband's friendship circle seem to be going through a midlife crisis at the moment, mostly involving affairs and separation. It seems so unfair that their wives must suffer the humiliation and repercussions of their actions. I'm on high alert, as I don't want my husband to be led down the same path, which would undoubtedly result in me sharing a similar fate to Mary.

'What a lovely outfit,' I tell Tallulah, who is wearing a dress clingy enough to leave little to the imagination. It's completely inappropriate for tonight's celebrations. As I guide Tallulah and Geoffrey to the Winchester Room, I wonder what poor Mary will be doing now.

'What an incredible hotel,' Tallulah says. Geoffrey, of course, has been here many times before and is familiar with Burcott House. She, however, is new to all of this. 'I picked the wrong man.' Tallulah throws back her head and laughs at her own joke.

Geoffrey gives me an embarrassed smile but I don't comment. A waitress moves towards us, champagne flutes at the ready.

'Enjoy,' I say, nodding to the glasses and taking this as an opportunity to leave them to it. Tallulah is brash and unpolished; I can tell she's not going to be easily accepted amongst the tight-knit circle of friends Geoffrey has. Judging by the look that Geoffrey just gave me,

I'm guessing this relationship may not last very long. Surely an annual event like this will make him realise how highly regarded Mary was. He's certainly going to have a different experience with Tallulah by his side this evening.

I can't dwell on these thoughts as there's already several people filling the room. I circulate, blowing air kisses to parents from the twins' school and thanking more of our business contacts for coming this evening. Half an hour flies by and the hotel fills up quickly. I alternate between greeting guests at the door and checking in on the party to make sure everyone has a drink in hand. I try to throw myself into my role as hostess but I can't shake the conversation between my sisters from my mind. The secrets of our family's past are already resurfacing.

It seems some things can't stay buried forever...

# Chapter Nineteen
## Leah
## Now

Of all the people to drop a truth bomb tonight, I didn't think it would be Sasha. Never in my whole life have I suspected that I have different parentage to my two sisters. Yes, it's true I'm the youngest by several years. There's a sizeable age gap between me and Erin of about four and a half years whereas there's barely two years between Sasha and Erin. I'd never really thought anything of this before. Mom always said I was her lovely surprise.

'Leah! Leah, wait!' Sasha's right behind me. I just slammed the bathroom door in her face; I don't want to look at her right now let alone talk to her.

'Just go away!'

'Leah, I'm sorry. That was dreadful of me to tell you like that.'

Sasha tries to put her arm around me but I shrug her off. She may have said sorry but I'm still mad at her.

'Let's go and sit in the Snug.' Sasha manages to cajole me into the cosy room with the roaring fire. I select a comfortable sofa in front of the fireplace and we both sit there for a bit as the flames crackle in the hearth. It's mesmerising watching the colours flash and the fire spit. Sasha puts her arm around me and we sit like this for a good fifteen minutes.

'I'm sorry,' she says again.

I blow out a breath.

'I sure picked my moment, didn't I?'

'You can say that again...'

'Can we make peace for tonight and then talk about it in the morning?'

'I guess so,' I reply reluctantly.

'Are you sure?'

'You're not just trying to shove this to one side, never to be spoken of again, are you?'

'No! I promise. We can sit down with Mum and discuss everything.' Sasha looks sincere about this.

'OK, deal.' There's so much I want to ask but now isn't the time. I'll store my questions up and quiz Sasha and Mom tomorrow.

'Let's go and make the most of this party then,' I say, standing up. If we're going to park this conversation, then I need a distraction.

Sasha and I go back into big expansive room at the centre of the hotel. It looks like it might have been a ballroom or something similar at one time. There's a little brass sign on the door that reads 'The Winchester Room'. I roll my eyes at this. Erin really is living in another world now. The majority of guests seem to be mingling in here. Lots of posh accents and fancy clothes. The DJ has just started playing and there are already a few people throwing shapes on the dance floor.

I take a selfie of myself and upload it to my social media. Then I cast my eye around for eligible bachelors but so far most men seem to be coupled up. I haven't seen one guy without a wedding ring on his finger yet and I'm beginning to think this party isn't going to be as fruitful as I'd hoped. And then I see him; tall, broad with fair hair and a dimpled chin, standing a few feet away from me in the doorway leading to the next room. There's definitely not a wedding ring on this man's finger.

'Sasha,' I nudge my sister in the ribs. 'Over there,' I give a subtle nod. 'What do you think of him?'

'She thinks her husband is standing right next to her,' Jesse jokes as he joins us. 'But ding dong, go for it, girl!'

The three of us laugh.

'I might just do that,' I say, gearing myself up for a bold introduction.

At that moment, Aaron joins our group. Sasha is looking glassy eyed and Jesse's attention is elsewhere, scanning the room of party-goers, so I ask our host about the handsome guy I've just seen.

'I thought I'd take you up on your offer,' I state confidently.

'What offer was that?' Aaron looks a little bemused.

'Your offer to introduce me to the eligible bachelors.'

'Ah, how could I forget.' The twinkle is back in Aaron's eye again.

'The tall guy, with the fair hair and the chin dimple. Who's he?'

'You've set your sights on someone already then. Quick work, I approve.' Aaron looks around the room. 'Do you mean him?'

'Don't point,' I say, batting his hand back down. 'Yes, it's him.'

'That's Xavier Knight. He's a good man.'

Well he has the surname to suggest he could be my knight in shining armour. But does he live up to his name?

'What's the full low-down?' I ask, cutting straight to the point.

Aaron grins wolfishly and then reels off everything that I want to know. 'Recently single after a lengthy relationship with the daughter of an ex-England cricketer. Xavier is the heir to a successful art gallery,

his family are wealthy, he lives a more laid-back lifestyle. What else...
He spends most of his summers in Ibiza and his winters in exclusive
ski resorts.'

'Bingo!' I give Aaron a megawatt smile.

He shakes his head, laughing now.

'Thanks for the information,' I say.

This party might not turn out to be so bad after all.

# Chapter Twenty
# Erin
# Now

The steady stream of arrivals begins to slow and I take a few minutes to check on the twins to make sure they're not getting too tired. Jasper is with a group of Aaron's family, no doubt getting quizzed about what he's learning at school and what he plans to be when he grows up. Aaron has high expectations for our son and I worry Jasper is starting to feel the pressure to fly high from both his father and grandfather.

'Erin, honey, how are you?' Aaron's stepmother greets me with a kiss on each cheek.

'It's so good to see you.'

'I wouldn't miss this party for the world,' she says. 'Are they here?' Melanie is quick to press the question upon me.

I nod. 'Yes, they came early. They're here somewhere.' I scan the room and I spot Sasha with a large glass of red in her hand, standing close to Leah and Jesse who are both knocking back shots of something.

'Over there, that's Sasha in the black dress, Leah in the red and Sasha's husband is with them.'

The three of them are standing close together, heads bent, and I'm certain from the way they're glancing in my direction that they're whispering about me.

'How did it go?' Melanie is not one for mincing her words.

'It went as well as it could,' I say honestly. I'm not about to elaborate on the meeting with my family or divulge the conversation I overheard between my two sisters.

Melanie looks thoughtful. 'It was very brave of you. I hope it all turns out the way you want it to.'

I give her a faint smile, not quite as certain anymore that things will go to plan.

'I must go over and introduce myself, after all your family is my family.'

I'd prepared myself for this. Melanie is technically Aaron's step-mother, although his mother passed away only seven years ago and Melanie came on the scene exactly one year after her passing. So Melanie married into the Scott family when Aaron was an adult with his own children. She hasn't had any motherly duties to perform and she has no children of her own, although she's very good with the twins. I thought at first that Aaron might resent her, but she so clearly made his father happy that Aaron quickly came to accept the new status quo and now she's very much a part of the clan. Melanie is hard not to like and I've always seen her as an ally, another strong female to join forces with in this very traditional and male-dominated family. It also helps that Aaron's father has been transparent that his only child, Aaron, is set to inherit the majority of his world possessions and there's a trust fund set up for the twins. Melanie has a small sum of money that is due to be gifted to her in his will, but she's not a threat to me in that way.

'Absolutely – and while you're doing that, I will supervise.'

She snickers. 'You know me too well.'

'I do.' I'm not really too worried about what Melanie will say, she's always been adept at extracting information from people in a way that they don't quite realise how much they've divulged until it's far too late. So I'm interested to see her in action where my family is concerned. We make our way over to where my sisters are standing.

'Sasha, Leah – I hope you're enjoying yourselves? The canapés will be out soon.'

They both turn towards me and smile politely. There's no trace of the argument in the bathroom visible on their faces. If I hadn't been hidden in the toilet cubicle at the time, I would be none the wiser.

'This is Aaron's stepmother, Melanie; I wanted to introduce you.'

'Delighted,' says Melanie, extending her hand in turn to Sasha, Leah, and Jesse. 'We're all so pleased that you came tonight. After all, there's nothing more important than family, is there?'

Sasha seems surprised at this introduction. 'Nice to meet you, Melanie. I completely agree.' She stares pointedly at me and I can feel the colour rise in my cheeks. My husband and his family know my mother and sisters haven't been in my life for the last decade. Although admittedly Aaron only got my version of events.

Melanie continues to make small talk, asking them about their lives. The confidence I felt earlier on has fallen away; I'm much more self-conscious now after hearing the conversation between Sasha and Leah.

'Leah, tell me about yourself. What's your story?' Melanie has a curious expression on her face as she says this.

'Well, I like to travel. I've just come back from Australia.'

'Really, how long were you there for?'

Leah is in full flow, telling us all about the places she's been to and the experiences she's had. As she's talking, I feel inexplicably jealous of her carefree lifestyle and the freedom she has. She's been globetrotting for most of her adult life, experiencing the world and all it has to offer, whereas my controlling husband is always watching me. Every shopping trip, every hair appointment, and every lunch out I've had in the last few years has been logged in our joint calendar. I stand and listen, holding back my thoughts and learning more about my little sister as she talks. I realise just how much we've grown apart and how different we both are.

For the first time, I wonder if asking my family here today was a big mistake.

# Chapter Twenty-One
## Erin
## Ten years ago

What do I do? What do I do?

I've run someone over. They're lying unmoving on the road. I've made a lot of mistakes in my life but I've never crashed my car. And I've never knocked someone down before.

I bend and fish my phone out of the puddle. It's water-logged and showing no signs of life, much like the body in front of my car. I stab at the buttons but nothing happens. The phone is very dead.

I cast around. To my left is a park and to my right is a little woodland area. There are a few houses a bit further up the road and my mother's house is at the other end of this stretch. I look back and I can just about make out a light in one of the windows. It's the light I left on in my bedroom. The other two cottages on either side are in darkness.

It doesn't look as though there are any witnesses. I could just make a run for it, drive off and try to pretend I wasn't here, this didn't happen, it wasn't me.

Except I can't just leave whoever it is in the middle of the road. They could get run over again. They might be OK, just a little shaken. Or they might not.

I steel myself and move towards the shape on the ground. I kneel down and let my eyes adjust to the darkness. I can make out a blue coat. I put my hand out and gently roll the body towards me.

I shriek.

The person lying on the ground is... is my sister.

Leah.

# Chapter Twenty-Two
## Leah
# Now

The tall, good-looking man has disappeared. I may have lost my moment but then, scanning the room again, I reassure myself that most of the women here are coupled up. Melanie is asking polite questions and I get drawn into an exchange about travel. I show Melanie my Instagram photos and she asks me for tips on a few destinations. Erin slides away, so I also attempt to detach myself from the rest of the group. I want to go and find the hot guy but this woman Melanie can talk for England. It seems like there's going to be no chance to escape any time soon.

Then I hear the clinking of a glass. A call for hush. We all turn towards the raised platform of the DJ booth and see Aaron and Erin standing next to each other. Aaron has a microphone in his hand.

'Thank you all for coming here tonight,' Aaron's voice booms across the mic. He fiddles with the setting and gets the sound level just right on his next attempt. 'It's wonderful to see you all here, for the Bailey-Scott's fourth annual Christmas party.'

A whoop goes up from the crowd. I take a photo of Erin and Aaron standing together, hand in hand. How did my sister manage to bag such a catch?

'Erin and I have been looking forward to this celebration. It's an event in our calendar that means a lot to us and, I hope, for those of you who have been coming for the last few years it's become an occasion to enjoy. For those of you here for the first time,' Aaron nods towards our group as he is saying this, 'I hope that this will also become a yearly feature in your own diaries.'

Erin sends a big smile in our direction as well. Aaron continues on, thanking people individually for their efforts in making tonight happen – the flowers, the food, the specialist gin. It's like he's at the Oscars or something. I think it's a little bit over the top but Aaron seems to like the sound of his own voice. He keeps going, pointing out that there will be a buffet and later on fireworks. I can't even imagine how much all of this is costing them. Aaron begins to wrap up his speech by sending a heartfelt thanks to his children and his parents for all of their help. He pauses for a beat and I hold my breath; it seems like he is going to miss Erin out. But then he grins widely.

'Of course, not forgetting my brilliant wife. She is the reason this party came into being in the first place. It's her drive, creativity and organisation that ensure everything is planned down to the finest detail. Thank you, my darling Erin.'

Everyone claps and Erin raises her glass to the crowd.

'So from my wife and I, Merry Christmas to all and to all a good night!'

Everyone is clapping again and raising their glasses to the festive toast. I'm a little surprised Erin hasn't said her own piece, given how much she loves to be the centre of attention. Perhaps she's met her match in Aaron, because he seems to love the spotlight too.

So far the interactions with Erin haven't been as excruciating as I'd imagined before we arrived. I'm actually looking forward to chatting to her more as the night goes on. Despite the public displays of affection with Aaron and the pair of them being more than happy to flaunt their success, there's so much more to find out about Erin. Now I'm here, I'm curious about her life and how she came to meet Aaron. And I could quite easily spend more time in this gorgeous house.

While the majority of guests are still captivated by Mr and Mrs Bailey-Scott, I scan the crowd and quickly locate Xavier Knight. He's a couple of inches taller than the average person and therefore easy to spot. I weave my way past women in sequin dresses and men in immaculately pressed suits until I'm at Xavier's elbow.

'Hi, I'm Erin's sister,' I say, snagging Xavier's attention straight away. I'm used to travelling solo and I've had a lot of practice in introducing myself to new people.

'I'm Xavier Knight,' Xavier shoots back. 'Nice to meet you.'

I smile sweetly. 'Likewise.'

'Having a good night?'

'I think it's only just getting started...'

# Chapter Twenty-Three
# Erin
# Now

I always feel a little out of place up on the stage, in front of all of Aaron's friends and family. It's silly really, as Aaron is the one doing all the talking. All I do is stand there next to him, playing the attentive wife, the perfect accessory. We discussed this before the first party we hosted four years ago. I wanted to add my voice to the toast but Aaron was insistent that he would do all of the talking. He's used to public speaking, given his prominent role in his father's shipping company. We've kept the same routine every year since. Aaron does the speech and I stand next to him, silently.

I would actually feel less exposed if I were speaking. At least I'd have something to do. Instead I try to stay poised, making sure I nod and clap in all the right places while everyone's eyes are on me. I always think Aaron's speeches are a little dry, although I'd never tell him that. Every year I rehearse my own party speech in my head; it will never be spoken out loud but at least I know that my version is a lot more fun.

I scan the crowd as Aaron's speech comes to a close and my gaze lands on the cluster of women who are the wives of Aaron's golf pals. They're a mixture of clients and influential businesspeople in the area and Aaron always impresses upon me the importance of this friendship group and the connections they have. Every one of the six women standing there will be staying in our hotel tonight with their partners, free of charge. I've made sure there are fresh flowers in their rooms and a complimentary bottle of bubbles in an ice bucket. They have brand-new robes hanging in the bathrooms and I've inspected every inch of their rooms to ensure they're as perfect as can be. I watch as Lucinda, the unofficial queen bee of the group, claps at something Aaron says. I automatically do the same, even though I've now zoned out of my husband's monologue. At least the golf wives all seem to be happy, for now. I catch sight of my nine-year-old daughter standing on the other side of the room, one arm around the girl standing next to her. The girl with curly auburn hair and big green eyes, the girl who looks so similar to her they could be twins. My sister's child.

I'm relieved to step down from the stage tonight, relieved that this part of the evening is over. I could see my family watching me as they stood together: my mother, Sasha, Jesse and Leah. I thought I was ready for this reunion but maybe I was wrong. I've spent a lot of time – and money – with my therapist, preparing me for this meeting. My therapist thought that it was a good idea to organise the reunion on neutral territory but I wanted to do it on my own terms.

Except all the feelings and thoughts from ten years ago have come flooding back to me. Those first few weeks after I walked away were so lonely, I spiralled into a dark place. I had no idea how I would carry on without them all. On more than one occasion I nearly went running home with my tail between my legs. But my pride kept me from doing that. I knew if I did go back then I would be seen as the one in the wrong, and no one would let me forget it. So instead I concentrated on moving forward on my own.

Aaron was my shoulder to cry on. He was a client for the bank that I worked at. He was so kind and listened to my troubles. He took me out for dinner, distracting me from my sadness. Gradually it became a regular occurrence, a highlight in my week. He never let me foot the bill and treated me like a princess. Our friendship developed quickly and within a few weeks our evenings out became dates and our dates turned into something more. I knew Aaron was wealthy, I could see his accounts. Although I didn't know that was only the half of it; he had plenty of other investments, a thriving business, he came from the kind of money that I couldn't even imagine to begin with. His family were extremely well-connected, his mother's side English aristocrats and his father's side entrepreneurial Americans.

When Aaron leaves the stage, he strikes up a conversation with a guest and I can tell he immediately has the woman under his spell. Aaron isn't a tall man but he has a strong presence about him. He is naturally good-looking and the flecks of grey that are starting to pepper his hair make him appear all the more suave and sophisticated.

I knew all those years ago that I'd lucked out. I also knew I'd never meet anyone quite like Aaron again. He was my dream come true. My chance for a better life. We got engaged really quickly. When, after a few short months, I discovered I was pregnant, it was the cherry on the cake. I was worried about telling Aaron but he was overjoyed, completely besotted with me, especially when we found out I was expecting twins – a boy and a girl. It was all so perfect. We had an unforgettable wedding in Paris, surrounded by Aaron's close family, the twins already an obvious bump in our wedding photos. It may have been a small affair but it cost a fortune. I glance down at the ginormous rock of an engagement ring complete with a matching diamond-studded wedding band on my ring finger. This is my security.

Aaron sees me looking over at him and makes his way towards me, to give me a long, lingering kiss. He likes to put on public displays of affection, to reinforce the idea that we're the perfect couple. I respond, kissing him back, but he pulls away swiftly, straightening his suit jacket and giving me one of his trademark winks.

There are so many things I'm thankful for. Aaron is a good husband in many ways, he makes sure the children and I have everything we want. He showers me with gifts and I've got used to being spoiled by him. Just like I've got used to the skiing holidays, the long summers in Italy and never having to worry about money. It's a far cry from my own childhood, where we had a weekend away in a caravan if we were lucky and my mother was always scrimping and scraping from one month to the next.

My husband rejoins me and tucks my hand in his arm and we walk amongst our guests, smiling so wide my face aches, all the while I'm displayed at his side. The trophy wife.

We stop when we come to Aaron's father, Hugo.

'Hugo, how are you?'

'All the better for being here.' Hugo shakes Aaron's hand and kisses me on the cheek.

His father was worried about our marriage to begin with. He thought I lacked the pedigree to be a suitable wife to his son, so I had to work hard to win him over. I showed them all that I was a fast learner. I observed everyone and was quickly able to imitate the language and the behaviour of the privileged set of people that Aaron called friends. My love of acting has come in handy. Now, my father-in-law is my greatest champion. He sees how I support his son in every endeavour. And both Hugo and Aaron are proud of my achievements with the hotel. I've transformed an old family home, that was a drain on their finances, into a thriving business that has more than reinforced his family's place at the heart of the social set they belong to.

I'm proud of how far I've come as well. But that's not to say everything has been sugar-coated. My husband may be charming, gentlemanly and refined when we're out in public but things aren't quite so easy behind closed doors. Aaron is often stubborn with me, a result of being the sort of person who has glided through life without any resistance. I'm far from a doormat and there are things we lock horns over. I'm sure every couple has their ups and downs but Aaron expects perfectionism every single day. There's no such thing as a bad day, he wants the children and me to behave to his high standards all of the time. Aaron always tries to control what we're doing, who we're seeing and how we're behaving. I'm sure the teenage years for our twins are going to be interesting as, one day, they will want to spread their wings. I'm not sure if Aaron would be able to cope with that.

After nine years of living like this, my gratitude to Aaron and the life he's exposed me to is starting to wear thin. Yes I have a millionaire lifestyle but my relationship with my husband is deteriorating with every passing month. And I'm certain my husband is playing away, like his golf buddies. It's something I've been paranoid about for a while now. Another subject my therapist has been paid a tidy sum to discuss. However much she tries to convince me to trust my husband, I know I'm the only person I can truly rely on.

For now, I'm going to keep playing the dutiful wife. And I'm also going to keep watching my husband's every move.

# Chapter Twenty-Four
# Sasha
# Now

Now the speech is over, the party is in full swing. The DJ set seems to be going down well with a mixture of club classics and cheesy festive songs that everyone knows the words to, whatever age they are. The room is huge, with a high ceiling making it feel even more spacious. The amount of effort and expense Erin has gone to is mind-blowing. It's like a wedding, with a Christmas guest book to sign, a sweetie station and a photo booth in one of the connecting rooms.

I keep getting glimpses of Erin flitting from one little group of people to another. She knows how to work the room. Leah has slipped away and is now chatting to a cute-looking guy near the DJ booth. Judging by his body language, it seems Leah has got him drawn in hook, line, and sinker. She always was a fast mover when it came to potential love interests.

Melanie is still jabbering away; we're on the subject of schools now and I'm seriously regretting telling her I'm an assistant headteacher because her thoughts on how schools are run seem endless. I take another big glug of wine and nod my head in agreement with her latest statement. Out of the corner of my eye, I see Leah and the hot guy move to the dance floor. At one time Jesse and I were like that. We used to be first on the dance floor and the last to leave. That all seems such a long time ago now.

Jesse seems to be thinking along the same lines and asks me if I'd like to go and dance. Melanie takes the hint.

'It was just divine talking with you both. I'm sure I'll see you again. I'm off to find my husband so we can have a go in the photo booth. He won't want to of course, but it's such fun!'

Melanie dissolves into the crowd. She was hard work. I take another gulp of my wine and realise there's not much left in the glass.

'Well, how about it?' Jesse repeats. 'Shall we hit the dance floor, like old times?'

I'm trapped in this room, surrounded by a sea of strangers. Unfamiliar faces flash by me and I feel unsafe, unprotected, vulnerable.

I shake my head and his face falls. 'I need another drink.'

'No you don't.'

'What?'

'You don't need another one. Just slow down.'

'I'm going to the bar.'

I stalk off, with Jesse following in my wake. As I do, I feel myself sway unsteadily but manage to right myself again before I trip.

'Let's take the weight off our feet.' Jesse guides me to a barstool and I plop down on it.

'A bottle of red,' I tell one of the bar staff.

'How about a glass?' Jesse suggests.

'If you're that worried, share it with me,' I retort, annoyed that Jesse's hovering over me like I can't make my own judgements.

'I'll have a glass to go with it as well, mate,' Jesse instructs the barman.

I knock back another drink, not really noticing the taste anymore. I'm sure this stuff is expensive, just like everything else around here, but the quality of the wine is lost on me right now. I'm in my own little world, the thoughts in my head the only things I can focus on.

I can't believe I let slip to Leah the truth about our DNA. As far as I'm aware, Erin still doesn't know that Leah is our half-sister and we have a different father to the man who helped bring us up during our younger years. Simon died in a tragic car accident when Leah was just four, Erin was eight and I was ten. It was a difficult time; I remember Mum crying every day. Our nana, Simon's mother, stepped in a lot to help after that. I can imagine Mum not wanting to taint our memories of Simon, he was an excellent dad to us and the only one I've ever known. She's going to get a shock when she finds out I've let Leah in on this family secret.

I drain my wine glass and feel Jesse tensing at my side but I ignore him, going over and over the same thoughts in my mind.

I'm fed up with the whole situation. I completely understand why Mum wanted to protect Leah when she was younger but Leah is thirty-two now and it's crazy that Mum still hasn't said anything to her. I didn't mean to blurt it out but it happened and it's something we all need to talk about properly.

'So what do you think of Burcott House?' Jesse asks. 'It's like a millionaire's mansion, isn't it?'

I can't answer him. I don't want to make small talk about Erin's fabulous hotel. She always did have a knack of getting exactly what she wanted when she was a child and it seems this has followed her into adulthood. I'm not a jealous person but I'm grinding myself into the ground, working every hour of the day, and Erin is swanning around living the high life. It's hard not to feel like Erin had the winning dice roll.

'Sasha, did you hear me?' Jesse sounds annoyed.

'Yeah, she's done well for herself,' I reply, not wanting to get drawn into this line of conversation further.

I refill my wine glass. I'm feeling guilty and afraid of the consequences of my actions tonight, so drowning my sorrows seems to be the best of my limited options. After all, I can't drive my car away after the amount I've drunk and Jesse has forbidden me to get a taxi. Not that I'd probably be able to get an available one at this time on a Saturday night in December anyway. Burcott House is so rural. And everyone will be at some Christmas do or another, with taxi drivers making a killing on double fares.

I feel panicky and shaky, I'm losing control. I hate not having a handle on situations. I hate that I don't have a plan b, an escape route.

It's the most breathtaking hotel I've ever stepped foot in, with its plush furnishings and perfectly coordinated festive decorations. Everything about it is spacious and inviting and yet I feel so claustrophobic. I don't want to be here.

But I'm trapped with no way out.

# Chapter Twenty-Five

# Jesse

# Now

This place is truly incredible. From the fully stocked bar to the chandeliers hanging from the ceilings, it's got everything you could ever want and more. I got chatting to one of the bar staff and they told me there's an indoor pool here, a home gym and even a cinema room in one of the outbuildings. I've never stayed somewhere as lavish as this before. Even the city guys who use the health centre I work in don't own property like this. It's on another level.

I wish my wife wasn't so stubborn. If Sasha and Erin had kissed and made up years ago, then we could have been experiencing this lifestyle too. I'm sure Erin would include us in the Sunday lunches, the birthday gatherings, the Friday night drinks. We could be enjoying a slice of all of this alongside her. I just hope Sasha isn't going to ruin my chances of checking out the pool and gym tomorrow morning. She's been so quiet so far that I'm feeling jumpy: it's as though I'm waiting for the ticking bomb to explode. It doesn't help that she's been knocking back the drink tonight. I mean, I'm all for making the most of a freebie but Sasha's going too fast. It also hasn't escaped my attention that she's been having a drink or two more than usual at home recently as well. Whenever I come back from the health club, she's got a glass poured – some nights to the brim – as she tap, taps away on her laptop.

'Have you seen Freya?' Sasha asks me, her voice sounding slightly slurred. The dress she's wearing is unflattering, it's baggy around her frame and hangs in a way that makes her appear bulkier than she actually is. Her lipstick has worn off and she has a tell-tale red wine stain on her mouth.

'No, not for a while.' I take this as my chance to go for a walk around. Sasha is irritating me and I need a break from her. 'I'll go and find Freya.'

'Thanks,' Sasha says, her eyes a bit too unfocused for my liking.

'Just go easy on the wine,' I tell her.

'What do you mean?' Sasha snaps and I wish I'd never said anything.

'Why don't you grab some of the food, sober up a bit...'

'Oh and it's all right for you to have glass after glass.'

A waitress walks towards us with a plate of food. 'Ah, look, what have we got here?'

'These are mushroom duxelles, sir.'

I have no idea what a duxelle is and, by the looks of them, they're not going to soak up as much alcohol as cheesy chips but, as it's the best we've got, I claim two of them.

'Here you go,' I say, shoving them both in Sasha's direction. To my amazement, she doesn't protest and just takes them.

'I'll bring Freya to you when I've found her.'

It's a relief to escape from Sasha and her unpredictable mood swings. She never used to behave like this. When I first met her she was fun and flirty. She used to laugh at my jokes and gaze at me like I was the only thing that mattered. The minute she started working at that school everything changed. I've only stuck things out as long as I have because of Freya. Well, that and because Nadia has made it crystal clear that she'd make my life hell if I left Sasha. But life isn't exactly a bed of roses anyway, so I'm beginning to think that it's worth risking the wrath of my mother-in-law.

I catch up with the waitress and nab a few of the mushroom canapés for myself. I may not be able to pronounce the name of them but I can appreciate the fact they melt in my mouth.

'Tasty!' I exclaim, my mouth still half full. The waitress giggles and gives me a little smile. It's good to know I've still got it. Even though I'm approaching the end of my thirties, I still work out as much as I did in my twenties if not more.

Scanning the growing groups of people, I spot my daughter standing over by the window with Ophelia. Ophelia is holding Freya's hand and whispering something into Freya's ear. Weaving to the other side of the room, I can't help but notice that there's a different class of women here. They're doused in perfume and expensive clothes. I can see a few of them looking my way, probably intrigued as to who I am. Most of the men are older and greyer than the women. It seems the cliché of rich men and attractive women is very much at play in this room.

'Freya!'

'Hi Dad,' my daughter says.

'Are you having a good time?'

'Yeah, look at all the pretty dresses. I feel like I'm Cinderella.'

'You're not Cinderella,' I say, picking her up and swinging her round. 'You're already my princess.'

Freya laughs.

'How about a dance with your dad?' I suggest. 'Not too old for that, are you?'

An Ed Sheeran song is playing and I whirl my daughter round again before setting her back down on the floor. We do an exaggerated slow dance, punctuated with me spinning her round as she laughs in delight.

I can see a few of the women watching us, and I hear a few comments too.

'Isn't that sweet?'

'Adorable.'

'Who are they?'

I smile. 'I think they like our dancing.' Freya loves to be the centre of attention and she's noticed it too.

'Come on, Dad!' She pulls me from the side of the room, towards the middle, and as the song closes we have a little half circle audience around us. Freya is lapping it up, her dance moves becoming bolder.

The song comes to an end and we receive a round of applause. Freya does a little curtsey and I follow suit with a small bow. The group dissolves and we make our way back to Ophelia. She's sitting sullenly in the window seat, her arms folded.

'Isn't my dad the best?' Freya crows, on a high from her little performance.

Ophelia doesn't answer.

'Would you like to dance with us?' I say, aware that she might be feeling left out.

Ophelia shakes her head.

'OK, well Freya, your mum wants to see you. Let's go find her.'

Freya looks at Ophelia. 'Come with us, come on.'

Ophelia seems as though she's going to refuse but Freya gives her a winning smile and tugs on her hand and the two of them follow me.

'Remind me to book you for the entertainment next year,' Erin says as she meets us walking across the dance floor. 'I'd forgotten that you like to dance, Jesse. Freya has followed in your footsteps.'

'I love dancing!' Freya twirls around to make her point.

'Well you danced wonderfully. Perhaps you'll help Ophelia and Jasper to come out of their shells.'

Erin is talking as though the three cousins will be great friends and I take this as a good sign for things to come. I could quite easily make myself at home here.

Erin pushes her hair back from her face, looking directly at me. 'Freya is delightful, you've done a great job with her.'

Her comment rocks me. It's not often anyone praises me on my parenting skills. I'm more used to Sasha nagging at me for all the things I haven't done or Nadia giving me one of her withering stares when she thinks I'm being too silly with Freya. It's nice to have a compliment for a change.

'Thanks, I try.'

And it's true, I do. Where my daughter is concerned, my heart is in the right place. Even if things with her mother aren't exactly rosy at the moment.

'I'm looking for Sasha, have you seen her?' I ask, scanning the room but not spotting my wife.

Erin narrows her eyes. 'Um, she was over there with Leah.' She waves towards the corner of the room.

I give a cheesy thumbs up without thinking, then realise what an idiot I must look to this woman who is probably used to much more sophisticated behaviour. But Erin laughs.

'You don't change, Jesse.'

Erin used to hang around with me and Sasha when we first got together. It wasn't unusual for us to invite Erin and Leah along to a cinema date or night out. The Bailey girls came as a trio and I knew that if I was going to win Sasha's heart then I needed her sisters on side too. Those days seem a long time ago now.

'Thanks for getting Sasha to the party. I'm guessing she wouldn't have come without a little encouragement.'

I'm aware of little ears listening, so I just say, 'Well she's here now, so over to you.'

We part ways and I almost walk into Sasha, who's tottering along very unsteadily on her heels.

'Hey, are you OK?'

'Whaaat do you thiinnk?' Sasha asks, her words more slurred than earlier. The posh mushroom bites haven't done the trick then.

'Sasha, I think we should sit you down and get some water.'

My wife sways a little more and I put my arm out to support her. Great, the night isn't even in full swing yet and Sasha has got herself wasted.

'I want to go home,' she states in a louder voice.

'What? We've not been here long.'

'I said... I want to... go...'

'Sasha, come on. Freya is having fun. The night is still young, let's get you straightened out and we can still enjoy the evening.' I don't really believe a word I'm saying but I have to try to get things back on track.

'I hate Erin. I hate this house. And I want to go home.' Sasha's words are all too clear now and the people standing to the left of us turn to stare at the drunk woman who's bad-mouthing the hostess.

I attempt to shuffle Sasha away from the group of aghast onlookers, but she digs her heels in and refuses.

'Jesse, get your hands off me!' my wife exclaims, pushing me away from her.

And just when I think the evening can't get any worse, it does.

# Chapter Twenty-Six
# Leah
# Now

'Jesse! Sasha! Are you OK?'

I arrive breathlessly after witnessing Sasha trip over her own feet, crash into her husband and take them both down onto the floor.

'Oh! I can't believe I just did that!' My eldest sister is lying in a heap, a tangle of limbs, as people around us murmur and point. I pull Sasha up to standing and help to brush her down.

'Jesse, what's going on?'

Jesse springs to his feet, embarrassment written all over his face.

'She's drunk, that's what's going on,' he hisses so only I can hear.

I can smell the alcohol coming off Sasha's breath. I'm shocked. She's always so strait-laced and she's not normally a heavy drinker. At least, as far as I'm aware. But then, I'm not around that much. And, if tonight's news is anything to go by, there's plenty I don't know about my family.

I'm furious about the revelation in the bathroom, and the way Sasha dropped it on me out of the blue. It's literally turned my world upside down. My sisters are my half-sisters. That's a massive piece of news, at least to me.

Even though I'm mad at her, I couldn't leave Sasha there on the floor after she'd fallen down. Jesse looked so dumbfounded – if it had been anywhere else, it would've been funny. But here in this grown-up house, with all these grown-up people, what just happened feels far from funny. I'm sure Erin is going to be mortified when she finds out.

I turn and realise both Freya and Ophelia are watching us, eyes wide and mouths agape.

'That's your mum,' Ophelia says, in a voice that sounds a little too unkind for my liking.

Freya mumbles in response.

'Right, let's get her sat down.' I support Sasha's weight as I guide our small group out of the Winchester Room and onto the terrace outside. There's a chill in the air and I'm hoping the change in temperature will help to sober Sasha up quickly.

There are several sets of tables and chairs out here, so I lower Sasha down into one of them.

'Look, a full moon!' Freya points up into the sky, distracted momentarily from her mother's out-of-character behaviour.

I pull my mobile out of my pocket – a dress with pockets is a rarity, which is why I love this one so much – and send a quick text to Mom, hoping she will see it and come out to assist. I don't really want Freya seeing her mum in this state for too long. And I'm even less keen for Ophelia to be witnessing this.

'I've just texted Mom,' I tell Jesse. 'How much has she had?' I point to Sasha.

'Well, she had most of a bottle of red wine to herself when we first arrived. I tried to get some canapés down her earlier but she must've had some more to drink in the meantime. I thought she was with you?'

'No, we had words earlier so I haven't exactly stuck by her side all evening.'

'What did you have words about?'

'Oh... nothing. It doesn't matter now.' I don't want to go into it all with Jesse. Although, he might already know about me having a different father; it's something Sasha could easily have shared with him. As usual, I'm probably the last to find out.

'I want to go home,' Sasha is mumbling over and over again. She's starting to shiver violently.

My phone vibrates and I pull it out of my dress pocket. But it's not Mom. It's the person I least want to hear from in the world and the message flashing up on my screen is more unnerving than the last.

*IF YOU DON'T PHONE ME THEN I WILL COME AND FIND YOU. I KNOW EXACTLY WHERE YOU ARE.*

My jaw tenses but there's no way I'm replying. My fingers fumble in the cold and I block the number and hit delete. I'm not giving into these messages and I'm going to get rid of this phone as soon as I can. I just hope they're bluffing.

'Was that Mum?' Sasha asks.

I shake my head and move closer to Jesse. I put my hand on his arm and whisper to him, 'The girls are getting cold. You take them inside and find some water and meet me back out here. And try and find—'

'Leah?'

I whirl around and see Mom there. She's got a strange expression on her face. I step away from Jesse and propel Freya and Ophelia towards her.

'Mom! Sasha's a bit worse for wear, can you take these two inside and perhaps get a glass of water?'

'Oh Sasha, are you OK?' Mom takes off her shawl and wraps it round Sasha, who is still shivering. Mom drops a kiss on her forehead.

'Right, there's buffet food out now so I'll get these two sorted and get a plate for Sasha. It's too cold out here, we should move Sasha inside as well,' Mom says, looking concerned.

'She's either going to be sick or fall over again, so I think it's safest to keep her where she is.' Jesse's tone is firm. 'I'm sure the shawl will help to warm her up.' A few flakes of snow have been fluttering down as we've been talking and my weather app predicted heavy snowfall over the next few days. But that's the least of our worries right now.

Mom looks back and forth between me and Jesse and then she reluctantly turns away. I watch her as she goes back inside, one arm around Freya and one arm around Ophelia. She's twittering away to them both as though she hasn't got a care in the world.

At least someone's enjoying this family reunion.

# Chapter Twenty-Seven
## Erin
## Ten years ago

'No!' I sob. How is this happening?

I roll Leah towards me and cradle her in my arms. There's a sticky, wet patch on her head. I think it's mud. I brush her short blonde hair out of her eyes and I discover it's blood.

I whimper. The rain is still coming down, pooling all around us. My jumper is already sticking to my skin. I remember reading something about not moving injured people. But if I lay her back on the floor she'll be soaked through in no time.

'Leah! Leah!' I call her name loudly and shake her, trying to wake her up.

It doesn't work.

'Leah!' I give her cheek a gentle slap.

Her eyes flutter and my heart leaps. She's alive.

'Leah,' I try again, slapping her cheek a little harder now.

Her eyes fly open.

'It's OK, it's OK,' I say to her. Leah's eyes are wide and scared.

She moans in pain.

'What hurts?'

'My head.'

'Anything else?'

Her eyes have closed again and there's more blood oozing from the gash in her head.

*Think, think, think.* What do I do now?

I feel in Leah's coat pockets and thankfully find her phone in one of them. As my mobile is out of action, I use hers to call an ambulance, giving a hurried, hysterical account of what just happened. Then I call my mother.

'Mum, Mum, you need to come outside quickly.' I give another garbled account of the accident and, before I've finished speaking, the phone line has gone dead. My stomach drops as I imagine my mother running up the road to find us.

In just a few minutes she is here, crouching down beside me. She still has a kitchen tea towel in her hand and uses it to help stem the blood flowing from Leah's head.

'What did you do?' she wails at me, her blue eyes full of distress.

'I... I... I didn't see her.' It wasn't my fault. She came from nowhere. She must have stepped right into the road without looking.

Except it was my fault, I put my foot down and I was going too fast. I couldn't see properly out of my windows.

'If anything, *anything*, happens to Leah, I will never be able to forgive you!'

Her words cut through me like a knife.

'How many more things will you do to try and break this family apart?'

I bow my head, unable to speak. Her words cut through me a second time. I didn't mean for this to happen.

I hear the sound of sirens coming towards us.

As the flashing blue lights come into view I know that whatever comes next, nothing will ever be the same again.

# Chapter Twenty-Eight
## Nadia
## Now

My mind is all over the place: being with Erin again has been both amazing and heart-wrenching. It's been so good to see her precious face and I feel proud of the successful woman she has become. Although I can't help berating myself for this feud going on for so long. I regret some of the things I said and I wish I'd handled things differently. There's so much of Erin's life I've missed out on, as well as her children's baby years. I'm never going to get that back but I am determined to make up for it and enjoy the time we have. This reunion is a positive turning point. It's time to move forward. But I'm also curious about why Erin has agreed to be in contact now.

I was hurt that Ophelia and Jasper didn't come running into my arms but I understand why they were so reserved. It was an overwhelming moment after all and I didn't help things by being a blubbering mess. Ophelia seems comfortable in my presence now though, allowing me to put an arm round her as we make our way back into the main throng of the party. The smell of delicious food hangs in the air and we follow some of the other guests into yet another room downstairs. This place is a maze and I can't quite get my head around the layout.

The room we go into is another large space; it has a buffet table running almost the length of one side with all kinds of hot and cold festive food available. I see one man walk away with a plate brimming with Yorkshire puddings and turkey sandwiches. There are waiters serving so I join the queue with Ophelia and Freya.

'Do you think Jasper would like something to eat?'

'He's already got a plateful,' Ophelia says, pointing to her brother who I can now see is sitting alone at one of the tables. His plate is brimming with food and he is devouring a Yorkshire pudding.

'So he does!'

'Jasper is always first in line when there's food on offer.'

I love learning these new pieces of information about my new grandchildren. Ophelia sounds so grown-up, much more so than Freya, even though there's only a few months between them in age. I imagine Ophelia has probably heard her parents saying this and is repeating the phrase.

'Yum, there's pigs in blankets!' Freya says as we move towards the start of the queue.

'I'm not touching any of the pigs in blankets,' Ophelia comments in a scornful voice. 'I'm going to have steamed vegetables, just like Mummy does.'

Freya is confused at this. 'But they're so tasty.'

'That's all right, Freya,' I interject, steering the conversation. 'There's so much choice here, so you both have what you want.'

Ophelia has pursed her lips and is behaving in a very prim and proper manner. I guess because she and Freya look so alike I was expecting them to be similar personalities as well. But they're both very different. Ophelia's upbringing will have been worlds apart from

Freya's, and from the childhood my own daughters had. If Erin is happy for me to see Ophelia and Jasper going forward then maybe I can be a down-to-earth influence.

Freya and I pile our plates with roast potatoes, stuffing, and turkey sandwiches while Ophelia's plate consists of only salad and vegetables.

'It's good you eat your greens,' I say to Ophelia. 'But are you sure you don't want some chips?'

Ophelia shakes her head and I think how unusual it is for a child of her age to have such discipline where chips are concerned.

'Let's go and sit with Jasper.'

The three of us seat ourselves in the free chairs around the same table as my grandson. I was planning on having just a few bites to eat before I go back outside to check on how Sasha's doing. But just thinking about the state my eldest daughter is in makes me feel tense. The children seem settled enough so I will extract myself quickly and take some carbs out to help sober Sasha up.

'Mmmm.' Freya is noisily tucking into her pigs in blankets and voicing her appreciation. 'Nana, why aren't you eating any food?' Freya is nudging me.

'Oh, I'm just not hungry, love. Is your tummy full now, Jasper?' I ask. He hasn't even left a crumb on his plate.

Jasper nods slowly. The poor thing seems so shy. I just want to wrap him up in a hug, but I need to tread carefully and give him time to get to know me.

'Well, I best get this plate out to Sasha.' I stand up, not wanting to miss a minute with my grandchildren but knowing Sasha needs me right now.

'Is Mummy OK?' Freya questions.

'Yes, nothing a turkey sandwich won't cure!'

Checking my watch, I note that I've been inside for a good ten minutes, perhaps more. So I hurry out of the dining room, trying to remember my way back to the terrace. But I'm stopped abruptly by a male figure blocking my way. It's Aaron. He's standing in the doorway I was about to go through and practically boxes me into a deserted corridor.

'Are you having a good evening?' Aaron asks, a serious look on his face.

'Yes. Thank you again for inviting us,' I reply, feeling wary about where this conversation might go as the frown across Aaron's forehead deepens.

He doesn't respond so I fumble for something to say. 'It's probably quite strange to meet your mother-in-law at this point in your marriage.' I chuckle, trying to make light of the circumstances.

Aaron studies me. 'I can't pretend Erin hasn't been hurt by everything that's gone on but we both felt it was time to move on.'

His tone makes me feel like a child being told off and it catches me off guard. Earlier on he had been so warm and welcoming.

'I agree. We all need a proper chat but for now it's been wonderful to see my daughter and grandchildren.'

'Just don't hurt her again.' He leans forward, his face incredibly close to mine.

'Excuse me?' I think I must've misheard and his close proximity makes me feel intimidated.

Aaron is smiling a wide smile now, his pearly white teeth noticeable in the dimly lit space. 'Don't upset my wife again and I'm sure everything will be fine.'

He straightens up, cool and collected, and ends our conversation by walking away from me. I'm left flabbergasted. I wasn't expecting such a change in disposition from Erin's husband. On the one hand, it's good that Erin has someone fighting her corner but, on the other, I really don't like the way Aaron looked at me or the shiver that ran down my spine as he spoke.

I take a deep breath and then try to carry on as though I haven't just been threatened by my son-in-law. As I walk through the Winchester Room, I see Aaron again, standing in the middle of a group of polished and well-dressed people his own age. He's talking to a tall man who's wearing a flashy grey suit and a Santa hat. They laugh at a shared joke. As I watch him conduct himself so confidently, I have a frightening thought. What if Aaron had stopped Erin responding to all the messages we've sent over the years?

The thought sends shockwaves through me and sets my pulse racing.

I must admit, after the first three or four years after losing my middle daughter I had to take a step back from trying to make contact, for my own sanity. Although Sasha, until about eighteen months ago, still tried regularly to get Erin to reply to us. Despite going to the police, more than once, we were told they didn't get involved in family arguments. So we knew nothing about Erin's new life and I had to accept that not being in touch with us was her choice to make.

But what if it wasn't?

What if Aaron had something to do with it? He could very easily have persuaded her to cut all contact or poisoned her mind against us all. There were plenty of ways he could have turned her head and distracted her with all the wealth he has. The more I think about this, the more I'm convinced it could very well be the reason I've been apart from my daughter for such a long time. Yes, we argued, but so do all families. I've blamed myself for so long that I never considered any other possibilities. I take in Aaron once more: he's still holding court, the group of people around him are totally under his spell. He's charismatic and powerful. But beyond that, I know nothing about my new son-in-law at all.

What if my daughter is trapped in her marriage?

What if inviting us here tonight is a cry for help?

# Chapter Twenty-Nine
## Sasha
## Now

My limbs feel heavy and tired. I'm slumped in a chair outside and I'm finding it hard to focus. It's so very cold. I think I just fell over, but I'm not entirely certain. The only thing I do know is that I don't want to be here. I want to go home. This whole evening is a big mistake. I was so nervous I've ended up ridiculously drunk.

'Jesse?' I croak. 'Can we go now?'

I look up and see Jesse and Leah whispering together. They haven't heard me.

'Jesse!' My voice comes out louder than I intended but at least I've got his attention now.

'Ssssh,' Jesse scolds me. 'You've caused enough of a scene already.'

'Let's just go,' I protest.

Jesse is shaking his head. 'Your mum's gone to get you some food and water. Let's soak up some of that wine. If you need to you can go and lie down in the room Erin has organised for us.'

I pout. Jesse doesn't want to leave. He's made it clear that he isn't going anywhere.

'Leah, come home with me.'

Leah is observing me with a disgusted look on her face. I suddenly remember our conversation in the toilets earlier this evening and remember that I'm not her favourite person right now either. Jesse and Leah turn away from me and continue their hushed conversation. I can't follow what they're discussing, but it doesn't sound like a taxi is going to be booked any time soon.

'Sasha, here you go, love.' Mum is hovering in front of me with food and water. I take the ice-cold water and gratefully gulp it down.

'Jesse and Leah don't want to go home. I just want to go home,' I repeat to Mum, hoping she will wave a magic wand and send me to the comfort of my own bed.

'Sasha, just stop.' Jesse has whirled around and his face is contorted into an ugly expression. 'Just because you don't want to be here, it doesn't mean you can just ruin everyone else's night.'

I stand up at this. 'All you care about is yourself and having a good time.'

'Well it's better than being totally self-absorbed and miserable,' he barks back.

I'm suspicious of his choice of words, they don't sound natural in my husband's mouth. Even in the state that I'm in, the way he speaks jars with everything I know about Jesse. It sounds like he's repeating someone else's phrasing.

Leah is still standing next to Jesse, barely a slice of air parting the two of them.

'Oh, I see. Leah is mad at me; she's let off steam and told you what she thinks of me and you're now repeating her character assassination. Right?'

'Wrong!' Leah interjects, looking hurt. 'I would never say something like that.'

Jesse hangs his head guiltily. A silence falls over our group. Mum is standing rigid, as if bracing herself for what might come next. Jesse has his hands balled tightly at his sides, a tell-tale sign he's angry. Leah is flushed and her body tense.

'Sasha, let me take you up to the room Erin has offered us. You can go to sleep and we'll leave first thing tomorrow.' Jesse's voice is lower now, but he's still determined to get me to stay here.

I shake my head stubbornly. 'I'll call a taxi and take Freya back with me.'

'Sasha!' Jesse roars at me. 'No, you're too drunk to be looking after Freya.'

'What's wrong?' Erin appears suddenly. Looking totally flawless, her perfect hostess act is starting to grate on me.

'What's wrong?' I cackle loudly. 'What's right, more like!'

Erin looks baffled. 'What's she talking about, Leah?'

'Oh, don't listen to her. She's drunk. Let's just get Sasha upstairs now.' Leah tucks a strand of her blonde hair behind her ears and glances around us, obviously embarrassed that several sets of eyes have turned our way and are following the drama that's unfolding here.

But I can't stop myself now. The alcohol has made me bolder. 'Erin, do you even want us here? You say you want a family reunion but we've hardly seen you all evening.'

Annoyingly, I start hiccupping. This is not the time for the wine to repeat on me.

'Of course I want you here,' Erin says in an even voice. 'Please just quieten down, everyone is watching.'

It's true, all eyes are now on us. All the people out on the terrace, gathered in little groups of twos and threes, are now looking our way. Erin must be mortified but I couldn't care less.

'Oh, I'm so sorry,' I reply, my voice getting louder with each word. 'I didn't mean to embarrass you, sis.'

'Sasha, what's got into you?' Jesse pulls me roughly away from Erin and starts walking me in the opposite direction to the gawking party-goers. But I'm not done yet. I yell my parting line over my shoulder, projecting my voice as much as I can.

'I bet you wish you'd never invited your *family* to this Christmas party now.'

# Chapter Thirty
# Erin
# Now

I want the ground to swallow me up. I can't believe Sasha has got so trashed. For the second time tonight, I'm shocked by the viciousness of her words. If anything, I expected Leah to be the one to kick off. I guessed wrong. Leah is standing red-faced; she seems almost as horrified as I am. Except, she's not the hostess and these aren't all of her friends, family and acquaintances who are circling round us, wondering what is going on.

Jesse is hauling Sasha into the darkness as she continues to rant and rave. He's pulling her away from the terrace, towards the gardens beyond. It doesn't look as though she will be settling down any time soon. Snowflakes are swirling all around them as their figures disappear into the night. I can't just stand here, but I don't think there's any point in me going after the pair of them as I'm sure it will just antagonise Sasha further. Jesse is dealing with his wife, I need to leave them to it. There's a murmuring going round the cluster of guests out here and I need to smooth over the situation.

'Apologies everyone, there's always someone who has a few too many!' I make sure my laugh sounds as genuine as possible.

'Let's head back inside, it's cold out here.' I move away from Leah and Nadia and begin to encourage the others back into the hub of the party. The beat of the music has picked up and the dance floor is more crowded now that everyone has had their fill of food and drink.

I assess those who were clustered out here. A few of the school mums, which is highly annoying as I'm sure this piece of gossip will be spread amongst them all and picked over for weeks, along with two of Aaron's cousins and an elderly aunt. Thankfully none of the golf wives or any of our business clients witnessed the scene my drunken sister caused.

I successfully shepherd everyone inside before turning back to Nadia and Leah.

'Should I go after them?' Nadia is saying, wringing her hands. It seems odd to see her so uncertain, she was always so self-assured and assertive.

'No, I wouldn't Mom.' Leah's response is firm and exactly what I would've advised as well. 'They need to sort things out between them.'

'I just don't know what's happened to Sasha tonight. She was nervous about coming but I've never seen her behave like this.' Nadia is clearly worried. 'I'm sorry Erin, I had no idea she'd act this way. I hope we haven't ruined your party.' She looks back towards Jesse and Sasha, who are now outlines melting into the inky black night.

They have of course, that's the truth of it. I'm going to need to make sure the next stages of the evening – the fireworks display, the sparklers, the live band and the coffee liqueur and hot chocolate at the end – all go like clockwork. This has to be the last of the family drama and I need to regain control of the situation. My parties are always highly praised and this one can't be an exception.

'No, don't worry. It's fine. It's been a big moment for all of us. I'm glad you all came. Really, I am.' I reach out and squeeze Nadia's hand reassuringly. If life has taught me anything in the last decade, it's that keeping a lid on your true feelings and being a good actress is the key to getting what you want.

Nadia steps forward and cups her hands around my face, before kissing me on the forehead. 'I don't want us to be split apart again. We need to work out our differences.'

I nod, completely unmoved by my mother's emotions, but outwardly agreeing. It's going to take a lot more than words for me to trust her again.

'Why don't we start with telling the truth.' Leah has one hand on her hip and cuts a striking figure in her fitted red dress against the dark sky and falling snow.

Nadia appears confused and this seems to spur Leah on.

'It's not nice to be in the dark about things, is it?' she says, talking slowly and dragging out her words. 'Why don't we start with the fact Sasha and Erin are my half-sisters?'

Nadia and I gasp at the same time.

'You know?' Nadia says, sitting down heavily on the chair that Sasha was occupying minutes before.

'I only found out tonight,' Leah replies, her blue eyes focused on our mother. 'I'm always the last to know everything, aren't I?'

I can tell Leah is about to go off on a monologue about being the youngest and being treated like a child. This was a regular complaint of hers when we were teenagers, all living in the same squashed terrace house together.

'I didn't know,' I interrupt. Because no one has actually told me this information. It winded me to hear Sasha sharing this secret with Leah in the bathroom earlier. Little do they know, I actually discovered the truth about my father when I overheard a conversation between Sasha and Nadia ten years ago.

'Really?' Leah asks.

I nod, intrigued to see how this conversation is going to play out.

'Girls, sit down,' Nadia tells us, patting the seats beside her. We do as she says, both of us sitting down stiffly. My feet are aching in my four-inch shoes; they may look gorgeous but after several hours in them I'm glad to sit.

'I'm sorry, I'm so sorry, I've made a mess of everything.' Nadia shakes her head as she's speaking.

'Why didn't you tell me?' Leah questions, leaning forward, eager to hear the answer. Her flash of anger seems to have dissolved as quickly as it came.

'It's complicated,' Nadia sighs. 'I was embarrassed, I didn't want you girls to think less of me. And... it's stupid saying this now... but I didn't want the three of you to feel any differently about one another.'

Leah scowls. 'But we were arguing anyway! Do you not think this information might've been helpful?'

'I came so close to telling you, I honestly did, on several occasions. I just...' Nadia looks off into the distance, a lost expression on her face.

'We can't change the past now,' I say, trying to be diplomatic. Inside I'm seething, all the feelings of that time coming back to me, but on the surface I remain unruffled.

Nadia shakes her head once more and bursts into tears.

'Hey,' Leah says, putting a hand on Nadia's back. She looks like she's about to cry as well.

'You'll always be my sister, Leah,' I say, leaning forward and catching both Nadia and Leah's hands in mine so we're linked together in a circle.

'And you'll always be mine,' Leah says, tears beginning to fall down her face.

'It doesn't change who we are,' I say to Nadia.

A silence falls over us, each of us contemplating our own thoughts. I shiver as the wet snow starts to seep into my clothes.

'I would like to know though, not now, but at some point I would like to know who my real father is.' My voice is gentle and soft. Now is not the time to press this issue with my mother. But I want her to understand this is important to me and that she can't carry on pretending any more.

Nadia nods, wiping away her tears. 'Of course, of course.' She gulps in some air. 'From now on, no more secrets.'

'No more secrets,' I repeat. Leah is echoing the phrase too.

But do we all mean it?

# Chapter Thirty-One
# Jesse
# Now

I'm cold and I'm angry. Sasha has caused such a scene. This should have been a happy family reunion and a lovely moment for Freya to meet her cousins. She's the only child Sasha and I have together so I want her to have a good relationship with Ophelia and Jasper, so she has her own generation of family. But all Sasha is thinking about is herself. She's gone too far this time; she's embarrassed me and completely humiliated Erin. Our relationship is already cracking and tonight feels like a breaking point.

I had to pull my wife away from her sisters before she said anything else she'd regret. Before she said things that could mean there was no way forward with healing the family rift. Sasha screamed and hurled abuse at me. And then she ran off into the pitch black of the night. I can't find her.

Where is she?

I've been shouting her name, calling for her to come back, but she's not answering me. This is getting ridiculous now. Over fifteen minutes have passed and she's nowhere to be seen. My teeth are chattering and my clothes are soaked. The snow is really coming down, a thick layer of white covering the ground. It's making it even harder to see and I'm getting further and further away from the hotel behind me, the only guiding light and landmark I have.

I try ringing Sasha's phone but there's no response. She was in such a state she may have fallen and hurt herself. Or passed out from all the alcohol she's consumed. My own phone battery is low and I curse myself for not charging it fully before we left this evening. The grounds of this hotel are vast, I don't need daylight to see that. Sasha could be anywhere...

As I search for my wife, I think of all the arguments we've been having lately. Good parenting is one of the regular themes of our disagreements. Sasha always makes out like she's a saint and I'm a useless father. She's constantly sending me links to podcasts and TED Talks, encouraging me to 'review the way I interact with my daughter'. It's true I'm more laid-back, but I think Freya benefits from this. If she had two stressed-out parents then the child would be a total mess herself. Sasha being a teacher also doesn't help matters. I think she piles too much pressure on Freya to do well. The high-brow, academic route isn't always the answer. I do all right in my work as a personal trainer and it's a far healthier job than sitting at a desk all day or being a slave to a career that exploits me. I do things on my terms; I work the hours I want to. As our marriage has worn on, it's become more obvious that my wife and I have very different ways of living life.

I can feel myself getting more and more frustrated with Sasha as I walk round in circles. My teeth chatter and my fingers are numb. I'm at the end of my tether now and there's no point in me wandering aimlessly out here in this weather. If she doesn't want to answer me, that's her choice. There's also no point in us both ending up with hypothermia. So I turn and trace my steps back towards Burcott House.

In the distance and the snow, the hotel looks as though it's in one of those little snow globes that you shake and all the snowflakes swirl round in the glass. This evening feels a bit like that too, everything seems shaken up and uncertain. As I trudge back, I'm all too aware that I'm giving up on my wife, but it's exactly what Sasha would expect of me. And my mother-in-law too.

As I get closer to the building, I can't stop thinking that Sasha is alone out there in the snow. The temperature has really plummeted now and she isn't wearing a coat. Every part of my body feels numb and I've got a jumper and chinos on; my wife was only wearing a dress and thin tights. Sasha could end up getting seriously unwell – or worse.

Of course, she may have already made her way back to the party. She's probably back in the warm and dry, while I've been out here like an idiot. That must be what has happened, as I don't know why she'd go roaming off in the darkness. Yes, she'd had too much to drink, but Sasha is usually the sensible type. Even as I'm trying to convince myself of this, my gut is telling me my wife is still out here somewhere. I'm sure I would have seen her if she'd gone back to Burcott House, as I've been regularly turning back to check my position in relation to the hotel, still calling her name.

I resolve to get my outdoor things and then to gather a search party to find Sasha. It's the last thing I want to do and it's bound to spoil Erin's party even more but I have to do it for Freya's sake. I could never forgive myself if something happened to Sasha.

My wife is out there somewhere, lost in a snowstorm.

What if we don't find her tonight?

# Chapter Thirty-Two
## Sasha
## Now

*Run... run... keep running...*

My body is in flight mode. I'm frightened, adrenaline coursing through me. I keep putting one foot in front of the other, going as fast as I can to put as much distance as possible between me and my husband.

The ground is hard beneath my feet. I kicked off my high-heel shoes a few minutes ago, so I'm running in my stockinged feet. It's madness but I just need to get away from Jesse. From everyone. This whole evening has been a complete disaster. Jesse has never behaved this way with me before. He's never handled me roughly. So the grip of his fingers circling around my upper arm was alien and scary. I could feel the anger rippling off him in waves as he dragged me away from my family and into the darkness. I screamed and shouted at him to let go of me, but he just wasn't listening. His grip getting tighter and tighter.

I had to get away before his behaviour went too far. So I stomped on his foot, causing him to yelp in pain, and I ran. I ran as fast as I could. I have no clue as to where I am. The landscape of the hotel's grounds is completely unknown to me. The only information I have is there's a cottage out here, Erin's family home, set back from the grandeur of the hotel. I have no idea which direction to go in or any kind of plan.

As I press forward, hot tears stream down my face. I feel like I'm losing control of everything. My breathing is ragged so I finally have to slow down, my heart thudding against my chest as I suck in lungfuls of cold air. I register the snow is falling hard and fast now. I'm not wearing a coat, let alone a hat or gloves or a scarf. Snowflakes settle in my hair and my feet are like ice blocks. I'm completely at the mercy of the elements.

I look over my shoulder, expecting to see Jesse following behind me but he's not there. No one's there, all that's visible is a blanket of fresh white snow stretching out across the ground and the pitch-black sky.

I cast around and try to make out my surroundings. The snow flurries are making it tough to see anything but I can make out the glow of Burcott House in the distance behind me. I'm shocked at my behaviour. The alcohol has made me reckless. Then again, there were things that needed to be said so at least I've made my feelings crystal clear.

Erin, Leah and our mother are probably back there now, discussing my meltdown. I should feel embarrassed, but I'm not. Perhaps that's due to the effects of the amount of liquor I've consumed, I'm sure my thoughts might be different in the morning. Now I've calmed down, my heartbeat returning to a normal level, I spot a railing ahead of me. I walk over to it, my feet throbbing, and the area in front of me takes shape. Thank goodness I stopped running when I did because, ahead of me, is a large expanse of water. At first I think it's a very large pond but, as my eyes adjust, I see it's more like a lake. I'm not at all surprised that Erin has a body of water in her back garden.

There are iron railings running around the lake. I lean against them, my elbows resting on the icy bars. The reflection of the full moon ripples across the clear water in front of me. It looks like a painting and even in my inebriated state I can appreciate how beautiful it is.

I breathe in slowly and steadily, trying to shake the heavy-limbed feeling washing over me. I absolutely must sober myself up and figure out what the hell I'm going to do now. I'm relieved to be away from the party as I found the atmosphere too much. The crowd of strangers and the unfamiliar surroundings made me feel so off-kilter. I don't want to go back – and yet I can't stay out here all night long.

The white blanket across the floor, the falling snowflakes and my own dramatic exit make me think of Freya's favourite Disney movie, *Frozen*, especially the bit when Elsa runs away from her own sister and sings 'Let It Go'. Yet, unlike Elsa, the cold does bother me. I'm only wearing a dress and tights, not exactly the outfit for these arctic conditions. I'll have to go back soon as otherwise I'll freeze to death.

'Sasha! Sasha!'

I can hear Jesse's voice calling for me. Damn. I assumed that he wouldn't bother coming after me, that he'd stomp back to the hotel and leave me to it. Maybe I think too little of him, maybe he does really care. But then the expression on his face as he manhandled me earlier and the throbbing of my left upper arm remind me that Jesse didn't exactly stand in my corner. His behaviour wasn't acceptable but neither was mine.

My muscles tense, I can hear him calling my name over and over. His voice is getting nearer and nearer and I'm terrified that he will spot me standing here by the moonlit water. I wait for a few nail-biting minutes but then the sound of his voice grows fainter as he appears to be heading away from me, until it eventually stops altogether.

I exhale a sigh of relief. I want to allow myself a little bit more space before I return to the hotel and face the music – I'm sure Erin is going to be furious with me. I wrap my arms around myself and wish it wasn't so cold. Even if I hadn't drunk a drop of wine, there's no way I would've been able to drive home in these conditions. It would be too dangerous down those dark and winding country lanes. So I'm stuck here, forced into staying overnight in the one place in the world I least want to be.

I lean on the railings once more, for support now. I'm so drowsy. I'm tired from too many late nights, trying to wrap up and get every-thing done before the end of term, so I'm running on empty as it is. All I want to do is curl up in my nice warm bed and sleep for the next week.

My head is starting to droop, my eyelids rapidly blinking. I stamp my feet to try and get my blood circulating and tell myself to wake up. Falling asleep out here wouldn't be a good idea.

I hear a twig snap behind me and my heart jumps in my chest. I'm on high alert now, jolted awake by the distinct sound. A bolt of fear runs through my body and it's nothing to do with the temperature out here. There's a person behind me, I just know it.

I turn slowly and, sure enough, I can see a figure, not too far away, standing by a tree. The silhouette seems menacing, faintly backlit by the distant glow from Burcott House. I can't make out if it's a man or a woman. But I'm not going to stick around to find out.

I lurch away from the railings, tripping over my own frozen feet. I'm running again, back towards Burcott House, back towards the party, and back towards my sisters. That figure wasn't Jesse and I don't know why anyone else would be out here in the darkness. I can't hear anything behind me but that doesn't mean they're not following me.

*Run... run... keep running...*

# Chapter Thirty-Three
# Nadia
# Now

I wanted tonight to go perfectly, without an argument. I can see now that was a little too much to wish for, given the high tensions running between me and my three daughters. If I had a time machine, I would go back and change things. Sasha and I have both said this so many times over the last decade. But I don't have the ability to time-travel and so I have to face the mess my family is in.

And I wasn't expecting Leah to discover the truth about her father this evening. A part of me is relieved. Relieved it's all out in the open – but also ashamed of myself that I didn't tell them all before now. It has weighed heavily on me over the years, but I didn't want the truth to cause any problems for my three girls.

Leah and Erin and I sit together talking and paving the way for bridges to be built between us all. It's cathartic and it has to be done. I just have one more daughter left to apologise to. I check back over my shoulder but there's still no sign of Sasha. I'm starting to feel stressed that she hasn't reappeared yet.

'Look at the time!' Erin exclaims. 'The children are up way too late.'

'They won't sleep anyway with music from the party,' I comment.

'They will,' Erin says confidently. 'The Winchester Room and the dining room have soundproofing, so that soaks up most of the noise.

We'll be having fireworks out here in an hour, so I've made sure their room is at the back of the building.'

She has it all figured out.

'Such great planning,' I remark. In many ways, Erin reminds me of how I was as a mother with young children. I was always firm with my girls. For the majority of their lives, I was the only parent they had. So I had to be strong for them.

'Well, only if I can herd them up there in time. Shall I encourage Freya up the stairs as well? She can sleep in with the twins or in room twelve.'

I stand up. 'I'll come with you.' Freya should be fine heading up-stairs with Erin and the twins, she's no wallflower, but she doesn't really know them properly yet so I just want to check on her myself. I'm also far colder than I realised.

'I'll sort them out,' Erin commands. 'I'm sure it won't take long.' My middle daughter disappears back into the hotel before I can reply.

'Freya will be gutted to miss the fireworks,' Leah observes.

'I was just thinking the same thing. Surely another hour won't hurt them.' I remember the days when I had three children to get to bed. They either all went up like clockwork or they all played me up at once. There was never an in between.

'Jesse and Sasha haven't come back yet.' I'm freezing now but I want to make sure Leah and Sasha get inside to warm up. I strain my ears, hoping I can hear Jesse or Sasha.

Leah checks her watch. 'They haven't been gone too long. Jesse's with Sasha so don't worry.'

'No, I'm going to go and find them. I need to see that Sasha is OK.'

Leah seems uncertain and I can tell she doesn't want to join me. She won't want to get caught up in a potential marital argument between Jesse and Sasha.

'I won't be long,' I tell her.

'I'll stay here then,' Leah suggests.

'No, you head indoors and warm up, love. There's no sense in you being out here and catching a cold as well.'

I pull out my phone and switch the torch light on, following in the footsteps of my daughter and her husband.

I peer into the dark and the snow, trying to catch a glimpse of them, but I'm surrounded by the dark blanket of the night.

I have no idea what's out here, in the grounds of Burcott House. Erin mentioned her home was a cottage set back from the hotel, so I'm assuming the land here is fairly extensive. As I progress, my eyes adjust to the darkness. I can see that I'm walking along the edge of an ornamental garden. I'm glad I didn't traipse straight through it as it's well-kept and expensive, like everything else here.

I can hear an owl hooting in a tree somewhere and the twigs snapping beneath my ankle boots but no sounds to suggest that Jesse and Sasha are nearby. I turn and see Burcott House lit up behind me, looking even more impressive at this distance. I'm shivering now but I press on, wondering how much further the pair of them are. Surely they can't have gone too far; Sasha wasn't exactly in a fit state to be going for a long walk.

I come across a bench. It's covered in snow so I sweep it off with one hand. The wooden seat is still freezing and damp but I sit down heavily on it anyway. I'm grateful for the respite as my old legs are aching from walking so fast in my quest to find my eldest daughter. My phone light shuts off. Squinting at my device in the darkness and pressing all the usual buttons, I'm dismayed to find the battery has gone. This phone isn't switching on again any time soon. So I sit for a bit longer, my legs numb.

And that's when I see it. A movement ahead of me.

Burcott House behind me is still providing a bit of light and I can make out the shape of a figure out there in the dark and the snow.

My breathing kicks up a notch. I hate the dark and my brain goes into overdrive. What if it isn't Sasha or Jesse? What if someone else is out here?

I shake the thought from my mind and continue to try and focus on the person ahead of me. There's a set of steps leading down from where I'm sitting and beyond that some kind of railings and some water. A lake maybe? Or a large pond? The light from the moon is reflecting on the water and helping my eyesight to pick out what's going on.

It's definitely a female form and in a few more seconds I'm certain it's my Sasha. I can see the curls tumbling down her back and the sparkles on her dress. There's no sign of Jesse. He could still be close by though or, if they've quarrelled, it's possible he's gone back to the hotel already. If he has, I won't be too happy with him. It's a good job I did come out here to see what was going on.

I heave myself up from my sitting position and lean against the tree next to the bench, standing in its shadow and watching my daughter's movements. She's obviously heard me moving as she suddenly whirls around, trying to identify where the sound is coming from. I realise I've scared her. I'm just about to call out and tell her that it's me when she runs off, lurching forward and staggering unsteadily. She's heading back towards Burcott House, which is something.

I start to go after her but, as I move forward, I stumble over a tree root and twist my ankle.

'Ow,' I cry out in pain, falling to the floor, the sensation taking my breath away. The snow is beginning to build now and I'm wet through as well as hurt.

Sasha must have heard the sound I made, as she looks around briefly, before continuing her race back to the warmth and light of the hotel. The noise must've spooked her out. I pull myself up to sitting and then attempt standing on my ankle but a red-hot pain shoots up my leg as I do so. Twisting my ankle is the last thing I need right now. I lean up against the tree once more. What am I going to do? My phone is out of action and Sasha is now too far away for me to call for help and be heard. Everything happened so quickly.

I could be out here for hours before someone works out where I am and comes to find me. My hands are already like blocks of ice and my legs are numb from the cold. I let myself rest for a few minutes and then try putting my weight on my left foot again. Another sharp pain. Casting around for inspiration, I see a fallen branch not far from me. Cursing under my breath, I manage to hook it up from the ground and then fashion it into a makeshift crutch. Slowly hobbling back towards Burcott House, I try to focus on the goal of getting back to the hotel and I try not to think about the cold that's freezing my bones. Instead, I keep my eyes on the warm lights glowing in the windows and hold onto the idea of sinking into a soft mattress and sleeping my cares away.

I just hope I get back to safety soon.

There's been enough drama for one night already.

# Chapter Thirty-Four
# Erin
# Ten years ago

The last few weeks have been like living in a nightmare. Leah has been in hospital and it was touch and go for a while. I haven't been able to eat or sleep properly because I've been so worried about her. But we finally got some positive news this afternoon: her head injury isn't as bad as they first thought. She's on the first step to recovery.

I thought it would mean things could go back to normal. Then Sasha cornered me in the kitchen. She'd barely spoken a word to me since the accident happened so I was surprised. I thought she might want to talk things through. I was wrong.

She yelled at me over and over again. Snippets of her angry words come back to me. One sentence stands out the most: 'You're too reckless, you're dangerous... you nearly killed our sister... and you need to leave before you go too far. Get out of here!'

I've spent weeks loathing myself, but neither Sasha or my mother seem to care how I'm feeling. I understand why my mother is so upset but I can't believe Sasha hasn't even stopped to think about how I'm feeling.

I hate them both. And I hate Sasha more for pushing me out of my home.

My face is pressed against the window of the bus as I watch the streets I've known my whole life disappear from view. I have no idea where I'm going. I only have one bag of clothes with me and just a couple of hundred pounds in my bank account.

I don't know how I'm going to do it, but I'm determined to make something of myself. I'm going to show them I don't need them. I'm not going to let this break me.

# Chapter Thirty-Five
## Leah
## Now

Everyone else has dispersed and I'm alone with my thoughts and the constant beeping of notifications that have been building up on my phone. I'm still outside, sitting at the little table on the terrace, my mind turning over all the things that have been said this evening, when I suddenly feel a hand on my shoulder.

'Xavier!' I'm instantly pulled from my musings. The hot guy from earlier is in front of me and he really is just my type. He's a few inches taller than I am in the heels I'm wearing; I'd say he's just shy of six foot tall. He has fair hair and teasing blue eyes. I enjoyed the time I've spent with him so far. He didn't seem pretentious at all, despite his public schoolboy background, so it just goes to show you shouldn't judge a book by its cover. It didn't take me long to persuade him onto the dance floor. When 'Last Christmas' was playing, I took full advantage of the song and danced close with him, his muscular arms around me. Unfortunately, that's exactly when I saw Sasha and Jesse tumbling to the ground. I rushed to help them, leaving Xavier on the dance floor. It was not a smooth move for me just to run off like that, with no explanation.

'You must be freezing.'

The dimple in his chin is so cute.

I shiver. 'Actually, I am a bit.'

'I wondered where you'd got to. What are you doing out here?'

'You wondered where I was?' I say. 'So you've been thinking about me then?' I decide to go for the forward approach. I may not cross paths with Xavier again, so I may as well make my attraction to him obvious.

'Well, yeah.' He rubs his hand through his hair. 'One minute we were dancing and the next you'd gone.'

'Not used to members of the opposite sex running away from you then?'

Xavier gives me a sheepish smile.

'Sorry about that. Some family drama, all sorted now.' I cross my fingers as I'm saying this, willing it to be true. I look out into the darkness but I can't see Sasha or Mom at all. I'm guessing they must be having a heart-to-heart or something. I should go and find them, but they might not want me to interrupt if they're talking things through.

'Want to come back inside?'

My gaze turns again in the direction Sasha and Jesse went, followed by Mom. It's been a while, maybe I should do something? I could call Erin and get her to arrange for someone from her staff, who knows the hotel grounds, to go out and find the three of them. It's so cold now. But maybe they've already come back inside through the front entrance of the hotel?

Xavier pulls me up to standing. 'Or we could just dance out here?'

He certainly is a distraction. I shake the thoughts of Jesse, Sasha and Mom out of my head. They're adults, there are three of them: I'm sure I'm worrying for no reason. Xavier and I pick up where we left off, pressing close together, and we dance slowly. He's warm and smells good, so I lay my head on his chest. After a few minutes, we come to a natural stop. I tip my head up towards him and his mouth meets mine. In a heartbeat, we're kissing in the moonlight. I'm expecting him to be rough and passionate so it takes me off guard when it's quite the opposite, more tender and sensual.

I step back, breaking the spell.

'Are you OK?' Xavier asks, reaching out for my hand.

I nod. 'Yeah... a lot has happened tonight. I just wasn't expecting...'

'Me neither.'

I move back into his arms again and we're kissing once more. I'm swept up in the moment.

All thoughts of threatening text messages and family secrets out of my mind.

# Chapter Thirty-Six
# Erin
# Now

Playing the perfect hostess has been a challenge tonight. Having my family here has been a lot harder work than I imagined. There's so much tension between everyone, so much unsaid. It's cast a shadow across the whole night.

I search for Jasper, Ophelia, and Freya. They aren't in the dining hall or the Winchester Room, where the party is now in full flow. As I make my way through the bar area, I spot Tallulah entwined with someone who's definitely not Geoffrey. He's about two decades younger for starters. The duo are oblivious to everything going on around them, so I discreetly take a snap of their antics and forward the photograph on to Mary. After all, us first wives have to stick together. I leave the bar area and as I do I come face to face with Geoffrey, who's ruddy-cheeked and marching with purpose. I could stop him here and send him off in the opposite direction to Tallulah, but where's the fun in that? I possibly didn't need to bother with the photo evidence after all. Tallulah is being so blatant about cuddling up with the first younger man she's found that I'm sure Geoffrey was going to discover her true nature sooner rather than later.

I finally find the three children in the Snug room. They're all looking heavy-eyed and sleepy so I steer them towards their beds.

'Muuummm, can't we stay up a bit longer?' Jasper protests.

I shake my head. 'No,' I say firmly. 'This is way past your bedtime already.'

Jasper gives a little huff but then follows me, with Ophelia and Freya behind us. The two girls are holding hands, it's so sweet.

'Say goodnight to Gramps,' I instruct as we pass Hugo. Ophelia and Jasper wave their goodbyes.

We climb the steep twisting staircase leading from the main hallway up to the third floor of the hotel. There's a little room at the back of the building that I always use for Ophelia and Jasper when we stay here. Our cottage isn't too far from Burcott House but it's far enough that I don't feel they're old enough yet to go back and sleep there by themselves. It's also easier for us to stay here so we can have breakfast in the morning with our guests who are staying overnight.

I glance out of the third-floor hallway window at the snow. It's falling heavily now and there are already a few inches on the ground. I expect that we might have a few more of our guests staying than originally anticipated, it's going to be difficult to drive down those country lanes in the dark with the ice and the current reduced visibility. It's a good job all of the rooms are made-up and ready. The hotel has over forty bedrooms and we can sleep up to eight over at the cottage if we need to. There's around a hundred guests, so we should just about fit everyone if needed. Although it's going to take some organising, even with the help of the staff.

'Where's my mummy and daddy?' Freya asks, as she rubs her eyes sleepily.

I glance out of the window again, wondering if Jesse and Sasha have returned yet.

'They're downstairs,' I reassure her. There's no point in worrying the little girl before she goes to bed.

I unlock the door to the bedroom and the children scoot inside. There are two sets of bunk beds and this space is decorated in soft blues. It always feels calming and peaceful whenever I'm in this part of the house.

'Freya, do you want to sleep in here with the twins?'

'Yeees!' she shouts excitedly.

'Perfect, choose your bunks then.'

The girls select the bunk bed on the left-hand side of the room to share and Jasper retreats to the other one. I can see he's being a bit left out of Ophelia and Freya's bonding.

'Are you OK?' I whisper to him, pulling him close for a cuddle.

He nods and then yawns.

'OK, pyjamas on and into bed. Freya, there's a few sets of Ophelia's in the drawer over there. They should fit you, you're both about the same size.'

The children scramble into their nightclothes and into bed. I kiss them each goodnight and tell them to sleep well. Closing the bedroom door carefully, I tread quietly away. I'm drawn to the window once more and look outside to see the snow is still falling. I shudder.

Sasha's dramatics earlier were a stark reminder of our childhood, we used to argue and make up over and over. Except we're not kids any more. This was an important event and Sasha has completely embarrassed me in front of my social circle. To say I'm not happy is putting it mildly.

I try to centre myself before going back downstairs. Now the children are down for the night, I should be able to relax a bit more but in all honesty I don't believe the drama with Sasha is over yet.

As I walk down the softly lit hallway, I hear muffled noises. It must be one of our guests retiring to bed early. I'm about to descend the stairs and I can't help but admire the spectacular staircase, adorned with tinsel weaving along the bannisters. This is one of my favourite parts of the building and the inspiration for turning a dusty, out of use ancestral home into a thriving boutique hotel. As I'm standing here, I realise something feels off. Then it dawns on me the bedrooms on the top floor haven't been allocated to any of our guests. I'd placed them all on the first and second floors, keeping the rooms up here free. Maybe Aaron has already had a request from an additional member of our party to stay here, given the weather outside? It's likely we'll be snowed in by the time the clock strikes midnight.

I can't explain my sense of unease. So I backtrack down the corridor and pause when I get to the door where the noises are coming from. I catch a familiar voice and my heart skips a beat. My thoughts are all colliding into one another, my brain conjuring up all sorts of scenarios about what might be going on behind that closed door. I catch the voice again and realise my fears could be true. But I don't want to believe it.

I try the handle. It's unlocked, so I push the door open.

My body begins to tremble. I wish I could unsee what I'm seeing, but I can't. This scene before me turns my world upside down.

My husband is standing at the other end of the room, trousers around his ankles, his bare buttocks on display. Tipped over the desk in front of him is a dark-haired woman with her skirt hitched up around her waist. It doesn't take a genius to work out what's going on. And there's no mistaking the outfit the woman is wearing.

It's one of our regular waitresses, the black skirt and pinafore marking her out clearly. After another beat I realise it's Nia – my most trusted member of staff has betrayed me. My thoughts are muddled, I'm not thinking straight. My brain is screaming at me to turn and run but my body is in shock and isn't cooperating. In the next moment, my husband whips his head around and realises there's someone standing in the doorway. He realises that someone is me.

He curses loudly and pulls away from the raven-haired woman half his age. It should be me cursing. A younger woman, I could see that coming. But one of our staff? I always feared someone in our own social circles, a woman with wealth and standing to rival me, might ensnare my husband. But this I hadn't predicted. I'm aware that it's bizarre that my train of thought is even going in this direction but, somehow, I don't want to scream or cry or have any kind of outburst of emotion. A steely calm descends on me. Everything I do from this point will count.

So I'm not going to get my claws out, slap him – or her. I simply turn around and walk straight back into the hallway. My heart feels like it will burst but I can't let that show. I can't let either of them see any emotion from me.

'Erin! Erin!' Aaron is dashing after me, his trousers pulled back up, fumbling with his belt buckle.

'Erin, wait!'

I keep walking, deliberate and steady strides back towards the staircase.

'Erin, don't just go... we need to talk.' There's a pleading note in my husband's voice that I've never heard before. He is well aware that we have a houseful of our friends and family downstairs, not to mention important business clients.

Aaron grasps my hand, pulling me off course and spinning me round to face him. His grip is tight around my wrist. As I look past him, I see a dishevelled Nia appear in the hallway behind him. She's flushed and wide-eyed.

'Erin, I'm so sorry—' She begins her apology but my husband abruptly cuts off her sentence.

'Just go, Nia. Leave this house now.'

Nia's face looks as though she's been stunned.

'What? What... did you say?' She stumbles. It's clear from her appalled expression that she was expecting Aaron to defend what they were doing, I'm sure she had designs on my husband that were more than ambitious.

'I said go,' Aaron repeats coldly. His grey eyes are still on me as he's speaking. 'Go and we'll pay your wages for the next six months, but don't ever contact me again.'

I can see what Aaron is doing. He's trying to prove this liaison really did mean nothing to him. And given his harsh, knee-jerk reaction, I'm actually inclined to think it isn't some big romance. But, even still, the damage has been done.

'But the snow?' Nia looks crestfallen, unable to comprehend that the man she was having an affair with is not hesitating to throw her out in the middle of a snowstorm.

Aaron doesn't reply.

'How dare you use me and then think you can cast me away,' Nia says, her voice laced with hatred as she comprehends the truth of her interactions with my husband. 'I'll go now, but this sure isn't the last you'll hear from me!'

Aaron's cold eyes are still on me and he doesn't even flinch at Nia's poor attempt at a threat.

Nia turns on her heel and rapidly disappears down the corridor, heading in the direction of the lift.

I try to yank my wrist out of Aaron's grasp but he's not prepared to let go so easily.

'Erin, listen to me.'

I don't want to listen to Aaron's lies. To hear him try and twist the truth into something that fits his purpose. I know he'll use every trick in the book to try and get me to accept this and carry on with our marriage.

I recoil and jerk away from him, finally managing to pull myself free. As I do, I trip backwards and I'm tipped off balance. I can feel myself toppling and a surge of panic washes over me. We're right beside the staircase and there's a sheer drop below.

This thought is rushing through my mind as gravity pulls me off my feet and downwards. I throw my arms wide, afraid of falling.

I just manage to clasp hold of the wooden bannister and right myself so I'm back firmly on my feet. My eyes are drawn to the drop below. The bannisters are high for safety reasons because there's no way anyone would survive a fall from up here, down onto the unforgiving marble floor below.

Aaron is white with shock. 'Erin, are you OK?'

I'm not sure if he means from my tumble or from what I've just walked in on. I don't know how he can even ask that question after what he's done. My brain starts to speed up and all kinds of questions brim to the surface. Was this a one-off? Has he been seeing her behind my back? Is this the first affair or one of many?

'Erin, it's not what it looks like. I... I...'

'That was exactly what it looked like.'

This was the sentence that came into my mind. Except I didn't say it out loud, someone else did. Scanning the hallway I'm startled to find another person has been standing in the shadows behind us. Somebody else has witnessed everything that happened in the last few minutes.

And the figure is stepping towards us, with a manic grin on their face.

# Chapter Thirty-Seven
## Leah
## Now

'Well, that really was unexpected.' Xavier is looking at me with his sea-blue eyes, a crooked smile on his face.

'All the best things are,' I reply, leaning in to kiss him once more.

We've moved inside now, back into the warmth of the hotel. We're curled up next to each other on one of the squishy sofas in the Snug, the roaring fire a welcome source of warmth after being outside. Although that's not the only heat in the room – the energy between us is palpable. A clock strikes midnight in the background.

'So how do you know Erin and Aaron?' I ask, making small talk as we thread our fingers together.

'Aaron's a family friend. Our fathers know each other well.'

I nod my head, having guessed that the answer would be along these lines.

'What's the deal with being Erin's sister then?' Xavier says. 'I've never heard Erin mention that she had siblings.'

This stings. To think Erin cut us out of her lives so completely that she wouldn't even acknowledge our existence. I shouldn't be surprised, and I'm sure Erin didn't want people prying, but still.

'I'm her younger sister. I've been travelling a lot.'

'Oh yeah, where have you been?'

'Everywhere,' I laugh, relieved he isn't probing the sibling question any further. 'I'm just back from Oz.'

'Nice.'

'A bit of a change of climate.'

'Just a bit. So you're the eternal wanderer then?'

'You could say that. I took a gap year before going to uni and I got the travel bug. I never did go to uni! But I don't regret it. Sitting in a stuffy exam hall or sitting on Bondi Beach? There's no contest.'

'When you put it like that, it makes sense. So do you travel alone? With a group? Boyfriend?'

Ah, so that's what he's getting at. I giggle. 'No group, no boyfriend, just me.'

I lay my head back on the sofa and close my eyes. That's not the complete truth. I've flitted around with different groups over the years. Eventually they all disband and head home to grow up, get jobs, settle down. Not me, I'm Peter Pan. I never want to grow up. Travelling suits me, I can't imagine doing anything else. There was of course someone, not so long ago. I thought he was the one. Things changed quickly.

'Are you planning another trip?' Xavier questions.

'Mmmm, I don't really plan ahead. I just go with the flow.'

Xavier lays his head next to mine and a silence settles between us. He has a solid, dependable air about him despite his insane good looks.

'I might take a trip with my mom to Europe, although I'm not sure if I will be able to pull her away from grandparent duties.'

'And if you can't?'

I shrug. The answer is, *I don't know*. I really don't plan ahead.

'How does skiing sound?'

'Skiing?'

'Yeah, I'm skiing in France after Christmas. I've got accommodation, you could join me.'

I turn and study Xavier. His expression is sincere, but I've met too many guys who promise the earth and then don't follow through.

'You've only just met me.'

'I'd like to get to know you more.'

'Nice line.'

'It's not a line, I mean it.'

I prop myself up by my elbow. 'Possibly,' I say in a non-committal tone. I can tell Xavier isn't used to women who play hard to get. This could be interesting. I'm not saying yes, but I like him enough that I just might take him up on the offer.

'I'll go and get more drinks,' Xavier declares. 'Another shot before we hit the dance floor?'

'Ha! Go on then.'

He gets up and I check my watch. The night is wearing on. I suddenly wonder where everyone is. I haven't seen Mom, Jesse, or Sasha. But surely they're not still outside? I move out of the Snug and into the long corridor with the floor-to-ceiling glass windows dominating one wall; the wind is howling outside and the snow is coming down in sheets. I feel guilty for not accompanying Mom. I haven't seen Erin for a while either but I have been wrapped up in Xavier's arms so it's possible I've tuned out for a bit too long.

My phone rings. I snatch it out of my handbag, it could be Mom or Sasha. But the number flashing up on the screen tells me it's not. It's an unknown number but I bet I know who it is. I grit my teeth. I'm fed up with this now. The message to leave me alone obviously isn't being received.

I head in the direction of the loos. I'm going to flush the sodding phone away, that way no one can bother me anymore. I head determinedly in the direction of the ladies', a woman on a mission.

'Leah!'

It's Erin. At least one member of my family has materialised. Her green eyes are bright, her cheeks are flushed and her hair is slightly more dishevelled than earlier. She still looks good but now she has a few stray strands escaping her neat chignon, framing her face and making her seem younger.

'Erin, are you OK?'

Her lip quivers and she suddenly looks vulnerable. This whole evening she's appeared so poised and polished but now something seems to have created a chink in her armour and her mask is finally slipping.

'Hey, what happened?' I ask her.

She shakes her head and rolls back her shoulders. 'I'm fine, I'm fine.'

'Are you sure?'

She nods. 'Where's Sasha?'

'I'm not sure. I hope she's not still outside... Mom went after her and Jesse. I haven't seen any of them since. Everyone seems to have gone AWOL.'

Erin's nostrils flare slightly. 'I'd forgotten what the drama was like with two sisters.'

I giggle.

'I've missed you; you know?' I say softly.

'Me too,' she admits. 'Life is just not the same without my crazy family.'

I'm anxious and when I'm anxious I always subconsciously run my fingers over my scar, down from my temple to my ear. My make-up covers it well but it's still there, still visible. Still a reminder of that night.

'Oh Leah, I'm so sorry.' Erin catches my hand and pulls me into a hug.

These are the words I was waiting to hear from her. The apology she has never said to me.

'You know I never meant to hurt you, don't you? I'm sorry.'

'You and me both,' I say, my words muffled as we cling to each other. I feel as though a huge weight has been lifted off my shoulders. It shouldn't have taken this long but Erin has finally apologised for what she did.

I just hope she means it.

If she does, then we might be able to move on. Now the unspoken words have been said, Erin and I could work on a new relationship. I would like nothing more than to have her back in my life.

Besides, she really has done well for herself. The least my sister could do is give me a slice of her life of luxury.

Because after what she did, sorry only goes so far.

Her debt isn't paid. She still owes me.

# Chapter Thirty-Eight
## Erin
## Now

'Come on, let's go and dance,' I suggest to Leah.

I can't dwell on what's just happened with Aaron. I can't think about his affair with Nia, not now. Not tonight. I've got to try and get through the rest of the evening. I mentally shake myself, switching back into lady-of-the-manor mode, and drawing on every acting skill I possess to keep going. I can't let anyone see the turbulent emotions behind my calm exterior.

It's just gone midnight, the guests who weren't staying here and have decided to brave the weather have already departed. A few others have already gone up to their rooms to sleep. The remainder are set to be partying until the small hours and will no doubt crash out in the Snug. We have a small firework display arranged in the next half an hour and the live band are due to start soon and they'll be here until 3 a.m. So I've got to keep myself together for a little while longer.

Leah and I link arms and make our way to the dance floor, just as 'I Wish It Could Be Christmas Every Day' starts playing. I block out all thoughts of my husband. The dance floor is packed now, I'm pleased to see everyone enjoying themselves.

'There you are!'

Xavier Knight has appeared next to Leah and is passing her a shot of something that's radioactive green in colour. They clink the miniature glasses and tip them up to their lips in sync.

'Urgh,' Leah cries, 'what was that?'

'You don't want to know,' Xavier jokes.

I can tell by the way he's looking at her that Xavier is into Leah and she seems equally keen.

'Woah, didn't see you there, Erin. Sorry, do you want a shot?'

'No, no I'm good, thank you Xavier. I'll leave the shots to you two.'

Xavier assesses the situation and seems to understand he's intruded on a moment between siblings.

'I'll be back in a bit,' he tells Leah.

To my surprise, Leah leans in and kisses him before he disappears into the crowd.

'I know, I know,' she says, seeing the expression on my face. 'It's Christmas!'

'Xavier's a good guy,' I tell her. 'You could do much worse.' It's true he is a decent person, he's handsome and the whole package is made all the more appealing by his family's infinite wealth. I can see why Leah is interested. I look at my baby sister and recognise what a remarkable young woman she has transformed into. The scar on the left side of her face is barely visible now, thanks to some carefully applied make-up, and she looks so youthful and full of life.

'You know, we're not so different, you and I,' I remark to Leah. She could easily snare an eligible bachelor and follow in my footsteps to make a new life for herself.

Leah gives me a blank stare. It dawns on me that she could take this statement absolutely the wrong way. After all, I was responsible for the accident that left her in hospital and with a permanent scar. She didn't press charges, so I never had to face any formal consequences for my actions. But Leah was in hospital for several weeks and my mother was a mess. I can understand why, her youngest daughter had been run over, which is enough of a shock for anyone. But because Simon, Leah's dad and the man who raised me, lost his life in a car crash, our mother was even more distraught as a result. Even when we were told by the doctors that Leah had been very lucky and would make a full recovery bar a broken arm and a nasty scar along her face, Nadia was still a jittery wreck. And every time we spoke we ended up arguing. It was like she thought I'd done it deliberately. Sasha didn't help matters. She'd always had my back – I trusted her completely – but she turned on me. Her reaction was worse than Nadia's.

'If I end up with half of what you've achieved, I'll be happy,' Leah replies, before reaching out for my hands.

I spin with my sister in the middle of the dance floor, our hands clasped tight, whirling round to the music just as we did when we were children. The DJ is playing yet another classic Christmas tune and we both shout along at the tops of our voices, smiles wide, eyes bright, mirroring each other. Rainbow-coloured disco lights shine across the vast room and the crowd around us shimmers and sparkles.

As the song ends, I stagger, wobbling on my high heels and putting a hand to my throbbing head. I feel a steadying arm loop through mine and I'm guided along the edges of the friends and family gathered here to celebrate in this exquisite hotel. Everyone else seems to be in the moment, lapping up the festive atmosphere. A huge Christmas tree dominates one corner of the room, the warm gold and red colour scheme spills out across the rest of the space and throughout the multitude of plush rooms beyond. Everything looks perfect on the surface. But, right now, I need to get away from the party.

When I exit through the double doors, the noise instantly dims and I feel like I can breathe properly again. I make my way along a winding corridor, my sister's hand in mine, and then we swing open another set of double doors into the grand foyer. This is the dazzling focal point of the building, with its curved marble staircase and sweeping gallery complete with a sparkling crystal chandelier.

The first thing I notice is the strange silence in the room. The music from the party shut out by the soundproofing.

The second thing I notice is the dead body. Lying spread-eagled on the white marble floor, a pool of dark red blood surrounding the head like a halo.

Leah inhales sharply next to me. So I'm not imagining this. This is not a horrible dream. It's real.

Someone is dead, their blood pooling on my white marble tiled floor. This shouldn't be happening. Not tonight.

All of these thoughts are flashing through my brain. I can't allow myself to panic. I need to take charge of the situation. Damage limitation is important right now.

My heart is hammering in my chest. I lift my chin and make myself turn once more in the direction of the person lying on the floor. I immediately recognise the broken figure at the foot of the marble staircase. I recognise the shoes, the cut of the clothing, the ring on the finger instantly.

And I scream...

# Chapter Thirty-Nine
# Leah
# Now

I'm swept away by the party atmosphere around us. The night is definitely getting merry, stuffy businessmen are discarding their ties, perfectly applied lipstick is now smudged and many of the guests are dancing away with abandon. The DJ set has given way to a band, who are geeing up the crowd. It feels like Christmas.

I snap a few pictures of me and Erin with our arms around each other. I know my followers are going to love seeing images of me with my secret sister. This will be a nice little story to tease out, a Christmas reunion, a family together again. My fans will go crazy for it. As I'm singing along to the music, I make a mental note to ask Erin if I can film some videos here at Burcott House. The setting is just incredible and I can't wait to see more of the hotel tomorrow.

Erin and I dance together for one song, but I get the feeling she's not in the mood. 'Let's sit this one out,' my sister whispers in my ear as the band strikes up a new chord. She's a little unsteady on her feet so I loop my arm through hers and guide her along the edge of the dance floor.

'This way,' Erin points to the large double doors at the end of the Winchester Room. I'm starting to get a handle on the layout of the sprawling country mansion now. I notice that Erin is looking a little less sleek and a little more rumpled than she was at the start of the party. We head down a corridor, back towards the entrance of Burcott House.

The beat of the music has already faded by the time we reach another set of thick double doors. The Bailey-Scotts must have some seriously good soundproofing, but I guess it's a worthwhile investment when you have a function room and accommodation in one building. Erin flings open the doors and I find myself back in the magnificent foyer. It's a breathtaking room. The dazzling white staircase combined with the white walls and white floor makes you feel like you could be somewhere abroad. This is definitely a statement room and the statement is the Bailey-Scotts have money.

As I step into the space, my attention is drawn upwards to the impressive chandelier glittering overhead. The sweeping stairs curve up to the gallery corridor above us and they seem to go up and up and up beyond this too. It looks like there's three floors altogether but I can't be sure because of the way the staircase curves round.

Erin goes rigid next to me. Something isn't right. My eyes flick to the scene in front of me and my hand flies to my mouth.

There, smashed on the perfect white floor, is a body. A person who was once whole is now broken. I look back up to the gallery corridor above; there's no one else to be seen.

I immediately feel like I'm going to vomit. I press my fingers hard to my lips to stop the rising bile in my throat and shut my eyes tightly, to block out the reality before me. I've only ever seen one dead body before and that was enough.

I'm frozen to the spot, time is standing still, and I can't move. My brain is urging me to turn around and flee but I can't seem to move my legs. I don't want to look back at the poor soul whose life has just ended but I'm going to have to. I take a deep breath and steel myself. I've got to remain calm because this could be a crime scene now.

I open my eyes. Erin is no longer at my side; she's walking towards the body on the ground. Walking slowly and quietly, as if taking care not to make a noise in case the person might just be sleeping. If only that was true. Erin's hands go to her hair and she pulls at her copper locks, the chignon bun comes undone, her eyes are wild and her complexion is something akin to grey. She lets out a bloodcurdling scream and it pierces right through me. I've never heard a sound like it and I never want to again. She rushes towards the body, still a few paces to go until she reaches it.

'Erin, no!' I yell. My limbs wake up and I spring forward, closing the gap between us and yanking her back. She can't touch the dead person; I've watched enough cop shows to know she can't contaminate the area. Now my brain has kicked into gear, I'm certain this will become a crime scene and we will be the prime witnesses. How has this Christmas party ended in murder?

Erin is whimpering beside me, she drops to her knees, sinking down like a puppet.

'Aaron! Aaron! Aaron!'

I whip my head around, thinking I might see Erin's husband standing at the double doors we've just come through. My first thought is that he has stepped into the room and Erin is calling out to him. But no. There's no one else here. Just me and Erin and the body on the floor.

The body on the floor.

Erin's husband.

# Chapter Forty
# Erin
# Ten years ago

This is the perfect date night: candles are flickering, the music is low and our glasses are filled with expensive wine. The man sitting across the table from me is handsome, clever and rich. I'm not expecting him to get down on one knee tonight but I can tell that a diamond ring is within my reach. If I play this right, I could have a life of luxury.

Aaron Scott is everything I want. He's my ticket to a better life and I'm going to grab it with both hands. It helps that he's a smooth talker and a good kisser. The fact that Aaron's family has an ancestral home, acres of land, a ski chalet and their own yacht is even better. Not to mention an impressive lineage that dates back centuries.

I'll do anything to make sure I become Aaron's wife. It's a shame I can't fall in love with him but my heart still belongs to someone else. My first love. I can't shake him from my mind, even now as I'm being wined and dined by one of the most eligible bachelors in England.

But I can't allow my past to get in the way of this opportunity. I'm going to make sure this marriage happens. Then, once I'm wealthy beyond my wildest imagination, I'm going to start plotting my revenge.

Because my family may not have forgiven me but I haven't forgiven them either…

# Chapter Forty-One
## Sasha
## Now

I'm not dead. I'm still alive, although I'm exhausted, thirsty and colder than I've ever been in my life. I somehow managed to stagger back to Burcott House, constantly checking over my shoulder, the hairs on my neck standing on end. I couldn't shake the sense that someone was watching me. Someone was following me, I'm sure of it.

It felt like the longest journey of my life. I wanted to stop, but I was propelled forward by my own fear. When I finally reached Burcott House, I collapsed on the very same chair I was perched on over an hour ago. I'm sitting here now, my chest still heaving as I try to calm my tattered nerves. My feet are sore and painful, I daren't look at them as they've probably been ripped to shreds. I could do with a whisky or something equally strong right now but there's no way I can go back into the main hub of the party looking like this.

Gingerly I stand up, each step I take like treading on hot coals because my feet are stinging so badly. I'm drenched through, my dress hanging heavily on me. The snow and the sludge and the mud have left splatters all over me. My fingernails are caked with dirt where I fell over a few times. Two guests come out onto the terrace, the man takes no notice of me but the woman stares at me and curls her lip. I can't imagine what my overall appearance must be like, but it speaks volumes that she simply looks at me with disdain and turns away. There's no question as to whether I'm OK, if I'm hurt, if I need help. I choke back a sob before weaving unsteadily back into the hotel. I somehow find my way into the Snug. My head feels strange. I slump down onto a sofa and try to shake the odd feeling that's washing over me. My senses are dulled, the sounds around me are muffled and my legs feel far too heavy...

*** 

I wake up. I can hear a clock chiming midnight. The smell of coffee fills my nostrils, and a half-drunk cup is on the low table to the side of me. I don't remember drinking it. I don't remember much of the last few hours. I heave myself up and try to regain my sense of direction. I need to go to the bathroom, so I shakily navigate my way along the fringes of the hotel, trying to locate one. I keep my head down but the corridors are empty of people now. I'm grateful as I don't want anyone to see me in this state.

I find myself near the reception area, at the front of the hotel, and take the first door on my right. I'm disorientated and the bright lights are blinding me after being asleep. I make my way to one of the bathrooms and again breathe a sigh of relief when I discover this room is empty as well. Turning on the hot tap, I squirt some soap on my hands. The dirty water disappears down the plughole and I scrub my fingers until they're red raw. I dry my hands with a paper towel and then glance at my reflection in the mirrored wall next to me.

I sigh. The transformation in my appearance in just a few short hours is quite something. My curls are wild and frizzy, I have a leaf sticking out of my hair and the sleeve of my dress is torn. But this is nothing in comparison to my smudged, tear-stained face. My nose is red and I have a streak of mud along my cheekbone. The expensive make-up I purchased has not fared well in the outdoor elements. My branded waterproof mascara has run, my lipstick has smeared and the glitter from my eyeshadow now appears to be everywhere. I do my best to patch myself up in an effort to make myself more presentable, removing the leaf, wiping off as much of the make-up as I can and trying to flatten my unruly hair. There's not much I can do about the rip in my dress or the fact that it's even more shapeless than before, due to the amount of water it's absorbed. I turn my attention to my feet and notice I've left bloody footprints across the floor. I try to wipe down the trail I've left but end up getting red stains on my hands. I need a plaster or something to stop the flow of blood coming from a gash on my right foot. I try pressing a paper towel to it for a few minutes and it slowly eases up.

Next, I pat myself down and then resolve to find our hotel room so I can hide away from prying eyes until the morning. I stumble my way back to the reception desk, which is still empty, and go through another door. I'm certain this is the way we entered at the start of the night, but this place is so vast I'm not one hundred percent sure.

It seems like forever ago that I was first standing here, waiting to enter unknown territory before the party started, when in reality it's only been a few hours. I step into the magnificent foyer, relieved I picked the correct way to go. The room is striking, a centrepiece in the middle of the hotel.

'Sasha!' Leah's voice is calling me from across the other side of the huge room. 'Sasha!'

I survey the scene in front of me and rub my eyes. Maybe I've had so much to drink that I'm now hallucinating. My head is hurting like hell and I can't quite make sense of what I'm seeing. But when I look again, I'm met with the same scenario. Leah is holding onto Erin, rocking and shushing her like a child, while Erin sobs uncontrollably. Beyond them someone is lying on the floor, stretched out like a starfish.

'What's going on?' I manage to croak.

A strange look passes over Leah's face and she shakes her head. The world seems to go into slow motion as I make my way over to my two sisters. I see there's a trickle of red across the white marble floor; the person's head is at an awkward angle. They're not moving.

'What's going on?' I say once more, this time a little louder. Then, as my eyes begin to focus a little more, I see the figure on the floor is a man, quite clearly no longer alive. The world begins to speed up again.

'No, no, it's not Jesse, is it?' As the words leave my mouth, I realise it isn't my husband lying there. The shoes aren't his and neither is the shirt but there is something strangely familiar about the clothing.

'Aaron, Aaron...' Erin is crying softly. I just about make out the name she is saying over and over and my stomach drops.

'No, no... it can't be... it's not... is he really dead?' My voice is shaking, my whole body tingling with disbelief.

'He is,' Leah says, her voice cool and even.

'What happened?' I ask, trying to fathom how Erin's husband came to be prone on the ground, his life cut short before his time. I gaze up at the high gallery above and things click into place. 'Did he fall?'

Something breaks in Erin and she leaps up from where Leah has been holding her in a sitting position on the floor.

'Yes, he is dead!' Erin screeches at me, her voice high and unnatural. 'Isn't that obvious!'

'Erin, calm down!' Leah has sprung up now too, trying to gather Erin back into her arms, trying to contain our sister's emotions.

'How can I calm down! Aaron is dead.' Her voice is still at full volume and laced with aggression.

'I'm so sorry. I'm so, so sorry,' Leah says and then bursts into tears, backing away from the body, as if trying to put as much distance between her and what has happened.

Erin sobs.

'Was it an accident?' I question, my voice thick with shock.

Erin advances towards me and the expression she's wearing is full of hatred. She lunges at me and grabs me by my dress.

'No one could fall accidently over those bannisters. We made sure they were safe when we installed them. So...' Erin's eyes widen, her face inches from mine. 'You, where were you?' Erin spits the words at me.

I stammer, unable to reply before Erin is screaming at me once again.

'Where have you been?'

'I... I was...'

'You've had it in for me from the second you stepped through the door. You didn't want to be here.'

'Erin, what has this got to do with Sasha?' Leah has stopped crying now, wiping her tears as she comes to stand next to Erin.

'Where were you?' Erin is shouting for a third time.

I still can't answer, my brain feels fuzzy and my mouth is dry.

'It was you, wasn't it? You killed my husband.'

# Chapter Forty-Two
## Erin
## Now

'You killed Aaron!'

I'm screaming at Sasha, my throat feels like it's on fire but now I've started I can't seem to stop. A raging storm is going on in my mind, my thoughts crashing into one another.

'Erin, how can you say that?' Sasha is yelling back at me now, her face blanched, her whole body shaking.

'I heard you in the toilets talking to Leah. I heard the hatred in your voice. You're jealous of me and this is some sort of twisted revenge—'

'Erin, stop!' Sasha puts her hands over her ears like a child, as if this action will block out my accusations.

'You've been missing for ages and my husband is dead! He's dead!' I sound hysterical and that's because I am.

'I was outside. You saw me go with Jesse. I've only just come back in; I can't be in two places at once.'

'Is Jesse with you?' Leah asks, her voice also shaking with emotion.

'Jesse? No. I ran off. He was out there with me. I don't know if he's still out there. We argued.'

'So has anyone seen you in the last hour?' Leah questions, a hard look on her face.

'No...' Sasha pauses and reconsiders her answer. 'I mean, yes, I think so... My head hurts.'

Sasha looks at Leah and me and then back again. She seems bewildered and she can't seem to recall what she's been doing but I don't feel even a tiny bit sorry for her. Sasha doesn't have an alibi, there's no one to vouch for her. That's enough to label her guilty in my book.

I rub my forehead. So much has happened here tonight, so much to try and untangle and understand. I glance around the foyer; it was my favourite place in the hotel. It was the room that Aaron and I were most proud of. We spent hours designing and redesigning it and the result was perfect. It seems absurd that just a few days ago I was in here, putting the star on top of the Christmas tree. Never again will I be able to step in here without seeing the image of my husband's brains splattered across the tiles.

I look up to the floors above us. There's no way anyone could believe my husband's death was an accident. The bannisters are too high for anyone to fall over. We made sure they were safe when we refurbished the hotel. And everyone who knew Aaron will say he had no reason to take his own life. He had everything and no motive to end things. The minute the police get here they will see this as well; they will know straight away that they're dealing with a murder.

'Please believe me Erin, you've got this wrong. Things may be strained between us but I would never kill someone. Come on, you know me.' Sasha's dark hair is wild and frizzy and her overall appearance conjures up the image of a scarecrow, someone who has been outside and battered by the elements.

I shake my head, my lips pressed in a tight line. I haven't seen Sasha in ten years, I don't really know who she is any more. Her behaviour tonight has really hit that fact home.

'Leah, this is madness. You don't think I did it, do you?' Sasha is appealing to our younger sister now. A sweat has broken out on her forehead.

Leah looks Sasha straight in the eye. 'I don't want to believe you did it, Sasha. I love you. But...'

'Oh.' Sasha is wringing her hands now. 'Don't say it, Leah. Please, please don't say you think I could've done this.'

'I'm sorry Sasha. You've been acting erratically tonight. There's a gap in time that you're not able to fill. I'm not saying you did it – or that you meant to – but I can't take your side on this until we know more. A man is dead.'

Thank goodness Leah can believe there's a very real possibility that Sasha killed Aaron. Leah is squeezing my hand now in solidarity and I'm reassured that my baby sister is on my side. I vow that I won't let things rest until Sasha is behind bars.

I suddenly feel drained and I'm aware that I ache all over. The reality of what has happened is starting to hit me. I don't want to be here in this room with the broken remains of my husband. But I can't waver now, the aftermath is only just beginning.

I need to be strong.

And I need to everyone to believe Sasha is a murderer.

# Chapter Forty-Three
# Leah
# Now

I feel afraid. So afraid. If I'd had any inkling something like this was going to happen then I would never, ever have come here tonight. What happened all those years ago, the accident which led to our family being fractured, is nothing in comparison to the horrific way in which Aaron Bailey-Scott has fallen to his death.

I only met Aaron tonight, but he appeared to be decent enough. And Erin seemed happy, like she'd met her match. But in the blink of an eye she's been made a widow and those poor kids are now fatherless. My heart breaks for them. I've experienced what it's like to lose a father in tragic circumstances. I was sobbing earlier, not for Aaron, not for Erin, not for me, but for the twins. Their lives will change beyond measure now. I'm catapulted back to the spectrum of grief and loss that I went through as a young child after my dear daddy was taken too soon in a car accident. A freak accident is one thing though, a death like this is unimaginable.

My phone begins buzzing in my back pocket. I still haven't had the opportunity to dispose of it. I check the screen and, as I suspected, it's the same number again. My sense of fear is heightened and I wish I could just catch the next flight out of here and not have to deal with this intense situation any longer. Except, I can't leave this time. Erin's children are going to need all the support they can get.

I gasp out loud. *Freya*. I'd forgotten in all of this that poor Freya might lose her mother to a prison cell. My lovely niece, the little girl I adore. My mind is racing so much that her piece in this jigsaw hadn't occurred to me. I take in the bewildered expression on Sasha's face and I bite my lip. Erin is so sure that Sasha is responsible but it goes against everything I know about my eldest sister.

'Perhaps we've all been too hasty,' I say, backtracking on my previous statement. 'Sasha, you can see how this looks—'

'Leah, I can see how this looks, but I'm innocent. I would never have done this and you know why.'

'Freya,' we both say in unison.

As I say this, I know it's the truth. Sasha might not have an alibi. She might have been raging drunk but there's nothing she would ever do, whatever state she was in, to risk being parted from her only daughter.

'Leah, you just said she was guilty. How can you change your mind so quickly?' Erin looks outraged.

'I don't know. This is all so crazy. But I do know Sasha would never do anything to hurt Freya or to be split apart from her. This... This whole thing is insane.'

I look around at the lavish Christmas tree, the shocked faces of my sisters and the steep, curving staircase. My head feels as though it's going to explode.

'Insane? What's insane is that my husband is lying dead over there! We were so happy, we had everything—'

A noise comes from the gallery above. Amongst all of our arguing and pointing the finger at Sasha, I'd failed to remember that if Sasha wasn't responsible for Aaron's demise then someone else was. The killer could still be here, in this house. They could be coming back right at this very moment.

We could be next.

'Oh my god! Who is it? Who's up there?'

I'm really frightened now. I don't want to die. I don't want my life to end tonight. I have too many goals and dreams that I want to achieve, too many places that I haven't yet travelled to.

Erin clutches my hand and the three of us stand there at the bottom of the spiral staircase, collectively holding our breath. Someone is stepping out of the shadows, coming towards the top of the staircase. I'm transfixed, unable to move an inch. I have to know who it is.

'Run!' Sasha yells and bolts for the nearest door.

Erin is still grasping my hand and I can't take my eyes off the space at the top of the staircase. The space where the figure from the shadows above is moving to.

'Sasha do not go anywhere,' the commanding voice orders from above us.

Sasha stops, her hand inches from the door handle. She turns around, mouth wide open and visibly stunned.

The figure comes into view and I'm totally confused.

It's the last person I was expecting to see.

Surely this isn't the person who pushed Aaron to his death?

# Chapter Forty-Four
# Sasha
# Now

Our mother, Nadia, is standing at the top of the stairs.

'Mum? Mum, is that you?'

Mum is walking down towards us now, slow and deliberate steps. Her hand clutching the railing, as though she's all too aware of what might happen if she slipped. All three of us watch her descend. For a fleeting second, I'm scared that Mum is behind all of this. Did she end Aaron's life? But why would she? She's only just met him tonight. What possible reason could she have to kill a man she's laid eyes on only this evening? It can't be true. After all, this is my mother; she's kind, selfless and loving. She doesn't have a bad bone in her body.

Mum stops when she reaches the final step and stays there. Raised up, hovering just above us. She observes each of us in turn. I feel as though her eyes are boring into my soul, seeing through me and all my secrets.

Mum looks over at Aaron's body and shudders. I can't bring myself to turn in that direction again so I keep my eyes firmly on my mother, waiting to hear what she is about to say.

'Girls, you need to tell me what's happened. You need to tell me the truth.'

Her voice is firm. She's looking at us like we're all little children again, waiting to find out which one of us has stolen a cookie from the jar. Except now someone is dead.

I guess if she's giving us the third degree she can't be responsible. It was only a fleeting thought because I feel like I've been tipped into an alternate universe. I've just had Erin, my estranged sister, accusing me of killing her husband. Things feel like they couldn't get any stranger tonight but I have a sinking feeling this evening is about to get a lot worse.

Leah speaks first. 'Erin and I were dancing; we were dancing to a Christmas song. We were having so much fun...' Her voice trails off, disbelief written all over her face.

'What happened next?' Mum presses, her gaze concentrated on Leah.

'We decided to have a break. Erin wanted to freshen up. We came along the corridor and through that door.' Leah is now pointing to show which of the three doors they entered by. 'We walked in and... and we saw Aaron on the floor.'

At this, Erin covers her face with her hands and lets out a strangled sob. Leah rubs her back, trying but failing to comfort her.

'Did you see anyone? Anyone else at all?'

Leah shakes her head.

'Erin, tell me the truth.'

Erin brings her hands down from her face. Her cheeks are pink and her eyes are watery. 'What Leah said,' she stammers, before sobbing further.

Mum waits for Erin to calm down. An eerie silence settles all around us.

'She did it!' Erin finally screeches, pointing her red-painted finger-nail at me.

All eyes turn on me.

'Sasha turned up after us,' Leah says. 'That's all I know.'

'We asked her where she'd been and she couldn't tell us. She couldn't tell us who she'd been with either.' Erin's voice is sharp and laced with anger.

'I was outside, you all saw me. I went with Jesse and we argued. I stormed off. I needed some space. Then I walked back here.' I pause, mentally tracing my steps.

'There were two people actually!' I say, remembering the couple from the terrace and the woman who curled her lip at me. 'I don't know their names, but they were with me outside on the terrace when I came back. I'd know them if I saw them again.' As the words tumble from my mouth I realise this isn't true. I'm not sure I would recognise them both again. Maybe the woman but I didn't get a proper look at the man.

I thought Erin was just clutching at straws earlier but she's not about to let up. There's a body in this building so the police will have to be called. Erin could tell them I'm guilty. The wife of a dead man is hurling accusations at me and I don't have an alibi. Could her allegation be taken seriously? Could I go to prison for this?

I'm terrified that I'm about to lose everything: my child, my husband, my job, my freedom. All because Erin is determined to pin the blame for her husband's death on me.

I didn't do it.

I'm innocent.

# Chapter Forty-Five
# Nadia
# Now

'Have you told me everything?'

All three of them remain silent.

I study my girls one by one. Sasha is completely dishevelled. Her curly hair is static and frizzy, her dress is hanging limply on her frame and her eyes are puffy. She's shaking like a leaf and looks horrified by the claims Erin is making. Erin herself appears angry, her whole body thrumming with energy. Her face is tear-stained and she's clearly been crying a lot. Leah, like the other two, is pale with shock. Her white-blonde bob is still sleek and, of the three of them, she is the only one who seems as though she could still re-enter the party without anyone suspecting that she'd been involved in such dramatic events.

'This is ridiculous. It was *not* me!' Sasha is exclaiming. 'Erin, just stop saying that. I have no reason to want your husband dead. We're all wasting time when the real killer is still somewhere in this hotel.'

Sasha's words sink in. She's right of course. Then Sasha rushes towards me, taking the steps at pace and attempting to slide past me to go up the staircase. 'I just want to get my daughter and get the hell out of here.'

I catch her by the hand and pull her to a stop, wincing as red hot pain shoots through my swollen ankle.

'Sasha, do you not remember seeing me? We sat together on the sofa and dried out in front of the fire.'

Sasha's brow smooths out. 'Oh, yes! I remember now! Of course, we sat and had coffee. In the Snug.'

'That's right. So no more accusations Erin, Sasha was with me.'

Erin looks from me to Sasha and back again. 'And what time was that? For how long?'

I ignore Erin and move on. 'Right, here's what we're going to do...'

I raised my three girls, almost single-handedly, while juggling jobs to make ends meet. I've had to be tough and, when my back is against the wall, I'm prepared to do whatever it takes to protect my children. So I have to take charge and steer my daughters through this terrible ordeal. I made a mistake letting this feud with Erin go on for so long and now I'm going to make things right. I just hope that we can all get out the other side of this in one piece.

'We all have to work together,' I instruct. 'Erin, we don't want any guests wandering in here so that's the first thing we need to organise. Have you got a key to lock the doors down here?'

'There's one in reception.'

'OK, go and get it.'

Erin nods, glancing back at her husband's prone figure.

'Are you all right to go by yourself?' I ask, relieved that my children are listening to me.

'Yes. Although the fireworks will be starting soon.' Erin checks her gold watch. It's just gone midnight. 'Everyone will be wondering where I am.'

'At least that means most of the guests will be outside,' I say.

'That's true, but many of the older ones wait up for the fireworks and then want to head straight to bed. They can't come in here. They can't see Aaron!'

'Don't worry, if they're going outside we can make sure they stay outside or in one of the function rooms for as long as possible.'

'Oh my god, you're not seriously about to suggest what I think you're about to suggest, are you Mom?' Leah cries.

Before I can reply Leah is talking at top speed, without pause. 'You're not suggesting we get rid of the body? Pretend like this didn't happen?'

'What?' Erin is aghast at this comment.

'No!' I reply sharply. 'We need to call the police but it's going to take time for them to get here, isn't it? We're snowed in and miles away from the nearest town. In the meantime, we don't want anyone in here disturbing... the... the deceased. Or getting a shock for that matter.'

'Oh, I get it.' Leah deflates, reassured I'm not about to ask her to go and get a wheelbarrow and a spade.

Erin nods. 'I agree. I need to limit the damage of all this to my children. Losing their father is one thing but the scandal of a murder at Burcott House isn't going to be easy to live with either.' She rushes off towards the reception, clearly on a mission now to try and protect her family reputation as much as she can, her shoes clattering across the polished floor.

I turn to my youngest daughter and issue her with instructions. 'Leah, can you go and tell the staff to keep everyone outside for the fireworks. Tell them to take out blankets, hot chocolates, extra sparklers, whatever it takes to make sure the guests stay away from this area of the hotel. Go quickly and knock four times on the door to come back in.'

Leah spins on her heel and hurries off to do as I say.

'Mum, you don't think it was me, do you?' Sasha appeals to me now that we're on our own.

'Absolutely not,' I reply instantly, witnessing my eldest daughter's shoulders sag with relief. It's true, I don't think Sasha has it in her to end someone's life. And certainly not in the state she was in earlier. I give her a reassuring hug. I'm just so glad she's not still wandering lost in the snow. It's only now that I realise how worried I was about her.

I take in a lungful of air. I need to keep going and be strong for my girls.

Erin comes back into the room and locks all the doors. It's just the three of us now: me, Sasha and Erin. Well, the three of us and Aaron's body.

'Do you know if there's anyone upstairs who might come down?'

Erin goes to answer and then snaps her mouth shut, shaking her head.

'We need to call the police and get everything dealt with properly. But first of all, we need to get our stories straight.' These are words that I thought I would never hear myself utter, but it's necessary to protect my three daughters.

'I saw who killed Aaron.' I state this very clearly and wait for their reactions.

'You saw?' Sasha repeats.

'Yes, I saw it with my own eyes. I saw the person who pushed Aaron. The poor man was so taken by surprise that he didn't even have a chance to react.' I pause, letting my words land before continuing.

'Erin, I'm so sorry, love. It's truly awful but it was quick and he died on impact.'

Erin whimpers at this, burying her head in her hands once more.

'Who was it?' Sasha asks, holding my gaze.

And I say the words I wish I didn't have to say.

'It was Jesse.'

# Chapter Forty-Six
# Sasha
# Now

'Jesse? As in, *my husband*?'

My vision tilts and I stagger forward. My mother puts out a hand to steady me.

'I'm sorry, Sasha, but it's true.'

I feel like any minute now a game show host is going to jump out and yell that this is all just one big hoax, a game for TV audiences. None of this feels real. This doesn't feel like my life.

'Jesse?' I say again, my lip wobbling.

Mum nods her confirmation.

Jesse and I may have had our ups and downs but I just can't understand how he could be a killer. This is the man I fell in love with, the man I said 'I do' to, the father of my child. I conjure up the image of Jesse dancing, just a few short weeks ago, in the living room with Freya. How could that same man be a killer?

'What did you see?' Erin whispers, as though afraid to ask the question.

Mum looks down at her shoes, composing herself.

'I saw them arguing, up there, on the third floor. They were really laying into each other. One second they were throwing punches and the next second Aaron was mid-air.'

Erin gasps.

'I... It was over very quickly.' Mum repeats this again.

'Jesse was fighting with Aaron. Why?' This still doesn't add up to me. Jesse didn't know Aaron. They'd never met until today. There was no indication of any tension between them when they met.

'I don't know,' Mum replies.

'Maybe it was an accident? Maybe things just got out of hand?'

'It didn't look like that from what I saw. Jesse deliberately threw Aaron over the bannister. It may have been in the heat of the argument, but he knew what he was doing.'

I think about Jesse and what could possibly have caused him to behave so irrationally. Jesse is a gym-obsessed, health-conscious, people person and he generally gets on with anyone and everyone. So what happened between the start of the party and the fight with Aaron?

My mind is in a spin. I don't know what's worse, me being accused of murder or my husband and the father of my child being a killer.

'Are you sure?' I'm aware that I'm being very quick to believe the accusation against Jesse. A minute ago I was in this very position, so I don't want to be swept away by a different version of events. But this is my mum, I trust her more than anyone in the world. Why would she tell me this if it wasn't true? She and Jesse have had their differences over the years but I remember how proud she was of both of us on our wedding day. She wouldn't say this lightly. She wouldn't break up our family and accuse Jesse of something so serious if she wasn't certain.

'I'm sorry, but I witnessed it all.'

Erin is very quiet and still next to me. She's obviously trying to process this information as well.

I'm back to wondering how everything has unravelled so quickly. Did Jesse and Aaron have a disagreement? Did they somehow know each other before today? Is there a connection that I'm missing?

I wrack my brains for the answer but there is absolutely no way in which I can imagine Jesse's world and Aaron's world colliding.

'Did you hear why they were arguing?'

'No,' Mum shakes her head swiftly. 'I didn't hear what they were saying.'

Mum is certain in her responses. Enough that I'm convinced she did witness this. I'm convinced she saw my husband throwing Erin's husband to his death.

My mind is racing, my thoughts leaping forward to what happens next. I'm the wife of a murderer. Freya has a killer for a father. His reckless actions have shattered our lives forever.

'Where is Jesse now?' I ask, suddenly realising that my mother has omitted to tell us what happened to my husband after Aaron fell to the marble floor. I need to go and see him. I need to speak to him myself and find out what happened. Maybe it was an accident? The minute I look in his eyes I'll know if he's lying or not.

My mum opens her mouth to respond but we don't hear what she says.

Rap. Rap. Rap.

Someone is trying to get through one of the locked doors.

Rap. Rap. Rap.

'I told Leah to do four knocks,' Mum says, her forehead creased with anxiety.

'That wasn't four knocks. It was six.'

So who is trying to get in the door?

# Chapter Forty-Seven

## Erin

## Now

The knocking starts up again. Slow and deliberate.

Rap. Rap. Rap.

Nadia and Sasha look scared but I can't just stand here, wondering who's on the other side of the door.

'Who is it?' I demand.

A pause, no response.

'Who's there?'

Silence.

'Erin don't open the door! It could be the killer.' Nadia's forehead is creased with worry. I should be glad that she cares but I'm not. She lost her right to tell me what I can and can't do a long time ago.

I quickly fit the key in the lock and pull open the door.

'Oh!' I sigh, relieved to see a familiar face in front of me.

'Leah, you were told to knock four times,' I say sharply. My heart is banging against my ribcage. I'm just thankful it wasn't a member of Aaron's family. The thought of having to tell them he's dead sends a tremor of cold dread over me.

'What? Oh, sorry about that. I didn't remember.' Leah tosses her hair impatiently.

I sigh and usher her into the room. Pulling the door firmly shut once more and locking it once again. There are four of us back in the room with my husband's body and, despite the grandeur of the space, I'm starting to feel more than a little claustrophobic.

'What did I miss?' Leah says, with all the innocence of someone who's just skimmed past a plot twist.

'It was Jesse,' Nadia says sternly.

'What was Jesse?'

'Jesse and Aaron got into a fight and—'

'For real?' Leah exclaims. 'No! Shut up! Jesse can't be the one who did it.'

'It's true.' Nadia is firm, her words seem to hang in the air over our heads. 'I don't want it to be but it's true.'

Sasha is gushing hot tears, like she's the one who's just been widowed. Nadia and Leah flock around her, stroking her hair and helping her to wipe her face. Sasha always did have to make everything about her. And now, even with my husband's life extinguished, she's still doing the same thing.

I can't stand it any longer.

'Where were you?' I press Nadia. 'How did you see what happened?'

'I was sitting on the blue chaise lounge by the second-floor window, at the end of the corridor.'

'So you saw everything that happened?'

'Yes. Everything.'

I'm rocked by this revelation. What was Nadia doing up on the second floor? Why was she even there? Can I trust everything she is saying?

I'm surprised that Nadia is naming Jesse guilty so readily. After all, he is family. I thought she would've been more protective of her brood. I remember when Jesse and Sasha first got together. Nadia used to go on and on about how well-matched they were. She adored Jesse and welcomed him with open arms to the Bailey family. Jesse even took our family name. He didn't have much of a connection with his own parents and Sasha wanted to have a modern marriage and keep her maiden name. So why is Nadia so quick to call the police and shop her precious son-in-law?

I wonder if there's something she's not telling us.

If she was sitting by the second-floor window then it's likely she would've heard what the two men were saying. If they were shouting or raising their voices then it's even more likely she caught onto the subject of their disagreement.

Which means there's a very real possibility that Nadia knows exactly why Jesse pushed my husband.

# Chapter Forty-Eight
# Leah
# Now

I was not prepared for Mom to name Jesse as Aaron's murderer. I've known Jesse for forever. He's been like a big brother to me. We have so much in common, especially our shared passion for fitness, and I always felt like Jesse just got me. In a way that my sisters and Mom never really have. They're all so quick to view me as the 'baby' in the family and none of them take my career as an influencer seriously. The number of times Mom has asked me when I'm going to get a real job. She doesn't seem to understand that I earn far more than she ever did stacking shelves at a supermarket. But Jesse has always encouraged me in my rise as a social media star. He understands what I'm doing and respects it. He and Sasha may not be love's young dream but Jesse has always been so cute with Freya. He adores that little girl. So I'm finding it hard to picture him getting so wound up that he'd lash out in such a terrible way. I stare up at the gallery landing above us and it makes me feel queasy just thinking about the height Aaron fell from.

As I picture Jesse in my mind, it strikes me he is fit and wiry. He works out, lifts weights daily and has the muscles to prove it. I know Jesse but I don't know Aaron that well. Maybe Aaron provoked Jesse? Jesse is strong, perhaps he shoved him a little too hard? It had to be an accident. That must be how it went down.

'Maybe the fight went too far? Maybe it was an accident?' I voice my thoughts – it doesn't change the end result but if Jesse didn't mean it maybe the consequences won't be so severe. We've all done things that we didn't mean to. We've all made mistakes.

Yes, this would be a terrible error on Jesse's part but I just can't come to terms with what's happened any other way. This is Jesse. He's family. I'm devastated for Erin and her kids but I also don't want to see Jesse torn away from Sasha and Freya. I can't believe he did this, it's so unlike him. Jesse is the sort of guy who gets on with everyone.

'Where is Jesse?' I ask.

We all look at each other. Erin's arms are crossed in front of her body, Sasha is sitting on the cold floor with her head in her hands and Mom is leaning up against the stair bannister.

'I know where he is,' Mom says slowly. 'And he needs to stay there until the police arrive.'

'Where is he?' Sasha jumps up. 'I have to see him. I have to talk to my husband.'

Mom shakes her head. 'No, that's not a good idea, Sasha.'

'I need to find out what happened. Just let me have a couple of minutes with him,' Sasha pleads.

'Jesse is staying where he is and I'm calling the police.'

'Then can I talk to him?' Erin says sharply. 'I have a right to know what happened.'

Sasha looks aghast at Erin and I suddenly see them as they are, women cast once again on the opposite sides of an argument.

The accident which gave me my scar fractured the relationship between my two sisters but tonight could break their bond forever. My hand automatically reaches up to trace my scar. Both Sasha and

Mom were angry at Erin's reckless actions: she'd gone too far and shouldn't have been driving when she was so emotional. They were afraid I was going to die or be injured in a long-lasting way. Sasha has told me several times since that she will never forgive Erin for causing me harm. It took me nearly six months to get back to anywhere near normal. Thankfully the head injury was nowhere near as bad as it could've been. But I suffered with shock and fatigue as my body slowly healed. Erin caused even more trouble after the accident. After weeks of arguments with Sasha and Mom following the car crash, she packed her bags and left.

We still haven't healed as a family. The reunion today was meant to be about forgiveness and creating a fresh start. I can't see how we can come back from this. The first time Erin has seen us all in a decade and her husband ends up dead.

Nothing will be the same between the Bailey women ever again.

That's if we all get out of here alive tonight...

# Chapter Forty-Nine
## Erin
## Earlier that evening, 10 p.m.

I managed to slip away from the party. I escaped outside and now I'm at the very back of the hotel, sheltering from the snow by the fire-escape stairs. The moon is full and bright but the fog hanging thickly in the air is obscuring the full potential of its light. So I wait here in the shadows, away from my guests. I needed this time out. The party has been hectic and full-on. I'm not usually one to feel the pressure, but tonight I have. There's been a lot riding on things going smoothly and so far, so good. But, at any given moment things could start to go wrong. I need this plan to work. I've been waiting for this opportunity for months.

A figure steps through the darkness, solid and familiar. In seconds his mouth is on mine and we're kissing with the intensity of lovers who've been kept apart for far too long. My fingers go up to his face, tracing the features I know so well. His hands are in my hair, drawing me in closer and closer to him, our bodies melting together.

'Jesse,' I whisper.

'Erin.' He nips my bottom lip and a flutter of delight runs through me.

'What took you so long?'

'You said be discreet.'

'At least you're here now.' I wrap my arms around his neck and kiss him again.

'Not long now and we'll be together... finally.'

I nod. If everything goes to plan then in just a few short months Jesse and I will be official. We won't have to keep our love for one another secret anymore. And we can be together as a proper couple.

'Yes, and then we can both start living.'

The thought of being out of Aaron's controlling clutches once and for all is all I've dreamt of in the last few years. My husband has always been very particular, a complete perfectionist. I was never madly in love with him but I felt fortunate to be part of his privileged world. When I was pregnant he was attentive, catering to my every whim. I had whatever I wanted; nothing was too much for him.

The first couple of years of our marriage were full of first milestones, the luxury lifestyle he offered was still new and exciting to me. He unlocked the door to many opportunities and elevated me into a world I had longed to be part of. But, as the children grew older, his interest in me waned. He didn't want more offspring and neither did I. We had two, one of each, and that was enough for both of us. We should have been happy. The perfect family. I tried; I really did. But Aaron's need to control everything around him became more and more of an issue for me. He dictated how we raised our children and how I lived my life down to the very last detail. He didn't want me to have any freedom to think or feel anything different from the way he wanted me to think and feel.

But he picked the wrong woman to be his wife. I was never going to be the docile, patient female who put up with all of his demands. It infuriated him that I wouldn't bend to his will at all times. I've got the bruises to prove it.

At times I felt like I might crumble and just give in to Aaron's way of doing things. Instead, I learnt to play the game my way. I picked my battles. I let him think I was becoming more pliable. I found smart ways to give myself small snatches of freedom. I pretended not to notice his wandering eye. Or the way he behaved with his golf friends. All the time, he thought I didn't know his little secrets. That I was too stupid to see what was going on right under my nose.

He was the stupid one. He never knew about the man I fell for when I was just a young woman. The man I could never forget. The man I was still aching for on the day I married Aaron. That man was Jesse.

I never told Aaron the real reason behind the argument that led to Leah's accident and ejected me from my seat around the family table. I never meant to fall for my sister's boyfriend, truly I didn't. Just like I never meant for any of the things that followed.

My mother cottoned on to what was going on. She discovered Jesse and I had been seeing each other behind Sasha's back. Jesse and Sasha were months off getting married. He was going to come clean with Sasha and tell her the truth. He wanted to be with me. He promised me he would leave her and he meant it. But, unfortunately, things didn't pan out that way. Nadia made sure of that.

'We've wasted so much of our lives Erin, doing what other people have told us to do instead of making ourselves happy. The future is ours now.'

I smile, looking into his amber eyes. 'Everything will be different.'

I regret the years we've lost together because it wasn't simply some messy affair. Jesse just met the wrong woman first. I've often wondered why everything happened the way it did. Why couldn't I have met Jesse before Sasha? We can't change the past though, what's happened has already happened. Perhaps now Jesse and I will have an even better life together because of the fortune I have. We can live out the rest of our days in style.

'I love you.'

'I love you too.'

And it's true. Jesse and I do love each other. A love like no other. Our love has been like a red thread, stretching through the years of absence and binding us together. I tried to stop loving him. I pretended I didn't and for a while I was able to move on with my life. But it was always there, threaded in the background of everything I did.

We started seeing each other again almost a year ago. I was so lonely. Aaron was away a lot on some business trip or another. Over the years, I've often checked Jesse's online profiles. I got glimpses into his life and it broke my heart. I missed him every day. I found out Jesse worked at an exclusive health and wellbeing spa. So I decided to go there. I told myself if I didn't see him then I'd walk away and finally try to move on from him. If I did see him then I would view it as a sign we were meant to be.

I spent a whole morning there. In the pool, the steam room, the sauna. I used all of the luxury facilities but there was no sign of Jesse whatsoever. As the hours ticked by, I felt more and more heartbroken. I checked out and exited the building through the sliding doors at the entrance. I wasn't looking where I was going and I walked straight into Jesse.

We were meant to be.

Nothing is going to stop Jesse and I being together this time.

Not Aaron. Not Nadia. And not Sasha.

However, after a few months of managing to catch an hour or two in the daytime together, or a whole evening if we were really lucky, we both confessed that we wanted more. Jesse couldn't stand the thought of me having to deal with Aaron. And I hated it every time we had to say goodbye.

The problem is, Aaron would never allow me to leave him. If he ever found out I was cheating on him I would lose everything – my children, my wealth, my status, the hotel. He knows too many high-powered people for there ever to be a fair fight in the divorce courts. He would rip me to shreds. And that wouldn't be the end of it. He would never allow me to move on, to start a new relationship, because he'd always be there trying to control my life. I've witnessed how ruthless he is when it comes to business. He certainly has more than a few enemies. There's no way I want to end up on his hit list – I've seen how Aaron treats the people he dislikes. It's not pretty.

There's no way I could risk being found out. There is too much at stake. I'm terrified he will take the children away from me and turn them against me.

So there was only ever one possible way all this could end.

I didn't want to have blood on my hands but it's the only way I can escape my marriage.

# Chapter Fifty
## Jesse
## Earlier that evening, 10 p.m.

Erin is in my arms and everything feels right again. Tonight has been agony, having to pretend I haven't seen the woman I love for years and having to act like Erin isn't the most important thing in the world to me. I've nearly slipped up a few times. Nadia has had her hawk eyes on me all evening. But I don't think anyone suspects us yet and that's the way it needs to stay. Sasha certainly doesn't have a clue. She's so drunk that I doubt she remembers her own name.

How did things end up like this?

As Erin and I kiss, I want nothing more than to carry her as far away as possible from here and start again. To run away from our complicated families and begin our lives together. It's something I've suggested more than a few times. I've dreamt of us stepping off the plane somewhere hot and sunny. It's too difficult for Erin just to walk away though. She has a lot more to lose. She's worked hard to make a success of Burcott House and the kind of money she'd be walking away from would be like burning a winning lottery ticket.

We talked about the possibility of Erin filing for divorce. Erin has kept a stack of evidence of her husband's business misdemeanours so, in theory, she could gain the upper hand if she decided to divorce him. Except Erin says Aaron is too well-connected with people in powerful positions, including lawyers, judges, and barristers. She's convinced he would twist things, manipulate the situation and leave her with nothing. Because of the kind of man he is, Aaron wouldn't stand for Erin having a new relationship. Erin says he would find a way to punish her and would likely use the children as pawns to do so.

My heart cracked in two a few months ago when Erin told me I was Ophelia and Jasper's real father. She was showing me photos of the twins as babies, as toddlers and the age they are now. I couldn't get over how similar Ophelia is to my Freya. They look so alike with their long, curly, copper-coloured hair and green eyes. Both of their faces pale and their little noses dusted with cute freckles.

She doesn't want to tell Aaron the truth about the twins. She doesn't want him to know that Jasper and Ophelia are actually my children. They would stand to lose too much. I want to shout to the world that I have two more children but I can't. Erin says Jasper and Ophelia are set for life, they have everything they could possibly want and it would be cruel to pull them away from their lifestyles and deny them the fortune they are due to inherit. I don't like it but deep down I know she's right.

Erin breaks away from my arms and checks her watch. 'We better go back inside before anyone realises we're missing.'

I go to speak but Erin presses one of her manicured fingers to my lips.

'It won't be for long now. Our time is coming.'

Erin stands on her tiptoes and kisses me on the forehead.

'I'll see you soon.'

In the blink of an eye she's gone. Her figure melts into the darkness. I listen to the sound of her heels, the noise fading the further away she gets from me.

If I could change what happened ten years ago I would. I would've ignored Nadia's orders for me to stick by Sasha and marry her. I wouldn't have completely abandoned Sasha of course, I would have paid child maintenance and been an active father to our child. Sasha was pregnant with Freya at the time. That's the reason why I stayed with Sasha and married her. I'd always wanted children and I thought I was doing the right thing. Sasha was thirteen weeks along and we'd just been to her first scan together. I fell in love with the wiggling baby shape on the screen the second I saw it. At the time, I thought the baby would bring us closer together. How wrong I was.

I'd had no idea Erin was also pregnant. To be fair, she didn't find out until after she left. She was barely six weeks along the night she drove away and never came back. If only I'd known then that Erin had two of my babies growing inside her. A boy and a girl. Jasper and Ophelia. She called me a couple of months after she left, the night before Sasha and I got married, but I told her not to contact me. I said I needed her to stay away and refused to listen to what she had to tell me. I wish that conversation had gone differently. I've missed out on so much of the twins' lives and I want to be a father to them. Although Erin insists that's not possible right now. It's the only thing we've argued about. Erin has assured me I'll have more of a relationship with them in the coming years. And maybe someday, when they're adults themselves, I'll be able to tell them that I'm their biological father. For now, I've just got to keep quiet and carry on with the plan we've set in motion.

Snow has settled onto my shoulders so I shake myself down and take a slow walk back along the side of the building.

After everything Erin has told me about her husband, I'm convinced that if we don't take matters into our own hands and end things for Aaron, he will find a way to break us apart. He will make our lives not worth living and he won't give a damn about us. I had to grit my teeth tonight when I met Aaron for the first time. Shaking his hand made my skin crawl. Being in the same space as the man who treats Erin like she's dirt was hard. I wanted to punch him in his arrogant face. Instead, I somehow managed to keep my hands by my sides in order to bide my time.

I'm not a violent man. I've never deliberately caused another person physical pain in my life. But the way I see it, our actions are more like self-defence. Retribution for all of the suffering Erin has endured during their marriage.

I would do anything for Erin.

And I would do anything to enable us to be together.

That's why I've agreed to help her get rid of Aaron once and for all.

# Chapter Fifty-One
## Nadia
## Earlier that evening, 11 p.m.

'Here we go,' I say, taking one of the cups of coffee from a waitress and passing it over to Sasha. 'Just what we needed, thank you.'

I take my own cup and place it down on the low table in front of me. Sasha and I are sitting together in front of the crackling fire in the Snug. The fire is lower than it was earlier in the evening but it's still giving out plenty of warmth. I take a sip of the coffee, which is so hot it scalds my tongue. I grimace and place the cup back down on the table quickly.

'Not quite drinking temperature yet,' I inform Sasha. She's still shivering and feels just as soaked through as I am. I'm hoping the fire will help to dry us out quickly – we spent far too long trudging about in that snow.

After just a few minutes of sitting here, the feeling properly comes back to my limbs and my ankle is still throbbing. I managed to hobble back to Burcott House but it was a slow and painful walk. I realise it's going to take quite a while for the rest of me to dry out, and Sasha is in a similar state.

'Why don't we go upstairs and I can run you a nice hot bath?' I suggest.

She shakes her head. 'No, I'll be fine in a minute.'

We sit together in silence, the events of the last few hours running through my mind. I haven't seen anything of Jesse since I re-entered the hotel. I'm furious at him for leaving Sasha out there alone and lost in the freezing temperatures. Anything could have happened to her, especially given the state she was in. I put my arm around my eldest daughter and pull her close. I'm so thankful she's here sitting next to me and we're back in the safety of Burcott House.

I reach out for my coffee cup; it's cooled down now and I'm able to drink it, the liquid warming my insides. I encourage Sasha to drink her own coffee, which she does.

'Are you sure you don't want to get changed out of those wet clothes?'

'I'm fine Mum, they're drying quickly,' Sasha says. 'Why don't you go up, I'll be alright here.'

I don't really want to leave her on her own, not after she's had such a tumultuous evening. She does seem more herself now though. A few more minutes lapse in silence and I see Sasha start to nod, her breathing becoming heavy, and she nestles back into the comfortable sofa. She's soon fast asleep.

I look around us. There's a canoodling couple in the far corner of the room and a few older women seated in high-backed armchairs nearer to us. It's quiet and cosy in this little room in the hotel; I can see why they call it the Snug. I drink in Sasha's sleeping face and her dark hair tumbling around her shoulders. It takes me back to when she was a little girl – she was the sort of child who would fall asleep anywhere.

I brush the curls off her face and kiss her forehead. It won't take me very long to go and get changed, and Sasha probably won't even wake up in the time I'm gone, so I leave her where she is and make my way through the hotel in search of my room.

I find my way into the beautiful foyer. The white marble staircase winds up to three different floors. I'm sure there must be a lift somewhere but I haven't come across it yet. So I slowly ascend the staircase, my ankle still throbbing, my hand on the cool bannister. I reach the second floor, dig out the key to my room and step inside. This bedroom is far bigger than my one at home. It's exquisitely decorated, just like the rest of the house, and has the most enormous bed I've ever seen in my life positioned in the middle of the room. It must be king-sized, or queen-sized, I'm not sure which one is biggest. My little suitcase is propped against the wall; Erin had one of her staff bring it up to the room when we arrived. At the far end of the bedroom there's a door, which leads to the ensuite. This room is also white, with gold edging and gold taps.

I take a hot shower and then wrap myself up in a clean, fluffy towel. I lie back on the bed, feeling drowsy enough that I could easily drift off to sleep right now, but I need to go back downstairs and check on Sasha. I'm worried about her. She and Jesse have been having far too many arguments of late and tonight the cracks in their marriage seem to have grown even bigger. Sasha may be in her late thirties, but a mother never really stops worrying about her children, however old they are.

I ease myself off the bed and quickly get changed into the dress I had packed for tomorrow. It's a little more casual than the one I had been wearing but at least it's dry. I give myself a quick once-over in the long mirror. My short, spiky blonde hair is still in style – the beauty of only having a short haircut to maintain – and I feel pleased that I've managed to smarten myself quickly. I slip on the spare pair of shoes I'd packed and hurry back out of the room. Erin told us all about the spectacular firework display she has organised and I'm keen to see the show. I check my watch; it's 11.25 p.m.

I should go straight back downstairs but something has been bothering me all evening. I sit down on the chaise longue that's at the far end of the dimly lit second-floor hallway and try to sort through my scrambled thoughts.

It's happening again, I'm sure of it.

Earlier on, for the briefest of seconds, I looked across the dance floor and saw Erin slip her hand into Jesse's and give it a little squeeze. Freya was right by them but she was too busy taking in everything else around her to notice what her father was up to. It wasn't the secret hand squeeze that bothered me though. It was the way Erin and Jesse looked at each other. Like they were the only two people in the room, like ten years had fallen away and they were caught up in their mad infatuation once again.

I wish now that I had just made Jesse leave our family a decade ago. As the years have gone by, I have often questioned if I did the right thing by keeping Jesse by Sasha's side. Maybe my caring, intelligent Sasha would have had a better life without him? It would've been hard when Freya was a baby, but that time flashes by in a blur. Perhaps Sasha might have found someone more supportive, someone who loved her and who was worth her love in return? There are too many what ifs to unpack though.

I shake my head, telling myself what I saw was a trick of my imagination. I've been trying to convince myself it was nothing but perhaps I should have just gathered up Sasha, Leah and Freya and whisked them back home earlier. It's too late now: I can see out of the little window behind me and the snow has piled up. There's no way we're going anywhere tonight, we're completely snowed in.

'What are you doing here?'

I jump up, confused, looking all around me to locate the voice I just heard. It was loud and aggressive, and it sounded as though it was close by to me but there's no one here.

I open my mouth to speak but then I hear it again. The voice repeating the same sentence over again, laced with even more threat this time. I realise that directly opposite where I am, and a little way up, is the third-floor landing. The staircase curves back on itself and, where I'm standing on the second floor, I can see through the bannisters. In my eyeline, I can just about make out two pairs of legs, one pair in a smart suit and the other wearing a distinctive pair of Jimmy Choos.

There's a response from another male voice, no more than a low growl. I can't make out the words but they're followed by the unmistakable noises of two people fighting. The pair of Jimmy Choos have moved away from the bannister now and instead I see two pairs of male legs. My heart speeds up and a wave of fear washes over me.

It's Jesse and Aaron. They're throwing punches at each other. Aaron's fists are raining down on Jesse and he seems to be getting the better of him. And then I hear Erin's voice.

'Are you going to let him beat you?' Her voice isn't high-pitched or charged with emotion. It's worse than that. It's hard and it's calculated.

I was a fool to believe I'd put a stop to the feelings between Erin and Jesse all those years ago. I was also a fool to think that Erin had changed, that she'd grown up and genuinely wanted to reconcile with her family.

I hear the clock strike midnight just as Aaron fells Jesse with an almighty blow. He goes down hard and I watch as Aaron begins to slowly walk away. He is shaking his head. He's obviously found out something is going on between Erin and Jesse. This means I'm going to have to come clean with Sasha and explain the secret I've been keeping. I am going to have to tell her that her husband is in love with her sister. I didn't want her to have to go through the struggles of being a single parent but, looking up at Jesse now, I feel nothing but hatred and disgust for the man who has caused so much trouble for my family.

Then Erin's voice rings out once again. 'If you want me as much as you say, then prove it. Now.'

Jesse somehow lurches up from the floor. He's unsteady on his feet but his target is clear. Aaron hasn't noticed that Jesse is standing up again. I want to call out but I'm paralysed to the spot. Jesse hurls himself across the space between him and his love rival, arms out in front of him. And Aaron is suddenly on top of the bannister, his torso suspended in mid-air, his legs struggling to reach the floor. Jesse steps towards him and I think he's about to pull Aaron back from the brink, back to safety. He doesn't.

Jesse grabs Aaron's legs and tips them skywards. Gravity does the rest. Aaron is falling through the air. It's all happening so quickly; I can't do anything to stop it but I also can't look away. I witness every detail of the poor man's downward fall. And then Aaron's body hits the ground with a sickening thud.

I sink back into the shadows, shaking.

'Damn, what have I done?' Jesse cries immediately.

I can just about make out Erin's instructions, low and frantic. 'Quickly... wash your hands and face... take off your jumper... use the fire exit to escape... come back to the party.'

There are more muffled words and I can't quite hear what is being said. And then, to my astonishment, Erin glides down the marble staircase. Down all three flights of stairs with a determined expression on her face. She passes her husband's body without a glance, she doesn't even check to see if he's still alive, and disappears through one of the doors leading off the foyer.

I stare over the railings at Aaron's broken form. There's no movement and nothing I can do to help him now. It's clear from the angle he's landed at that he's dead. How could Erin possibly behave so calmly? She's just witnessed her husband's death and she showed no emotion whatsoever.

Without thinking, I softly make my way upwards, up to the third floor, up to where Jesse is.

If Jesse is prepared to throw Erin's husband to his death then I dread to think what he might do to me – the mother-in-law who separated him from his lover. But I push that thought to one side and creep along the corridor as quietly as I can. There's a glow coming from a room half way along the corridor, and the fire exit is just a little further along. I get closer to the open door, light spilling into the corridor. The key is hanging from the lock.

I don't hesitate. Moving quicker than I have in years, I slam the door shut and swiftly lock the door. I wait for a second.

It doesn't take long for Jesse to discover what has happened. He's hammering on the door now, shouting to be let out. So I was right, he was in the room. Well, he shouldn't have waited around after what he's done. The door is made of thick, solid wood and no matter how many times Jesse throws himself against the frame, there's no way this door is budging. There's no escape for him.

'Jesse, this is Nadia,' I say. Somehow, I manage to keep my voice steady, despite the fact I'm still shaking with nerves. 'I know what you did. I saw everything.'

Jesse roars on the other side of the door.

'If you want to keep Erin out of this, you'll do as I say. For the sake of her freedom. And for the sake of Freya. The police are on their way. You can't escape now.'

Of course, I haven't called the police yet but my words seem to have had the desired effect. Jesse is no longer bellowing. There's no noise at all from him now.

I have no idea if he has a mobile on him or if he's able to get out of a window. Although given how high up we are, I think that's unlikely.

'Do you understand me, Jesse? Erin is to be kept out of this.'

'This is all your fault!' Jesse shouts. 'Why did you have to come between us?'

'Jesse, swear it. Swear you won't say a word about Erin being with you when... when...'

'I swear it,' Jesse says instantly. 'Despite what you think of me, I love Erin.'

Everything goes quiet again. I've done all I can.

Jesse will pay for what he's done to Aaron and what he's done to my family.

I will do everything in my power to stop Erin going to prison. She is my daughter after all.

And I will deal with her myself.

# Chapter Fifty-Two
## Nadia
## Now

'Hello, police? I'm calling to report a death. A murder. I need someone here quickly. It's Burcott House...'

In a remote place like this, it could take a long time for the police to get to us. There's a small, quaint old English village a few miles away but it's tiny, with only a handful of shops, a pub and a village green. I didn't even see a phone box, let alone a police station. The next town of any notable size is at least an hour's drive from here. We could be trapped here in this house for quite a while before the police come to our rescue.

'We have a house full of guests and the man who... the man who caused the death is still here.'

I grip the phone to my ear; it's the landline phone in the reception area as my mobile is still out of battery. I'm hovering in the doorway to the foyer because I don't want to let any of my three daughters out of my sight. Tensions are understandably running high and one wrong word could make this whole thing blow up even more.

'Thank you, thank you. Please hurry.' I switch off the portable phone and return it to its charging dock. I run my hands through my short, spiky blonde hair and try to figure out what to do next.

I have to keep my three girls safe and I have to make sure that we all stick together. It's crucial we support each other because, if we don't, one of my beloved children will end up behind bars. Because I know that only two of them standing in that room are innocent.

The other one is guilty as hell for Aaron's death.

When I said I saw everything I meant it. Jesse did deliver the final blow that sent Aaron spiralling to his death but one of my darling daughters was the catalyst for his actions.

But, despite what she's done, a mother's love is unconditional. I just need to manage this nightmare situation and then deal with my daughter in my own way. I feel responsible – after all, I'm a mother whose child has just been involved in a murder. What kind of parent does that make me? I've always tried my best; I may not have got things right and that's clearly had an impact on one of my offspring. So I need to sort this out. But first I need to get rid of Jesse.

No one else was there the moment Aaron Bailey-Scott was killed so I could be thrust into a situation where it's my word against Jesse's. In my experience, authority figures tend to listen to men more than women, even in this day and age, so already the balance is not tipped in my favour.

Jesse could deny it; he could say I'm lying. He might even turn the tables around and try to accuse me. I know he hates me enough to try it. The relationship with my son-in-law started out positive and I welcomed him with open arms to our family. I should have been more cautious. If I had my time again, I would send him packing before he had the chance to charm my eldest daughter. Jesse has caused so much heartache over the years for me and for Sasha. He's never been a good husband. He shouldn't have married; he lives the life of a carefree, single bachelor and that's just not fair on Sasha or Freya.

The image of him wrestling Aaron will be one I won't be able to shake easily. The determination was written all over Jesse's face. He knew exactly what he was doing. He meant for Aaron to go over the top of the bannister and the death was premeditated.

I know exactly why he did it.

He may have been the blunt instrument, but one of my daughters was the puppeteer.

It's the reason we should've all stayed away from the party tonight and let things be. I realise now too much has happened, there was too much water under the bridge and too many unresolved emotions. It's my fault; I was the one who wanted this reunion, more than Leah or Sasha. Finding out about my two grandchildren wore away the last of my resolve to stay out of Erin's life. I should have stayed stronger. And now a man is dead.

My three daughters are all looking to me for guidance. Waiting with bated breath to hear what I say next. Never before have I felt the responsibility of parenthood weighing so heavily on my shoulders. I notice that Sasha's eyes keep flicking to the broken figure on the floor. She looks bewildered. I've just told her that Jesse is a killer. What must she be thinking? How must she feel?

Leah is antsy, pacing up and down, tossing her hair around and glowering. I'm sure my youngest daughter is cursing her decision to come back home for Christmas. She could be anywhere else in the world right now – Sydney, Paris, Milan. Instead, she's locked in this nightmare. Thrown into the midst of another family drama. Except this time someone has died.

Erin has her arms wrapped around herself as though she is cold, her eyes downcast, fixed on her Jimmy Choos, lost in thought. I study my middle daughter and she must feel my eyes on her because she jerks her head up and stares back at me. Of my three girls, Erin is the one I've always felt the least connection with. Not just in the last ten years but throughout her childhood as well. She is very much her father's child, both in looks and temperament. I found that hard after the breakdown of the relationship with my first love and the father of my two eldest daughters. In those dark years after Craig first left, Erin was a constant reminder of him. She is Craig's 'mini me'; she was back then and she still is now. Every photograph I took of her reminded me of him. Her mannerisms, her eyes, her hair are all so similar to those of the man I loved and lost. The gulf between us seems even wider now Erin has risen in class and material possessions.

I've never really understood Erin and I have no idea how she can stand there crying, after everything she's done. Jesse did push Aaron – I saw it with my own eyes. But Erin isn't as innocent as she looks.

Erin is beautiful; she knows how to get what she wants, and she knows how to wrap people around her little finger, me included.

I sweep my eyes across my three daughters and, in that moment, I realise Erin has always been the problem in this family. In every argument, in every disagreement.

The rose in the middle was actually the thorn.

# Chapter Fifty-Three
## Erin
## Now

I stand alone in the big room, my arms crossed. I'm cold and tense. Being in the same room as my dead husband, however much I hated him, is a chilling experience. Nadia is pacing up and down, waiting for the police to arrive. The snow outside is so thick now and the nearest police station is more than ten miles away, so we could be waiting a long time until they reach us. Sasha is in shock and her hands are trembling. Leah is leaning up against a door, clearly desperate to escape.

But Nadia has told us we're to stay here until the police arrive. It's like some kind of hellish limbo, just waiting to see what will happen next. My thoughts rewind to another accident and another night that will forever haunt my dreams.

As I reflect on that accident, I accept that I was foolish and I was reckless, but I never meant to hurt Leah. It all started because of that stupid argument with Nadia. I replay our heated exchange in my mind. The conversation that led to me storming out of our family home and into my car, my heart pumping and my emotions raging.

'You can't see him again,' Nadia had shouted at me. 'Just leave well alone.'

I can see the scene as vividly as if it were yesterday. I can remember our disagreement word for word.

'I love him!' I shouted back at her.

'You don't love him. You just want him because he's Sasha's fiancé.'

'How do you know how I feel?'

'Would you even be interested in Jesse if he wasn't Sasha's fiancé?'

'I'm not even going to answer that!'

'You can't see him again. You'll break your sister's heart.'

'You can't tell me what to do!'

'If you do this, it will be the biggest mistake of your life.'

'At least it will be *my* mistake!'

I was in love with Jesse, it wasn't just an infatuation. We were the real deal. He was going to leave Sasha to be with me. But then Sasha found out she was pregnant. I felt awful; I didn't want to cause my sister unhappiness but she needed to know how Jesse and I felt about each other. I didn't see the point in everyone living a lie.

Nadia disagreed. She told me to stop seeing Jesse: that's what started the argument off on that disastrous night. I was livid. My own mother was asking me to lie about my feelings, to carry on as if there was nothing between Jesse and me. She'd also threatened Jesse with all sorts of things if he didn't marry Sasha and stand by her. She blackmailed him and told him he wouldn't see his baby if he carried on seeing me.

I can picture his face now as he looked at me with his amber eyes and told me we needed to stop seeing each other. I was completely crushed. Jesse was staying with Sasha and the baby. Jesse chose Sasha over me.

It hurt like a physical pain. I was heartbroken.

That's why I was a mess. That's why my foot was down on that pedal. And that's why Leah's accident happened.

No one cared about my feelings or my heartbreak though. Even after the accident, my mother insisted that I kept my love for Jesse a secret and forbade me to try and restart our affair. And Sasha made it clear she never wanted to speak to me again because I'd put Leah in hospital. So I created a new life for myself.

And I plotted my revenge...

# Chapter Fifty-Four
## Erin
## Five years ago

As I walk through the lavender field, I breathe in the calming scent in the air and brush my fingertips over the soft flowers. I find this spot in the grounds of Burcott House so soothing; the tranquil scenery allows me to clear my head so I can focus on what's important.

This field of purple and green is so different to the white mountain slopes that have been my view for the last week. We've just come back from an incredible skiing trip, staying at Snowfall Chalet in the French Alps. Throughout the entire seven days, Aaron's smile has been wide, his eyes have twinkled and he's been attentive to me and the children. But it wasn't real. It was all for show on our winter vacation with friends.

No one really knows what Aaron is like – except me. He comes across as a decent guy, a family man, an upstanding member of the community. Underneath his impressive tan and designer clothes the truth is much darker. He likes everything to go his way. If it doesn't, his temper flares.

Aaron reeled me in. I had an ulterior motive but so did he. He wanted to marry a trophy wife, someone he could control, someone who would be the perfect spouse.

Life as Erin Bailey-Scott has been more challenging than I thought it would be. The first few years were a whirlwind of nappies and no sleep and as the children have grown, so have the cracks in our marriage. Aaron doesn't like me trying to carve out a career for myself; he reluctantly let me get involved in the running of Burcott House. He thought he was giving me an impossible task when he asked me to renovate the crumbling manor house but I've proven to him and his father that I'm more than just a pretty face.

In the distance, I see Aaron's car coming along the gravel driveway. My mouth goes dry as I think about the expectations he piles on me and the twins. I can't keep living like this – something has to change. That's why I've booked an appointment this afternoon with someone who might be able to help me. Butterflies flutter in my stomach as I consider the possibilities this meeting might lead to.

It could set me on the path to freedom. It could open the door to a new life for me and my children. And it could enable me to right the wrongs of my past.

# Chapter Fifty-Five
## Leah
## Now

'Listen girls and listen to me carefully.' Mom is talking in a low voice now, the three of us gathered around her.

'The police will be here soon and then things will move quite quickly. I want you to know that I will protect all three of you as much as I can, I don't want any of you getting into trouble for this so we have to stick together.'

'Why would we get in trouble for this?' I ask, feeling confused. Mom has said Jesse pushed Aaron. She's locked Jesse in a room upstairs, surely it's case closed?

'The police... they will want to question all of us. They will try to trip us up, ask tricky questions. You have to be on your guard and stick to what we agree.'

Mom draws herself up to full height. 'Above all else, do not go pointing the finger at anyone else.' She gives us a stern look. 'Promise me?'

'Promise,' I say. Erin and Sasha mumble the same.

I'm reminded what a powerhouse she is. She had to be tough when we were growing up. She raised us as a single mother for most of our childhood as well as balancing more than one job to keep a roof over our heads. My Mom may have softened as she's gotten older, but she has an iron core. She's the strongest person I know.

'Sasha, there's just one more thing I have to tell you.'

'Oh no, why do I feel like this isn't something I want to hear?' I say under my breath.

'Wait—' Erin interrupts. 'Let's just leave things as they are.'

'No, we need to talk about this because otherwise the police will spring it upon Sasha.'

'But—' Erin tries to stop Mom again.

'Let me handle this,' Mom says to Erin. 'Sasha, I'm sorry I have to tell you this on top of what Jesse has done but I'm sure you're wondering why he pushed Aaron.'

Sasha nods her head slowly and uncertainly.

'The thing is, Jesse was infatuated with Erin.'

I observe Erin and notice her blinking rapidly, but she doesn't seem at all shocked.

'Infatuated? What do you mean?' Sasha's voice is high-pitched.

'He was obsessed with her. He thought there was something between them, he kept telling her he loved her. That's why Erin was so upset when she got in the car that day.'

I gasp and Sasha does too. We don't need to ask which day she means.

'Erin was driving away in the car because Jesse was harassing her?' My eyes fill with tears. So Jesse was the cause of Erin's distress. He's the reason why Erin wasn't in control of the car when she hit me.

'Yes,' Mom confirms.

I'm astonished by this revelation. For so long, I've laid the blame squarely on Erin's shoulders. During my initial recovery, my hatred for my sister burned bright. If I'd known Jesse was pursuing her and she was emotional for that reason, I may have felt differently. My whole perspective on the day of the accident distorts and shifts.

'He... he loves her?' Sasha has a lost expression on her face. I can't imagine what she must be thinking right now. First of all Mom tells her Jesse has murdered Erin's husband. And then she tells her that Jesse was obsessed with Erin, like some creepy stalker.

'Is this true?' Sasha turns to Erin.

'I'm sorry...' Erin says, tears gleaming in her eyes.

'Oh my God, I can't believe this. Jesse... what kind of a man did I marry?' Sasha is pacing the room now, hands in her hair, going out of her mind with the new information she's trying to process.

'Sasha, slow down.' Mom grabs Sasha's hands and makes her stop. 'It's a lot. I know it's a lot but please just promise me that you'll keep calm when the police get here.'

Sasha goes still, breathing in and out deeply.

'We can talk about it properly when we're in private but I needed to tell you before someone else did. You've just got to keep strong, for Freya.'

Sasha is still concentrating on her breathing, but it's better than her marching around the room like she's lost it.

'And Erin,' Mom says. 'Do not point the finger at anyone else. It was Jesse. End of.'

I think it's strange that Mom repeats this specifically to Erin, but then Erin was shouting her mouth off earlier at Sasha. I'm not looking forward to the police arriving but at least then we will be able to get out of this room. It seemed so big and impressive when we first arrived. Now I feel confined in here. Aaron's body is unnerving me; I try to look anywhere but where his broken frame is but my eyes keep getting drawn back to the other side of the room.

So many things feel different now, after all the truths that have been laid bare tonight. I'm scared in case any more secrets are unravelled. And I'm frightened in case our fragile family is shattered, like a broken Christmas bauble, beyond repair...

# Chapter Fifty-Six
## Sasha
## Now

'Police.' The man in uniform flashes an ID card at me. 'We've been informed there's been a death here tonight.'

I step to one side and let the first police officer through the door. He's followed by two other men in uniform and a woman in plain clothes. She flashes her ID card at me and I see the title *Detective Inspector*.

Everything feels so unreal, like I'm outside my own body watching everything unfold. All I want to do is go and find Freya and get the hell out of here.

'Can I go and get my daughter?' I ask one of the officers. He is fresh-faced and looks barely old enough to be wearing a policeman's uniform.

'We need everyone to stay where they are.'

The detective inspector is standing near Aaron's body and speaking with my mother. She's frantically scribbling something down in her notepad and then beckons two of the officers to follow her. They all walk up the marble staircase together, leaving just the fresh-faced officer standing beside me.

'There's more of us on the way,' he says. I'm not sure who he is trying to reassure, me or himself.

It looks like I've got a long few hours in front of me. I stand, fiddling with my charm bracelet. I'm feeling twitchy that Freya isn't with me. Although she might be better off sleeping through all of this. How am I going to explain to her that her daddy is a murderer? My charm bracelet jingles on my wrist and I bring my hand closer to my face, running a finger over each charm in turn. All the little symbols signify major moments in my life: my engagement, my marriage, Freya's birth and moving to my own home. Mum had gifted me a little charm at each new milestone. At the time all of these events were cause for celebration and happiness. How can I ever wear this bracelet again? My whole life with Jesse has been a complete lie, a sham marriage. Did he ever really love me? Or did he use me to get close to Erin? I have so many questions. The biggest of them all is why didn't anyone tell me? Why didn't Mum let me in on what was going on? And why did Erin run instead of confronting what was happening? None of it makes sense.

I can't bring myself to be anywhere near Erin right now. I feel sorry for her: her husband is dead, she's a stranger to her family and all because of my husband. I can't even begin to process that Jesse was so infatuated with Erin that he'd kill someone. I feel so stupid. I was completely in the dark. I didn't see any of the warning signs all those years ago and I didn't notice anything tonight either. What kind of sister am I?

The minutes tick by. They seem to stretch on forever. Leah, Erin and I are all still here, trapped in this space with Aaron's body. Eventually there's some noise from the reception desk area and a number of other uniformed officers come to hover by the door. The young policeman beside me visibly relaxes, his shoulders untensing as he greets his colleagues. I can hear the static and crackle of their radio devices. Distorted voices flying through the airwaves, reporting on the crime scene. Sharing information about our lives.

A female uniformed officer steps into the room and starts chastising the young policeman, telling him we should have all vacated the area of the crime scene by now.

'What are you doing letting them stand about here,' she scolds him under her breath. 'Come on ladies, come out here and let's get you some strong tea and a blanket each.'

Leah doesn't have to be told twice, she automatically follows the instructions and disappears into the reception area. I hesitate and I can see Erin doing the same. She's looking towards the stairs, waiting for the same thing I'm waiting for.

'Let's go, ladies,' the police officer repeats. But she's too late.

Jesse is being led down the white marble staircase, his hands cuffed in front of him, two officers either side gripping his biceps. His head is bowed and he seems to be watching his every step. It's weirdly ironic that they're proceeding so slowly and Jesse looks as though he's being careful not to slip on the polished steps.

Then he lifts his head. His amber eyes lock with mine. He looks so familiar and yet so different. His face is drawn and he has tear streaks on his cheeks. I'm not sure what I expected, for him to be led out protesting his innocence? To deny it? To say he's sorry? Or even ask me to take care of Freya? But he says nothing at all to me and his focus moves to Erin. He's looking at her like a lovesick teenager; he's completely besotted with her. How did I not see this before?

'Erin, this isn't the end for us. I did it so we could be together. And we will be together. I love you.'

Jesse has confessed. I gulp. He's actually confessed in front of all of us, including the police. I realise that I'd been holding out for another answer, for Jesse to deny everything, for all of this to be a nightmare that I wake up from.

I'm literally gaping at my husband as he passes me. He's so close I could touch him. He doesn't look at me again. Finally, it sinks in that everything Mum said must be true. Jesse's obsessed with Erin. And he's killed her husband. What kind of man am I married to?

Erin starts sobbing all over again. Her grief is loud and noisy. I wish I could cry right now as well, let out all the frustration and anger. Instead, I feel like my body has turned to stone. Mum puts a hand round both of us and steers us out the opposite door, where we're ushered away from Jesse and the body on the floor by an officer.

Tonight my life as I know it has ended. My whole world has fallen apart.

My husband is a murderer. The father of my child is a liar.

My mother is a secret-keeper. And Erin too.

Can I ever trust anyone again?

# Chapter Fifty-Seven
## Erin
## Now

Jesse is being led down the marble staircase, flanked by two police officers. I blanch. My stomach is in knots and I feel sick. I have no idea how Jesse is going to react. I have no idea what he will say or do. He promised he would protect me in whatever way he could. But will he stay true to his word?

'Erin, this isn't the end for us. I did it so we could be together. And we will be together. I love you.'

Jesse has confessed. He's told everyone in the room he is a murderer. The police have his admission. But will he say anything else?

Jesse is hauled past me and looks at me with longing. The police officers push him roughly out the front door of Burcott House. He doesn't say anything more and, from the look in his amber eyes, I'm now certain that he will not give away my part in tonight's events.

I sob noisily with relief.

Even though my secret lover, Jesse, pushed Aaron to his death, I'm just as responsible for my husband's demise. I encouraged Jesse to help me get rid of Aaron. And when Jesse found out about how Aaron had been treating me, he was more than willing to do whatever it took to get my twisted husband out of our lives. Aaron was always charming, always courteous and always calculated in everything he did. He wanted me to be his perfect wife. He tried to silence me in every possible way. There was no escape from his meticulous designs for me. I was trapped in a luxurious prison.

For years, I dreamt of Jesse and what our life might have been like if things had turned out differently. Instead, I had all the material things I could wish for but I didn't have a life of my own. Once I reunited with Jesse, everything began to change. Aaron was away on a lot of work trips at the time and, under the guise of looking after my wellbeing, I managed to keep going to the health club on a semi-regular basis. And that's when I realised there was a way to change my life for the better.

But Jesse has been pushed into a police vehicle.

Nadia steers Sasha and me out of the grand foyer and into my office. A police liaison officer follows and begins to gently tell us what will happen next. But I can't concentrate on the words the young police officer is saying. My thoughts are a tangle of the past and the present. My family is complicated and it's not just my fault that things have turned out this way. I think of everything that led to this messy, murderous evening.

My mother puts her arm around my waist, displaying her maternal support in front of the police. But she's just lied again, telling everyone Jesse is infatuated with me. She's still trying to keep the truth from Sasha. My mother's actions pushed me to become the woman I am today.

She made me lie about my relationship with Jesse back then. But that wasn't all.

There were more lies.

Leah had no idea that Sasha and I are her half-sisters, that we have a different dad to her. I had no idea either, until I overheard Sasha and Nadia discussing it one day, about six months before Leah's accident.

It was a summer's morning and Nadia and Sasha were out in the garden having a coffee. I'd had a heavy night and slept in bed until mid-morning; I awoke and went in search of water because my mouth tasted like sawdust.

The back door was open and I could hear Nadia saying, 'Leah is too young and she's just lost her nana. The truth would be too much for her right now.'

'She's twenty-two. I get she's upset but maybe in a few months she should know,' Sasha replied.

'Why? There's no need. Don't push it, Sasha.'

'Because Erin needs to know too. She has a right to ask where she came from. I'm not bothered about finding out about my biological father but Erin might be.'

A cup clattered to the floor outside. 'Simon was your father, that man did everything for the two of you. That's all you need to know.'

Another lie.

This isn't true.

'OK, if that's what you think is best. I won't tell her.' Sasha's voice again.

I remember every word of that conversation – because if our mother had told Sasha and me who our father really was, then this whole mess could have been avoided. I would have trusted Nadia. If Sasha hadn't kept the truth from me, I might not have been angry at her. But I was. So I was reckless. I did something I shouldn't have. I kissed Jesse.

And then of course I fell for him. I fell in love with my sister's boyfriend. Those feelings resulted in the late-night argument with my mother and then Leah's accident. A chain reaction of events. Sasha told me to leave our family home. I had to go and make a life for myself. I met Aaron, I married him. That should have been my happy ending but it wasn't because of the man my husband was.

If my mother had told the truth all those years ago, none of this would have happened.

Every action has a consequence.

# New Year's Day

# Chapter Fifty-Eight
## Leah

This will be a Christmas that I never forget but not for the right reasons. I'm still shellshocked by everything that's happened. Sasha is an emotional wreck, alternating between sobbing and snapping at everyone. Erin is the polar opposite to Sasha in all ways, she's been so quiet this last week, retreating to bed early and spending hours just gazing out of the window. The snow is still falling. I've never seen so much at one time in England; it feels like it's never going to stop. The blanket of white that we're waking up to every day is making me feel more and more claustrophobic. Mom has been getting on my nerves; she's been ceaseless in her fussing around all of us. I was tempted just to get myself out of here, before I got sucked into this mess even further, but the police informed us we all had to stay put while they were taking our witness statements and gathering evidence. So I had no choice.

We spent Christmas Day at Mum's house. All three Bailey sisters and the three grandchildren too. Mom was being too forced, too bright, and too over the top in her efforts to give the children an ordinary Christmas Day. *Would you like another mince pie? Who wants turkey sandwiches? Which movie shall we watch?* She's been relentless in her quest for a normal family Christmas. As if things could ever be normal again. I feel for the kids. Ophelia and Jasper have been so reserved but it's understandable, they've been pulled out of their privileged existence and told their dad is dead; it must be such a shock to them. Freya hasn't been her usual bouncy self. She's missed Jesse over Christmas and keeps asking when she can see him.

'Come on, kids!' I yell along the hallway. 'How long does it take to get your boots on?'

Freya comes tramping towards me first, a battered old pair of wellie boots on and a coat that looks one size too big.

'You OK?' I ask her.

She nods in response but her mouth is tugging downwards, not like the Freya I know at all.

'Come here.' I draw her into a big hug. 'All of this sucks, but it will get better,' I say to her quietly.

Jasper and Ophelia join us. They're wearing matching green Hunter wellies that don't look as though they've been worn before.

'Let's go, you two,' I smile, trying to inject some warmth into our little group as we all pile out into the crisp, winter afternoon. 'I think we need a rematch as I'm not sure yesterday's snowball fight was fair.'

Freya and Jasper visibly perk up at this. I've been trying to get all three of them outside each afternoon for a long walk. My plan has been to distract them with building snowmen and snowball fights and I think I'm slowly starting to make a connection with Ophelia and Jasper. The twins' discomfort at being at Mom's house with a bunch of strangers is so obvious to me. I've been the kid who lost her dad in a terrible situation, so I can relate to what they're going through.

'Hey Leah!' Freya shouts. I look in her direction and get pelted in the face with powdery snow.

'I can't believe I fell for that!' I groan, scooping up a ball of snow and aiming it at my niece. But Freya dodges out of the way just in time. She sticks her tongue out at me but, before I can react, Jasper has slipped a handful of ice down Freya's back.

'Aaarrggh! It's freezing!' Freya screeches, running around in a circle and trying to shake the ice free from her coat.

Jasper proper belly-laughs and doubles over. I smile. I'm so pleased the two of them are getting into play mode a bit quicker than yesterday. They run off together, blasts of snow being thrown between them.

Ophelia is still walking beside me, head down, watching her boots making footprints in the snow.

'You don't want to join them?'

'No, not today.' Her answer is firm.

'That's OK, wanna talk about it?'

'Do I want to talk about Freya's dad killing my dad? Yes, I do. Especially as it was kept a secret from me.'

My jaw drops. 'Ophelia!' I place my hands on her arms and look into her face. 'Who told you that?'

'No one. I heard you and Sasha talking about it last night.'

I clap my hand to my mouth. 'Oh, Ophelia... I wish you hadn't found out like that.'

'You mean you wish I hadn't found out at all?' Her arms are crossed against her body, her face thunderous.

'It's all so complicated. Let's talk it through with your mum.' I pause, giving her space to respond but she doesn't. 'Please don't say anything to Freya right now.'

'Why? Her dad is still alive.' Ophelia pouts in a way that makes her look exactly like Erin.

I sigh. 'I don't want to tell you to do something if you don't want to. But Freya isn't to blame. She's your cousin, she wants to be your friend. Don't push her away.'

Ophelia doesn't say anything for a minute. The yells and laughter of the other two children float back to us. Finally, she says, 'OK, I won't say anything. But please can someone tell me what's really been going on?'

I take her hand in mine and we carry on walking together. 'Let's talk to Erin – your mum – later when the other two are in bed.'

By the look on Ophelia's face, she doesn't seem content with this answer but she stops asking questions and falls silent as we walk along, beneath the bare tree branches and into a large park where Freya and Jasper are still chasing each other. I feel more worried than I have in days. I hadn't thought about Jesse's actions impacting the relationship between Freya, Ophelia and Jasper but of course it will. Another generation of our family could be destroyed by lies. Freya will be completely devastated, she's such a kind, caring girl and we haven't told her where her dad is yet or why. Just that he's gone away for a bit. She asked us if he was dead like Aaron and we reassured her that he wasn't but she's an intelligent girl, she can tell something is up.

My phone vibrates in my pocket, so I check the message out of habit, expecting it to be another threatening tirade from my least favourite person. But it isn't: instead I find myself reading a sweet message from Xavier, wishing me a Happy New Year. I smile to myself and make a mental note to reply later. I don't want to respond straight away and seem too keen but I would like to see him again. Perhaps something good might come out of the Christmas party after all.

When we get back to the house, the kids take off their outdoor things and troop into the lounge, red-cheeked and tired. Mom has made popcorn for them and they're all set up for a movie afternoon. I go through to the kitchen, where Erin and Sasha are sitting at opposite ends of the little dining room table.

I relay the conversation with Ophelia to them. They both look horrified.

'She heard you?' Erin says, a scowl on her face.

'Oh no.' Sasha's face is white. 'I was hoping not to tell Freya just yet.'

Mom sits down at the head of the table. 'If we've learnt anything from all of this, it's that keeping secrets leads to trouble. Let's tell them sooner rather than later, all out in the open, and we can discuss any questions they have.'

Erin looks concerned at this. 'I'm just not sure discussing it all together is the right thing to do. I've booked Ophelia and Jasper in for counselling sessions...'

'Let's deal with this as a family,' Mom says firmly.

The room goes quiet for a bit and the unmistakable dialogue from the *Home Alone* film filters into the kitchen. I envy them. I wish I could be sitting down with the kids and not having to deal with all the adult stuff.

'Erin, do you want to share your idea with your sisters?' Mom says gently, laying her hand on Erin's.

'Yes... I was thinking we could go to my chalet in the French Alps. It would be a change of scene, a chance to get away. There's plenty of distractions there. The scenery is stunning and the snow is excellent for skiing... What do you think?' Erin looks up from her mug of tea.

'Are you sure you want us to come?' Sasha asks tentatively. 'I'd understand if you'd rather Freya and I didn't join you.'

'I want you to come,' Erin says. 'Like Nadia— Mum just said, we've got to deal with this as a family.'

Sasha's eyes water and she nods in response.

'Sounds like a good solution,' I say. I mean it. I'd never say no to a holiday. And I wonder if it might be the same ski resort that Xavier is heading to.

This could just be the answer I need to put some distance between me and my own troubles. My phone hasn't stopped pinging in the last week. As much as I love my job as an influencer, it comes with lots of downsides too. People being able to contact you whenever, wherever is one of them. I'll be relieved to put some more space between me and my past. Because the truth is, Erin and Sasha aren't the only ones with secrets. I have enough of my own.

I retreat to the lounge and put my feet up on the low footstool as I open my phone messages. I re-read the latest threat from my stalker.

*I HOPE YOU'VE HAD A MERRY CHRISTMAS, BECAUSE I'M COMING TO FIND YOU IN THE NEW YEAR.*

The words swim before my eyes and I feel sick.

I thought I was set for life in Australia, with my influencer career flying high and a romance with a hunky Australian surfer called Shane. It was all going well, until his wife Lindsay found out and I discovered my boyfriend was already in a relationship. Ever since then, Lindsay has been stalking me. She's been threatening to expose my secret to my fans, and demanding that I give her financial compensation for what her marriage has been through. The thing is, Shane never told me he was married. Not until a long time after we met, and then he promised me they were separating. The oldest trick in the book, but it's given me a lot of hassle since.

I wish his wife would just leave me alone but she keeps persisting. I made the mistake in giving her some money to begin with, but she keeps demanding more. And things have been getting even weirder lately. She sent a Christmas card to Mom's house, signed from Shane and Lindsay. It unnerves me that she knows where I am. I always keep the address of where I'm staying off my social media accounts so I have no idea how she found me.

I would have paid her off by now if I had the cash but I don't have a huge amount to my name in terms of money. A lot of the time I'm getting freebies from companies rather than payment. I might not have the money to pay the crazy cow but I know someone who does...

The holiday to France will give me the chance to move location again and hopefully this time I'll shake off my stalker. It will also be the perfect opportunity to reconnect with Erin properly. I want to get to know my sister all over again and my goal is to make myself part of her world, her inner circle, someone she can trust. Hopefully that trust will earn me connections and rewards. I can see a life for myself beyond my influencer travels now. One that involves a French alpine lodge, a massive country house and staff at my beck and call. I want a lifestyle just like Erin's.

So the longer I can persuade Erin to stay at the ski resort, the better.

# Chapter Fifty-Nine
## Jesse

What a fantastic start to the new year this is. Erin and I were meant to be jetting off to Greece together, for a month on the secluded island of Kefalonia to get properly reacquainted with each other again. Jasper and Ophelia were due to be back at boarding school and we had so many plans for our first few weeks together as an official couple. Not to mention all of the hopes and dreams we had ahead of us for the rest of our lives. We wanted to get married, have another child, set up a home together. All that has been taken away now, along with my freedom, my reputation and my precious Freya as well. I've lost absolutely everything.

The bench is hard underneath me and I'm already fed up of staring at the same four walls of this cell. Within days of being here I felt like I was going stir-crazy. I'm used to running for miles, swimming in a luxury pool and working out for most of my waking hours. Now I'm nothing more than a caged animal.

I'm not too proud to admit that I've cried, cried for all that I've lost and for the dismal situation I'm now in. But I quickly came to the conclusion I would drive myself mad with thinking. What if I hadn't had an affair with Erin? What if I hadn't gone to the Christmas party?

What if I hadn't pushed Aaron? It's too late for what ifs now, what's done is done. What I need to do now is figure out how I survive this.

The magnitude of my action is also starting to hit me. A man's life has ended and mine has been put on hold. I could be in prison for years, the stretch of time before me still undecided. The question of what's going to happen in that courtroom is hanging over me. And each night when I close my eyes all I see is Aaron's face as he tipped over the bannister.

So I've started working out in here, doing as much as I can to keep my body active and my mind engaged. I'm focusing my thoughts on what happens next. Soon I'll be standing trial and I've got to play the game to make sure my sentence is as low as possible. My track record is clean. I was drunk, in a fight, I didn't mean for it to happen. All of these things might help my case with a jury. Then again, my solicitor says if I hold my hands up and say I did it and I'm sorry and just plead guilty that could swing the sentencing in my favour as well. There's a lot to decide, so it's a good job I've got time on my hands.

Whatever happens, I have to keep my body and mind strong to get through the next few years. I've reframed the situation in my head and, actually, I'm still young so when I get out of here there will be time for Erin and I to create a life together and make all of our dreams come true. It's going to be tough but Erin and I are meant to be. She helped me up on the third-floor landing, after it happened, to act quickly and to cover my tracks. She tried to save me from being caught. It didn't work out but I know she did her best. She also told me that she loved me even more for getting Aaron out of her life. And she said that, whatever happened, she would wait for me. We had an agreement that if one of us got caught for Aaron's murder, we'd try to protect the other. There's no point in both of us being behind bars. I know she'll be there on the day I'm released from prison and then we will have the rest of our lives together.

I'm not sorry that her brute of a husband is dead, I'm just sorry I've ended up behind bars because of it. If Erin asked me to do the same thing again I would, in a heartbeat. That's how much I love her.

I would do anything for Erin.

# Chapter Sixty
# Sasha

I still haven't come to terms with what happened at the Christmas party. And I'm not sure I ever will. Freya realises that something is wrong. But what should I tell her? It's all over the news and I've had to keep the TV remote away from her. How can we face our lives? Return to school? Carry on as normal...

I requested leave from work in January, citing personal circumstances. The school board aren't happy; they know they're losing more than a cog in a wheel with me out of action for the first half term. And, who knows, maybe it will be for longer. Perhaps it's time for me to resign, to move away from the career that put so much distance between me and my husband and to start again. I need to think about what's best for me and Freya now.

Erin has actually been quite sweet to me over the last few days. She could have reacted in a very different way. After all, my husband killed her husband. That was not something I saw coming. I would understand if she didn't want to see me again. It must be hard to look at me and Freya, knowing the man at the centre of our lives took the life of her husband.

Somehow, the knowledge of Jesse's obsession with Erin is even harder to reconcile with than the actions that led to Aaron's death.

Every night, when I lie in my bed tossing and turning, I keep delving back to the past. Things between Jesse and I may not have been brilliant in recent years but when we first got together I really loved him. He was so excited when he found out I was pregnant with Freya and our wedding day was filled with joy. I'll never be able to look at those photographs again in the same way. How could Jesse deceive me for all this time?

I had no idea that he harboured feelings for Erin. I feel guilty that she had to put up with his advances and even guiltier that she cut ties with our family because of him. Now it makes sense why she didn't respond to my messages. She was trying to do the right thing and let my marriage have a chance. If only she'd told me what was going on. My relationship with Jesse may not have survived, but blood is thicker than water and I would rather have had my sister in my life than a cheating husband.

All the Christmas decorations at our house have been packed away in the attic. I took them down as soon as I could, on Boxing Day. I don't know if I will ever be able to view Christmas in the same way, or bring myself to hang another trinket on a tree, or play 'Merry Xmas Everybody' ever again. Because I'll forever be reminded of the Christmas party that destroyed my marriage and changed my daughter's life, my sister's life and the rest of our family forever.

When Erin suggested we all get away from England and go to her lodge in the French Alps, I was pleased she'd included me and Freya in the invite. I didn't hesitate to accept. We all agreed a change of scenery is exactly what we all need. The way Erin described the lodge made it sound like heaven: a cosy hideaway, blissful mountain views and complete tranquillity. The photos of the lodge are breathtaking, set at the edge of an exclusive ski resort. I didn't think it would be possible, but I can feel the tiny blossom of hope.

I wouldn't wish these circumstances on any family.

But maybe there is a way forward, the three of us together again, with Mum looking out for all of us and our children.

# Chapter Sixty-One
# Nadia

I pull up outside the prison, parking my car in my usual spot. I flip the car mirror down and apply a fresh coat of lipstick. My hair is freshly blow-dried, my nails newly painted and I'm wearing an outfit that looks good but is also comfortable. The number of women who come to prison visiting hours dressed up to the nines, as though about to go out on the town, with the high heels and long hair extensions, is ridiculous. I've been coming here for too many years now and I'm more than familiar with the drill. The bag checks, the pat down, every humiliating little moment of these visits is ingrained in my mind.

I stand in line, waiting my turn to go into the room filled with rows of little tables. It looks like the set-up for a school hall, except brawny grown men are sat at childlike desks, appearing even bigger in stature because of the miniature furniture they're forced to sit at. I spot him at the furthest end of the room, which means I have to weave between all of the tables, squeezing by men with convictions that would turn your stomach, and the women who come religiously, every week, to see them.

I'm not so dedicated, I only come to this place when I absolutely have to. It gives me the chills every time I step foot in here. Coming face to face with him is not my idea of a good day out – far from it. Every time I see his tattooed arms, his thickset neck, his leering expression, I want to run straight back out to my car. But I don't, because we have an agreement and it's not worth my life to break it.

I sit myself down at the table, fold my arms and wait to see what Craig Turner has to say to me today. He doesn't change – he never seems to age – and being in his presence makes me feel so jittery. Craig is my first love, the father of Sasha and Erin, and the feature of all of my nightmares.

I didn't want Sasha and Erin to know who their biological father really is because he's in prison, behind bars. For murder.

'Hello Nadia, long time no see.'

Craig says this to me every time I come to visit him and it always makes me feel nauseous. The shape of these visits can vary wildly, depending on what mood he is in. I get one of three personas: angry Craig, amorous Craig or sardonic Craig. And I'm not sure which is worse. Time and time again, I wonder what on earth I saw in him when we first got together.

It all seems so long ago now. I was young and desperate to be in love. Craig had a magnetic personality, he was a few years older than me, and exciting to be around. I never quite knew where we'd end up on a date – he was full of life and adventure. I thought he was my happily ever after, but Craig was good at keeping secrets and portraying the image of someone carefree and uncomplicated. The truth was far from it. Being the sheltered young girl I was, I cottoned on only when it was far too late. I was already pregnant with Sasha when the penny finally dropped and I realised that Craig wasn't funding our lavish lifestyle with his own business, he was paying his way using other people's money.

Craig leans over and grasps one of my hands in his. I come only a couple of times a year to see him now but I always dread being here with him, because being near him makes my stomach churn.

'How's life treating you, princess?'

What do I say to that after everything that's happened? 'Oh, you know, still getting older.' I chuckle, shrugging off the question.

'You still look as sexy as the first day I met you.' Craig is squeezing my hand so tight it hurts.

Back then, Craig had a knack of getting away with petty crime after petty crime, mostly small robberies. He was a gentleman villain, just like his father before him. It seems shocking to me now that I was so blinkered to what was going on. But when I found out, he promised me that he'd never get involved in anything really bad. He tried to convince me he was a modern-day Robin Hood and I was his Maid Marion. And it worked for a while.

Until it didn't. A robbery went wrong and Craig got into a fight. He knocked a bank manager through a glass window and the poor man died. I had eighteen-month-old Sasha at the time and I was pregnant with Erin. My own mother had passed away several years before and I hadn't seen my father since I was a teenager. He and my mother had separated and not long after that, he had disappeared. I had a couple of cousins living in London but I was too embarrassed to open up to them about what was going on. So I fled from our flat in the city and moved away, further south, in the hopes of creating a new life for myself and my three small children.

I'm jerked back to the present when Craig says, 'A little birdie told me an interesting story the other day. About this rich guy who plunged to his death at a Christmas party.'

Craig always has a way of finding out what's going on in my life. I'd hoped this would take a bit longer but I'm not surprised the events have reached his ears already.

When I first escaped from our flat in London, it took him a while but he found me. So I moved again and again, getting closer and closer to the Cornish coast. I thought I'd finally shaken him off or he'd lost interest. Things settled down. I created a life for myself, I had a job, friends and the girls were beginning to thrive. Then I met Simon. It was love at first sight. He was the complete opposite of Craig – kind and honest. I hoped that the past would stay buried and that we could all live as a happy family.

But Craig's shadow was still there, hanging over me. I could never truly let myself relax.

Eventually, I told my lovely Simon the truth. I cried on his shoulder and he held me all night long. I remember things felt so different the next morning, like a weight had been lifted off my shoulders. We decided to concentrate on our future. We got married, just a little service with our friends, and then I fell pregnant with Leah. For a few short years we were so happy.

I should have known it wouldn't last.

Craig found me again and then the letters and the threats started. It wasn't so easy to move this time round; Sasha and Erin were settled in school and Simon was adamant that we were staying put. He wasn't going to be bullied away from his home. I begged and pleaded with Simon to move. I even suggested going to America or Australia. As far away as we possibly could to be out of Craig's reach. Simon didn't understand. He thought that because Craig was behind bars he couldn't hurt us. But he was very wrong.

Leah was only four when Simon died on an icy road at the end of the worst January of my life. At first the police said it was an accident, a case of driving too fast in difficult conditions. If it hadn't been for the eyewitness who came forward, it may have been left at that. I didn't need the eyewitness to understand the truth. Craig's circle of influence extended far beyond the prison walls and he was able to arrange Simon's murder.

It all came out in the end. Craig was charged with more time behind bars, for organising the car accident that resulted in Simon's death, and he was moved to a higher-security prison. At the time I didn't care about any of that, all I cared about was that my Simon had gone. The years that followed were dark, a haze of antidepressants and sleeping pills. I missed some of the most important moments of my children's lives and there were times when I felt like I couldn't carry on. Simon's mother saved us all; she was there for every school pick-up, every birthday, every January that rolled by. She could have pushed for custody of Leah and left me without support, but she was like Simon. She adored both Sasha and Erin like they were her own. She was such a generous woman. I always felt so guilty that she lost her only son because of my deranged ex-boyfriend.

I can never, ever forgive Craig for what he did. But I must try to keep him sweet so he doesn't hurt anyone else close to me.

'So you're not going to spill the beans then?' Craig barks, bringing me back to the present.

I try to give him a nonchalant, innocent look in response but he's not going to be dissuaded.

'The guy's name was Bailey-Scott. Apparently, his wife is called Erin. It wouldn't happen to be our little Erin, would it?'

I gulp, knowing there's no way of denying this.

'So it's true then? Erin is sitting on a fortune now her hubby's six foot under?'

'I have no idea,' I try to breeze my way through my response. 'Erin and I don't see much of each other these days.'

Craig leans forward, I can smell his stale breath. 'What happened? A chip off the ol' block?'

I blanch, he's skirting far too close to the truth for my liking.

He laughs. 'I'm right! Good girl Erin! She's not got caught though, has she?'

I shake my head. 'It's nothing like that. Erin wasn't involved.'

I can tell Craig won't give up on this until he's got the answer from me or someone else. I decide it's better coming from me. 'There was a misunderstanding, an argument. Sasha's husband, Jesse, pushed him.'

There's an unsettling gleam in Craig's eye.

'For all we know, it was an accident. Let's see what the verdict is when it goes to court.'

'I'll be following with interest,' Craig laughs, rubbing his hands together. 'Who knows, I could have my son-in-law in the cell next to me for company.'

My stomach flips, I hadn't thought about this. It's highly unlikely though, given the high-security measures Craig is under. But it does mean Craig could have contact with Jesse through the prison grapevine. It's not a pleasant thought but it's not something I can dwell on. I'll deal with whatever comes, when it comes.

'I'd like to see the posh pile that Erin's ended up with.'

Craig promised me that he would never contact Sasha or Erin while he was in prison. It was a promise that was made a very long time ago but he's kept to it. Why, I don't really know. The arrangement is that I still come to see him, I bring him photographs and news of what his girls have been doing. He has a small window into their lives; I don't like it but it's a small price to pay for him not reaching out to them directly. It also means I can select the information about our children that he has access to. I made the mistake of telling him Sasha was pregnant. I haven't told him too much about Erin, only that we'd lost touch. He's threatened to go back on his word more than a few times, but so far he hasn't done so. I just hope the news about Erin's fortune doesn't change things.

I pray that Craig will never be allowed beyond prison walls again. But prisons are overflowing these days and Craig knows how to get what he wants. I can tell by the way he's treated by the prison guards that he's made friends with all the right people and he's sure to use that to his advantage. He's always harboured this dream of being released from prison and returning to the outside world, like some kind of hero, to his daughters.

I live in fear of the day he tells me he's being let out.

So far that day hasn't come. I just hope it stays that way.

# Chapter Sixty-Two
## Erin

The Christmas party is over, my home is a crime scene and my husband is dead. I can't say things went exactly to plan. That was not the way I'd plotted for my husband to die. It was not meant to happen at the party. It was not meant to be so public. Jesse and I had agreed on a different way of ending Aaron's life: we were going to spike his drink at the end of Christmas party with a large quantity of crushed up sleeping pills. We'd got the same brand of pills that Sasha uses and we were going to set her up to take the blame. We'd intended for his body to be found in the Snug the next morning. There would have been enough people at the hotel to ensure multiple suspects, including business clients and even Nia. But Jesse couldn't wait. He acted sooner than we'd agreed and things got a lot messier than I'd expected.

But we had to take the opportunity as soon as we could. I'm free of my controlling husband and I can't say I'm sorry that he's gone. The possibilities for my new-found freedom are making me feel quite giddy. Everything Aaron owned is now mine: his cars, the hotel, the bank accounts, business assets. I have a hefty life insurance coming my way too. And all of his family money will eventually go to my twins. We're rich beyond my wildest dreams.

I regret it had to come to this, of course I do. If Aaron had been a different man we might've come to an understanding. If he was reasonable, I could've counted on a decent divorce pay out. But he wasn't, so it had to be this way.

Am I sad Jesse got caught?

Jesse rejected me ten years ago. He chose Sasha over me. He broke my heart and that's something I'll never forget. Although, I must admit, at points I got caught up; I was almost under his spell once again. I really did love him once and things could have turned out very differently. Instead, I deliberately put this plan into motion and it was a bonus that I got to steal him from Sasha and have some fun along the way. It all worked so seamlessly. Jesse is so gullible; he had no idea whatsoever that he was being played by me as well.

I even told him that Jasper and Ophelia were his children.

Not. True.

Jesse believed me hook, line and sinker. I can see why, Ophelia and Freya bear an uncanny resemblance to one another. The timing of the twins' births just about works out, except Jesse didn't bother to check if they were full term or premature. If he had stopped to ask a few more questions then he could have worked out that he wasn't their father easily enough. If he had asked for a paternity test I would have been busted. Jesse didn't do any of those things; he was too willing to believe my lies and too desperate to get away from nagging Sasha. He wanted to believe the twins were his, so I let him. I don't feel guilty in the least, this was payback for him breaking my heart ten years ago. I'm sure he had an agenda too – he was probably seduced by my good looks, but there's no doubt my wealth helped him to jump feet first into our affair the second time around.

There was just one other thing that didn't go my way. I wanted to take Sasha down with Jesse, two birds with one stone, because I'm desperate to be shot of my older sister too. Now I'm going to have to endure her reaction to what happened at the Christmas party and deal with her moping about now that she knows her husband is a cheat and a killer. But it can't be helped, I'll just have to put up with her for a little bit longer.

Did I have any help?

Of course I did. When I discovered ten years ago that my mother had kept the identity of my biological father under wraps from me I was astounded. I wondered who he might be and why she hadn't told us about him. When I had the time and resources I went looking for my real daddy. It took several years of searching but eventually, with some help from DNA searches, I found out who he was.

I was horrified at first to find out that Craig Turner was behind bars for not one but two murders. But five years ago I got in touch with him, we exchanged a few letters and then I went to meet him in prison. It was strange and surreal but I felt a connection with him instantly. It wasn't just because we looked alike – same hair colour, same straight nose, same smile – there was something more. I felt like he understood me at a deeper level, in a way that my sisters and mothers don't come close to.

My father asked me to tell him about my husband. I could have portrayed our life as idyllic but instead, for the first time ever, I told the truth about my authoritarian husband and the marriage I felt trapped in. Craig said he could sort things out for me but I didn't want that. I didn't want my father to be responsible for another murder and to have to do more time on my behalf. So we came up with a solution to bring Aaron down. And it worked.

Now, I can finally have some real fun.

I'm my own woman, with my own empire. I will charm all of the people Aaron charmed and I will make myself just as successful as he was. I will build on all the projects we had and put my own spin on them. And when Jesse is finally released from prison perhaps in ten, maybe fifteen years from now, if I've forgiven him I might consider us trying again. Third time lucky. The kids will have grown and I'll be looking for a new adventure. Or perhaps I'll have met a new man who truly deserves me. For now, I'm going to enjoy everything I've earned.

But I won't forget how Mum or Sasha treated me. They think I'm turning over a new leaf, being all generous and inviting them to my luxurious French cabin. A snowy mountain top they don't know the layout of could be just the place for us to get to know each other again. Although there are all sorts of things that can go wrong on holiday.

I might be prepared to make-believe at happy families for now.

But I can't promise it will last forever...

# Also by Mikayla Davids

## Prologue

Silence.

All I can hear is silence.

The world around me is hazy. Crisp, fresh snow, several inches deep, crunches under my heavy boots. The icy caps of the mountain peaks tower above me, appearing monochrome and chilling in the dim light. I inhale the cold air in short, sharp breaths as my eyes adjust to the gloom around me. The darkness of the night is only just beginning to lift and the sun is still yet to rise.

It's a long time since I've been up this early. And it's eerie, standing here by myself in the middle of this exclusive ski resort without a soul nearby. I'm used to seeing this scene brimming with people in colourful outfits, laughter and chatter swirling in the air around me. But not even the chalet girls are up.

Something jerked me awake from my warm bed, after a brief and fitful sleep. Only a few short hours ago, I was trudging up the hill to my family's holiday chalet, alcohol dulling my senses and urging me forward to the warmth of the luxury accommodation. I couldn't rest properly though, there was something on my mind, something that just didn't feel right.

I retrace the steps I'd trodden only hours before, making my way slowly down the slippery path. My mouth is dry and my whole body feels sluggish, but I keep going. I need to fill in the missing puzzle pieces of my memories from last night. As I slip and slide down the hillside, snapshots of the evening flicker in my mind...

I reach the large chalet and see there's a gap around the door, it's not fully shut. A shiver runs through me. It must be freezing inside. I push open the heavy wooden door. Stepping inside, I survey the scene. The wreckage of the night before is plain to see. Wine bottles clutter every surface, a chair is upturned and clothes are strewn everywhere. But there's no one here. There's nothing but silence. Everyone is long gone.

I'm turning to go, feeling foolish for coming back here, when I see something out of the corner of my eye, snagging my attention. I turn fully towards the heap of material in the centre of the room.

And that's when I realise... it's not just a jumble of clothing, there's a person lying there. I see who it is and I start to smile. I should've guessed who would be passed out in the middle of the floor after the heavy night we had.

I call out their name. There's no response so I drop to my knees and brush the hair off their face.

My jaw drops in shock.

This person is too cold, too pale, too lifeless.

The door is still open and a cold blast of wind sweeps into the room, causing snowflakes to flutter into the chalet. I feel numb. This can't be real.

I look back down and that's when I see it.

The knife. And the blood.

My worst fears are confirmed and I spring back with a cry. Panic grips me. I can't be found here.

I rush outside, my heart hammering wildly and my breath catching in my chest as I push myself back up the hillside. One thought circling in my mind:

What really happened last night?

**The Family Secret is available to read now.**

**The perfect vacation... or the perfect murder...**

**Alicia Silver** is spending her first Christmas holiday with her handsome new husband **Jack** and his family in their remote, luxurious lodge in the snowy Irish mountains.

The Silver family are wealthy and beautiful, and Alicia is determined to live up to their high expectations for her marriage. But with the festivities in full swing, Alicia quickly discovers that behind their perfect image, her new in-laws are hiding plenty of secrets...

**The gorgeous husband**
**The jealous sister-in-law**
**The glamorous step-mother**
**The controlling father-in-law**

Before the vacation is over one of them will be dead.

**Who would kill to protect their shocking secret? And will Alicia survive this Christmas holiday?**
***The Christmas Holiday*** **is available to read now.**

## Also By Mikayla Davids

*The Christmas Holiday*: A totally gripping and addictive psychological thriller

*The Couple on Holiday*: A completely addictive and gripping psychological thriller with a heart-stopping twist

*The Family Secret*: A completely gripping psychological thriller full of incredible twists (The Bailey family psychological thrillers Book 2)

Dear reader,

I want to say a HUGE and heartfelt thank you for choosing to read *The Christmas Party*. This is my debut novel and I'm so excited to share this story – which is the result of years of dreaming – with you! If you did enjoy it, you can keep up to date with my author journey and find out about my new releases, by visiting the contact page on my website and subscribing to my mailing list: https://subscribepage.io /MikaylaDavidsBooks

*Subscribe!*

I hope you were gripped and entertained by *The Christmas Party*. It would mean the world to me if you could write a review and post on Amazon.

*Write a review!*

I'd love to hear what you think, and reviews really help readers to discover new stories. If you'd like to get in touch with me you can do so via my Facebook page or through Twitter, Instagram or Goodreads.

All my thanks,

Mikayla Davids

Follow me on Twitter: @MikaylaDBooks

Follow me on Instagram: mikayladavidsbooks

Find me on Facebook: Mikayla Davids Books

Visit my website:

https://mikayladavids.wixsite.com/mikayladavidsbooks

ISBN: 978-1-7392278-1-4

eBook ISBN: 978-1-7392278-0-7

Printed in Dunstable, United Kingdom